ALSO BY ETHAN HAWKE

The Hottest State

ASH WEDNESDAY

ASH

WEDN

E S D A Y

A NOVEL

ETHAN HAWKE

Alfred A. Knopf   New York 2002

THIS IS A BORZOI BOOK
PUBLISHED BY ALFRED A. KNOPF

www.aaknopf.com

Knopf, Borzoi Books, and the colophon are registered
trademarks of Random House, Inc.

Library of Congress Cataloging-in-Publication Data

Hawke, Ethan, [date]
    Ash Wednesday : a novel / by Ethan Hawke.—1st ed.
      p. cm.
    ISBN 0-375-41326-X
    1. Absence without leave—Fiction. 2. Automobile travel—Fiction.
3. Unmarried couples—Fiction. 4. Pregnant women—Fiction.
5. Soldiers—Fiction. I. Title.

PS3558.A8165 A93 2002   813'.54—DC21   2002020811

Manufactured in the United States of America

First Edition

FOR KARUNA

"Let's do some livin', after we die."

—THE ROLLING STONES

ASH
WEDNESDAY

INTRODUCING
JAMES HEARTSOCK

I WAS DRIVING a '69 Chevy Nova 370 four-barrel with mag wheels and a dual exhaust. It's a kick-ass car. I took the muffler out so it sounds like a Harley. People love it. I was staring at myself through the window into the driver's-side mirror; I do that all the time. I'll stare into anything that reflects. That's not a flattering quality, and I wish I didn't do it, but I do. I'm vain as all hell. It's revolting. Most of the time when I'm looking in the mirror, I'm checking to see if I'm still here or else I'm wishing I was somebody else, a Mexican bandito or somebody like that. I have a mustache. Most guys with mustaches look like fags, but I don't. I touch mine too much, though. I touch it all the time. I don't even know why I'm telling you about it now. I just stare at myself constantly and I wish I didn't. It brings me absolutely no pleasure at all.

My fingers were frozen around the steering wheel. Albany in February is a black sooty slab of ice. The woman on the radio announced the time and temperature: eight-forty-two and twenty-three degrees. Christy and I had broken up fifteen hours earlier, and I was in a tailspin. I had my uniform on, the dress one; it's awesome. Military uniforms make you feel like somebody, like you have a purpose, even if you don't. You feel special, connected to the past. You're not just an ordinary person, a *civilian*—you're noble. The downside of this Walk of Pride is, it's a lie.

This is my story.

My orders were unbelievable, my lieutenant is an out-of-control high-speed prick. This was *his* job. I had to inform some dude's wife that her husband had been shot in the head. The soldier's name was Private Kevin Anderson, and he'd been killed outside of Paradise the night before. Paradise is a bar where all the black dudes hang: probably drugs or some kind of bullshit high jinks. I didn't know him at all.

Not to mention, I was all cracked up myself. I hadn't been to sleep, doing speed all night: crystal meth. Breaking up with Christy had been a giant mistake; I knew it the minute I walked away.

The army is more lamebrain than you can even imagine. My lieutenant sometimes has me and my men go into town and stand guard over parking spots: securing position. I joined up because I wanted to be of service to something. I'd tried college, Kent State, for two years but screw that. Who wants to pay all that coin just to drink beer and get VD? My dad had been in the army, and I grew up constantly drawing pictures of machine guns and soldiers killing the hell out of one another—shit like that—so I thought joining the army made sense. I figured it was my destiny, and it was, but just because something's your destiny doesn't mean it's gonna be any good.

I thought maybe someday I'd be in a Dairy Queen and some bonzo lunatic would whip out an automatic and start wasting people, and I'd be the one guy there who'd be able to stop him, who'd show some signs of personal heroism or integrity. There are a lot of people in the world. It's difficult to find a way to set yourself apart. When I was twelve, I built a working crossbow with bolts I could sink into a tree. That's about the coolest thing I've ever done.

Now, the only thing interesting or worthy of remark about me was my car. It was tits: silver with bold black racing stripes straight down the center. I never had any trouble getting laid.

I was hauling ass through north Albany into the "darker" part of town looking for this Anderson kid's address: 2376½ Hawthorne, apartment B. I had all his information in a folder on the passenger seat. The streets were icy and lined with piles of crusty pollution-stained snow. I found the house easy, a big old place divided up into eight apartments. All the homes on the block were done the exact same way. Once upon a time this was the swank part of town—about eighty trillion years ago.

I sat in my Nova under a tremendous barren old sycamore tree that grew adjacent to the Andersons' driveway. Trees are wonderful. My dad was a tree man. He planted and trimmed trees for a living. Sometimes he'd be 180 feet up in the air rappelling around with a spinning chain saw, dead and sick branches bombing down onto the ground. I loved my dad. If I could give you the sensation of being eight years old watching him up in some magnificent maple singing to himself and talking to the branches—if you could hear him yell down, *"Jimmy, when you're thirteen and you come live with me, we'll have ourselves some laughs then, pal, you can bet your sweet ass on that!"*—if you could be inside my guts for that moment, you'd know exactly what it is like to be me. Summers, growing up, I worked with the ground crews, chopping and clearing. I was Mr. Know-It-All about landscaping. This sycamore in front of me was close to two hundred years old. Unless some ding-a-ling cuts it down it'll be right there on Hawthorne Drive long after I'm dead. Can't tell you why, but that makes me feel good.

I checked my nose to make sure it wasn't bleeding. Four hours before, I'd blown my last line with Tony, Eric, and Ed. Ed brought the crank. I wasn't gonna do any, but they started chopping 'em down, and like I said I'd just broken up with Christy and—*bada-bing bada-bam*—next thing you know I've been talking about Patrick Ewing, John Starks, and the rest of the New York Knicks for nine hours. Tony, Eric, and Ed are a bunch of numb-nuts, but I hang out with them all the time anyway. It makes me sad to think I'm like them. "Better to be alone than to wish you were." My father used to say that, but I never listen to anybody. I don't say that with any pride. It's good to listen to people.

In no way did I want to get out of the car. My lieutenant is a motherfucker. When I think about him, my body palpitates with rage.

Only eight-thirty in the morning and already things were going terribly. THE ARMY. WE DO MORE BEFORE NINE O'CLOCK. Isn't that the ad line on TV?

I'd always considered the military, but that movie *Top Gun* put me over the edge. Tom Cruise on that Ninja, banging that girl. Fuckin'-A. That was me. Sounds idiotic, and I'm savvy to that now, but walking out of the dark theater into the mall parking lot, the blazin'-hot August sun screaming down, I felt that film move me like a calling from God.

Needless to say, I'm not among any elite faggy batch of specialized pilots. Drugs were by far the most invigorating thing in my life. At first, I had aspirations. I wanted to go into Special Forces, Airborne Rangers, eventually maybe the FBI. Now my confidence was broken. Christy had been responsible for all the best elements of my life. I missed her. I wished I'd never met her. I wanted to die, so the unavoidability of my disappointing her would be avoided.

"You're leaving me, aren't you?" Christy had asked.

She worked in the hospital, and we were on the seventh floor sitting in the cafeteria breaking up, both of us dressed in our uniforms. She was in her usual hospital garb, a blue skirt and blue blouse with her Social Services ID badge pinned to her chest, and I was in my normal office greens. Her tall lanky body was awkward in the small red metal chair, her skin was translucent, and her big apprehensive gray eyes were trapped underneath tortoiseshell oval glasses. God, I didn't want to hurt her.

"Come on, Jimmy, you're leaving me, aren't you?" she asked again.

"Yes," I said.

"You make me sick," she whispered. "People have always told me about this feeling, but I've never had it. It's awful." She spoke with empty eyes, as if it were already two years later.

We'd been going together for about eighteen months, and I don't know why but she loved the holy hell out of me.

"When you go back to your pea-brained friends and tell them how you've left me and how unstable I am, and they tell you what a psycho bitch I am and all that garbage, just remember that all they are is glad you're back drinking beer with them. They don't know you. They don't give a shit about you. And I do. I love you with my whole soul best, and if somebody else ever loves you as good as me, please remember there's nothing you have to *do,* just let them." She choked out a short laugh. "You're my greatest disappointment." She didn't kiss me good-bye, she just gave me another empty half-cocked smile, turned, and walked down the hall, her black leather shoes clacking on the shiny hospital floor.

A family was coming out of one of the neighboring houses and strolling onto Hawthorne Drive all dressed up in suits, dresses, and matching cute little outfits. They were heading off to church looking genuinely happy. I liked them. It's easy to like strangers, but difficult to like people you know well. I was sure I'd like the Andersons. Jesus, I didn't want Kevin to be dead.

Iowa University, my lieutenant went to Iowa University, that's all. Anybody can go to Iowa University. This was his job.

In one quick motion, I got out of my car and shut the door. I could hear how cold it was by the way the metal snapped shut. My body felt delicate, like if my fingers touched anything too hard, my whole hand might shatter. My head felt like a tarantula was gonna crawl out my nose. Things appear differently to me when I'm coming down off of drugs, like the kids climbing on trees are connected to the branches, and the tree is connected to the blowing breeze, and the breeze is connected back to me. If someone asks me if I believe in God, I shake my head like I couldn't give a shit, but the truth is, I do. I just don't know what to do about it.

The Andersons' front yard looked like a frozen-over version of Satan's lair. There were places the snow had melted and then frozen again in thin waves of ice. Weeds were poking their way through the ice out into the air. I could hear Ed's obnoxious laugh mocking me like a skipping CD inside my brain. What a moron. Walking up the driveway, I checked again to make sure my nose wasn't bleeding. The next drug test was in a couple of weeks. I was boned. Always, I had to push it. I tried not to be too mad at myself right then. There'd be plenty of time later.

The driveway was loaded with green bags of garbage. I wondered if the sanitation department was on strike or if Kevin had simply spaced on trash day. I didn't want to go inside. The front porch was loaded with broken toys—a Big Wheel with the front plastic tire worn through, action figures twisted with their legs curled up around their shoulders and wrapped around their backs in impossible positions. All kinds of pathetic playthings in neon colors were half buried in the icy snow.

The front porch was made of wood and had started rotting probably thirty years ago. It seemed to be held together by a half inch of ice. Somebody was bound to slip and crack their head wide fuckin' open. Why didn't Kevin shovel his front walk? He was obviously not an outrageously gifted soldier. Being dead should've been my first clue.

It was unfathomable that I had to do this. Ridiculous.

Recently, I'd been having a problem where I couldn't stop crying—more like weeping, really. The realization that I was not someone I was proud of would slap me in the face. I'd be in the Blue Sunrise laughing or drinking or smoking a joint, or rambling on about boats or cars or guns or pussy or some newfangled anything, and then I'd just go into the bathroom and sit in the stall and bawl my eyes out. I wanted to be alone, but I leaped at every bullshit opportunity to surround myself with more people.

There was this empty hole in my chest; I could almost hear it. Sometimes I'd think I was hungry, or that I had to take a shit, or that I needed to get laid or have a cigarette, or maybe if I drank five shots in rapid succession I could wet it and fill it up, but I'd do all that and this desolate hole under my rib cage would still be there: right above my stomach and below my heart.

If I sat still and took a deep long breath I could grab it or touch it— almost. But when I did that, I'd get scared like there was some big lie about to burst open.

God, I don't want to change, I thought. I just don't.

Turn on the radio, go to the movies, drive out to the drop zone, and jump out of a friggin' airplane. Do anything you want. Just don't sit still.

As I knocked on the screen door with my bare cold knuckles pain shot through my hand. I wondered what I'd do if Jesus Christ himself answered the door. My dad loved Jesus; he talked about him all the time, about the value of powerlessness.

For a moment I considered my appearance, brushing off my pants and jacket, running my fingers through my cropped hair, softly patting my mustache, checking again to make sure my nose wasn't bleeding. The wind blew through my rayon uniform, and my teeth started chattering. I knocked again, this time with the butt of my fist. There was the faint sound of cartoons coming from inside. When I was a kid, they didn't have cartoons on Sunday.

An older black woman with a long purple down parka hanging over a crimson dress opened the front door but left the screen door closed. Nobody'd put up the storm windows yet. A welcome mat at my feet read GO AWAY. The old woman had thick gray wool socks on over her black stockings and no shoes. She was overweight, with healthy bright skin. Her eyes were extremely light brown, the whites a faint yellow. Two children, a boy of about four and a girl barely old enough to feed herself, were seated behind her in the kitchen munching on Honey Nut Cheerios and watching a sixteen-inch television that sat on the plastic tablecloth.

"Yes?" she said. She had a soft rich voice, probably sang in the church choir.

I didn't say anything.

"Who is it? Who is it?" the elder child shouted out.

"It's nobody!" she yelled back. "Eat'cher breakfast and watch the TV." She turned back to me and smiled. "If you're looking for Kevin, he's not here."

"No," I said, "I'm looking for his wife. Is that you?"

"No, sweetie, I'm his mother. Tangerine's upstairs asleep, but I wouldn't recommend waking her up for no reason." She smiled, expecting me to leave.

"Well, that's OK. I guess I can talk to you if that's all right?" I didn't have the first idea how I was going to go about doing this. This wasn't my job.

"Sure, come on in," she said, pushing open the screen door. "Is everything OK?"

"Yeah, sure," I lied, quickly concealing Anderson's folder.

"Well, you don't look too good, darlin'."

"Oh, no. I'm just cold." I checked my nose again. It still wasn't bleeding.

"Kevin's not in any trouble or anything, is he? You're not with the MPs?"

"No. No, I'm not with the MPs." I laughed, as if it were nothing all that serious. The heat inside their place was oppressive, I thought I might pass out. My head began to swell, and I was forcefully aware of its weight.

"Does this mean we don't have to go to church?" the little boy asked hopefully, looking up from the television.

"Does WHAT mean WHAT?" the old woman said, looking back over at the kid.

"You said if there was someone here to watch us, we wouldn't have to go to church," he said simply.

"This man ain't gonna save you. Your only hope was your father, and it don't look like he's gonna show up in time." She took the kid's head in her hand and rotated it back toward the television set. "Have a seat," she said, turning to me and removing some newspapers from one of the chairs around the table.

I sat down next to the boy. The table was littered with lottery tickets.

"What's your name?" I asked the kid. He looked up at me, handsome with cropped hair, light brown skin, and huge black eyes.

"Harper," he said.

"That's a cool name."

"I know." He nodded.

"So, what's your business?" the old woman asked me. She was standing by the refrigerator lightly rubbing her arms over her parka. The kitchen was pretty clean. The walls were painted blue. There were too many knickknacks and junk, but overall the house was well kept.

"I used to hate to go to church too," I said, smiling.

"And now you go all the time?" she asked cynically.

"No, I still don't go too much. Not at all, actually, but I would like to go sometime." In that moment I seriously contemplated the possibility.

"You might should try," she said. She was from the South. I wondered how she'd made her way this far north. "Why are you here, son?" she asked again. There was only a slight trace of impatience in her voice. The sound of the imbecilic television seemed to be growing in volume. It's amazing how immersed children can be in cartoons without laughing at all.

"Could I have something to drink? Would that be all right?" I asked, touching my face. There was something wrong with my mouth. That always happens to me when I do drugs, like I'm trying to chew my own face off from the inside out. I can't stop cranking my jaw around and gnashing on the inside of my cheeks.

"All we have is tomato juice," she said, without moving.

"That would be great."

"You want tomato juice?" she asked incredulously, forcing me to meet her eyes.

"If you don't mind."

She opened up the fridge, took out a bottle of tomato juice, and poured me some in a small blue cup.

"Harper, take your sister in the other room."

"Why?"

His grandmother gave him a sharp look. "Are we not going to church?" he asked softly.

"Maybe not," she said, looking at me.

"Yes, yes, yes!" he cheered and grabbed his and his sister's bowls and put them both in the sink. *"Hot-diggity, dog-diggity, boom whatcha do ta me,"* he shouted at his sister, and then grabbed her hand and dragged her into the other room, chattering to her the whole time about the benefits of blowing off church.

"Uh, look, here's the deal," I said the millisecond we were alone, opening up the army file I had tucked under my arm. "Your son Private Kevin Anderson was shot and killed last night outside the base in an altercation that occurred in the parking lot of the Paradise Bar. His body is being held at the Medical Center, where the exact time of death, complete medical outline, and profile of any criminality are waiting for you." I was doing good, looking down at Kevin's folder and occasionally back up at her. "Kevin is owed a military funeral provided for by the U.S. Army. Other benefits and outstanding information will be given to you with the body. It is army priority and policy to inform the next of kin at the earliest possible conven . . . opportunity. And uh . . . that's my job today." All that crap jettisoned out of my mouth. I've been living with the army long enough that their whole mumbo-jumbo vocabulary comes pretty easy to me, even when I'm swishing my mouth around like a coke fiend.

There was a long silence as this woman looked me square in the eyes. I tried to sit still.

"Do you do this all the time?" she asked, with no visible reaction to the information I just gave her.

"No, it's no one's job. It rotates. This month the responsibility falls to my lieutenant, who in turn assigned it to me. In fairness, however, I should explain this is not supposed to be my job." I checked my nose again and took a sip of tomato juice. The juice was warm and gnarly-tasting. The refrigerator must've been on the fritz. "I'm awfully sorry," I added. I was feeling a tiny bit better.

"Are you on drugs?" she asked me.

My whole body tightened as if I were about to have a seizure. I shook my head no.

"Are you on drugs?" she asked again.

"Yes." I nodded meekly.

"Is my son really dead?"

"Yes," I said.

"GET THE FUCK OUT OF MY HOUSE," she shrieked, and threw the bottle of tomato juice at my head. It bounced off the table and rolled onto the floor without breaking. Violence is so tame in real life. The cap had fallen off, and there was tomato juice everywhere. The mess would take forever to clean up. Quietly, the two children crept up the hall behind their grandmother, grabbing her leg and the bottom of her parka.

"What's wrong, Grandma?" Harper asked, looking at me.

"Get out of my house," she said, this time quietly and sternly. I didn't move. I couldn't. I wanted to tell her I understood how she felt—I never wanted to be in the army, it was a whim that'd turned into two and a half years of drinking. I was better than this. This was the worst day of my life.

My father had committed suicide, and the life I was supposed to be living had died with him. I promised myself that if I lived till tomorrow, and if my nose didn't fall off my face, I would change. The first thing I'd do is get Christy back, and she'd help me figure out a way to make all this better.

Kevin's mother walked over to the door and opened it for me to leave. With the file still in my hand, I moved over to the door and went to step out. I turned around to tell her one more time how I was sorry, and she bitch-slapped me hard on the side of my head. My nose started to bleed. I stepped out, pushing open the screen door. The cold air numbed my throbbing face.

"Hey, you," she called out, pissed-off tears welling up in her eyes. I turned around. "What's your name?" she yelled through the screen.

"What?" I said, still holding my nose. Any second, I was gonna start sobbing.

"You never told me your name. You never even introduced yourself."

"James," I said. "Staff Sergeant James Heartsock Junior." My father would've been so disappointed in me.

"Well, Jimmy Heartsock, I will never forget you."

INTRODUCING
CHRISTY ANN WALKER

THE COLD AIR SNAPPED in my lungs as I walked across the gravel-pitted asphalt, bit my lip, and took that long step up onto the Adirondack Trailways bus.

O my holy, everliving, and gracious God, please help me.

I showed the guy my ticket and wondered if he could tell I was pregnant. I could feel Jimmy's breath behind me. *Don't go, baby,* I heard him whisper. *Let's make love.* His fingers, I imagined, gripped my biceps, tugging me, pulling my shoulder around back toward him. I stepped down the aisle, one foot at a time. He hadn't called; I thought he would have. I couldn't cry anymore. What would he say, I wondered, when he found out I was carrying our child, when he discovered I was gone?

Moving down between the rows of seats, I picked one in the middle by the window. The upholstery was a faded blue and green plastic. Fifteen years ago this bus was clean, with vibrant colors. Now, every aspect of it was dull. There were ashtrays that flipped open inside the armrests. I wanted a cigarette. I was dizzy with that desire. Opening my purse, I took out a cold fractured stick of spearmint gum and placed it in my mouth. I could feel Jimmy kissing me, the warmth of his tongue. He liked to approach a kiss from the side, starting with the corner of my lips. I could feel the soft hairs of his mustache, the roughness of his chin, tickling me. My neck would get blotchy and red whenever we made out.

When we were in a fight, or if I was scared he might leave, I'd take my comforter and a pillow and sleep on the carpet, with my back against the door. Oh, fuck, I'll miss him forever.

A man sat beside me, jostling me up and down. I didn't even look at him. He smelled slightly. I wanted to be alone. The plastic of the seat was hard and cold. My pillow, I thought; I've forgotten my pillow. The bus engine made those exhaling sighs, the wheels slowly started to spin, the world that I had known began to inch away, and in that instant I died.

You are nothing, I chanted to myself, and that made me feel better. I took a deep breath and ran my fingers through my hair.

Nothing you will ever do will matter. Your life, and that of everyone on this bus, doesn't matter any more than the trees outside. Earthworms matter the same as you. All our lives are passing. My child's life will come and go, as will my grandmother's. This bus will someday rest among a heap of other buses, and no one will know I sat here. Upon my death, my story will float out into such a mass of stories that my voice will be absorbed unheard. You are nothing. Nothing is important.

I said this over and over to myself. No awareness of identity existed inside me. For that instant I was dead.

The pisser is, I've died before.

We pulled out through town. There were still heaps of snow piled along the curbs, black and sooty from car exhaust and other miscellaneous garbage. The traffic signs were shaking in the wind. The whole of Albany was covered in a winter film of grime.

I had been awake seven hours and still had not smoked.

The man next to me shuffled in his seat. He was an attractive dark-skinned black man. He did smell slightly, not badly but soft and salty like I'd imagine a desert smells. His skin was a deep midnight black and his hands were strong, laced with wide veins that you could see slightly beating with his blood. He was wearing sunglasses with reflective forest-green lenses. The white February light was beaming intensely on his face but I couldn't see his eyes at all, just his high cheekbones and images in his glasses of the light moving outside.

We drove along slowly. The only time that I ever seem calm, and a gentleness eases the scratching under my skin, is when I'm moving. I'm like a baby that way. Some of my favorite memories were of sitting on the black vinyl bench seat of Jimmy's Chevy Nova as he drove us to get some videos. In his car there's nothing to do. There was the hum of the asphalt underneath us and the vibration of the engine. Everything else could wait till we got to the video store.

The bus stopped briefly at a toll booth and circled onto Interstate 87.

I took another deep breath, tried to relax my shoulders, turned, and stared out the window. Jimmy's Nova is silver with two black racing stripes down the center. It was difficult to keep from searching for him. Faintly, I could see my reflection in the glass in front of me. I'd cut my hair and dyed it raven black. It made me look more mature, but underneath I still felt like a teenager. I tried to sit perfectly still and not speak. I made a decision to be silent for the entire journey.

The man next to me took off one of his jackets, dug into the knapsack under his seat, bumped me hard several times, and sat back up with a 40-ounce beer wrapped in a brown paper bag. In between his thumb and forefinger, in green ink, on his black skin, was a tattoo of a half moon. You could barely make it out.

He muttered inaudibly a few words of what seemed like a prayer of gratitude and opened the beer. It popped and sprayed a mess dripping down onto his lap, but he didn't care. He casually wiped the spilled beer into his pants.

He was staring straight ahead, but somehow he felt me observing him. "You going all the way to Manhattan?" he said.

His voice was higher than I would've thought, not delicate or fragile but vulnerable and warm. He was wearing a thick wool cap with wide stitching and a down vest over a canvas jacket. The jacket was zipped right up to his chin; underneath I could see the edge of a beige turtleneck. He had a little scar on his forehead over his right eye. I could see the tops of his scraggly eyebrows sticking out from underneath his glasses. On one of his fingers was a large silver ring that read PROTECT ME FROM WHAT I WANT. His face and body were wide and powerful but also tender and round. He was big, taller than I am. He weighed a lot, you could tell. He had a short cropped mustache, like Jimmy's, only with a completely different kind of hair. Jimmy's mustache is a bit wispy. You can't say that to him, but it's true.

"First I'm going to Manhattan," I said, trying to be curt without being hostile. The light had now moved so it was shining directly in my face.

"Where you going after that?" he asked.

"Texas," I said, my vow of silence abandoned.

"I won't bother you if you don't want to talk," he went on. "I don't need to talk, is what I'm saying." He turned and looked at me. I still couldn't see his eyes. "If I could change one thing about myself, I would stop speaking entirely."

He was quiet. I clicked the ashtray open and closed.

"Why?" I asked finally. My hands were still cold. I warmed them by pressing them upside down along my neck as if I were choking myself.

"Well, because I've never said anything of any real value in my entire life." He smiled. "I can yabble on at the mouth, telling people how I *feel,* asking them how they *feel,* but it's just fillin' the world up with more noise." He was sitting perfectly still, his hands, centered in his lap, gently holding the beer can.

I had sex with a black guy once. He was skinny and neurotic, not like this guy at all.

"It's nice to be understood," I said quietly.

"Thank you," he replied. I wasn't sure what he meant.

I poked through my purse and dug out a matchbook and began apprehensively picking my teeth with the corner of the cardboard. I've always done that: picked my teeth with an inappropriate object. It's a habit that annoys Jimmy. He picks his ear and smells his finger. *That's* the most peculiar habit *I've* ever seen.

"If I could, I wouldn't even think," I said softly.

"You'd be like an animal?" He turned to look at me again. All I could see were his green glasses and a mutated reflection of myself.

"Well, yes—like a good animal. An owl or something."

"Owls are good?" he asked.

I nodded. There was a long pause. He turned away and looked straight ahead. His movements were calm and deliberate. He had beautiful lips.

"An owl is wise, correct?" he asked.

"Correct," I answered. "Wise and good."

"I'd be a bear," he said definitively. "Nobody eats a bear. Top of the food chain."

"Nobody eats owls. I don't think." I'd never heard of anyone eating an owl. There was another long silence between us. It started to seem as though our conversation had ended.

I wished I'd had more friends. I don't know what happened; in high school it seemed like I had so many. The only person I'd been close to in Albany, besides Jimmy, was my old roommate, Chance. She was married now, with a baby son, and our friendship had altered into something I didn't recognize.

The bus moved down through New York State. On the right side of the highway you could see old weatherbeaten mountains, the

Catskills. Sometimes a gust of wind would hit the side of the bus so hard I could feel it shove us inches over into the next lane. We were passing farm after farm. At the turn of the last century, 80 percent of Americans were involved in agriculture. Now there's less than 10 percent. Jimmy talks about that all the time. He loves history.

"Thoughts have value," the man next to me said, breaking the quiet. "They shape what we do. I wouldn't give up thinkin'. You never do something without thinking about it first."

"Still, if I could, I'd behave with more spontaneity, not second-guessing myself all the time, you know?"

"Thank you," he said again, only this time a little too loudly, and slowly dragging out his speech. Then he was mute again. I still wasn't sure what he meant.

We sat for a long while without speaking, as we passed exit after exit on the highway. The bus was about half full. All of a sudden I felt hot and took off my jacket and my sweatshirt. They crackled with static electricity. Cooler now, I sat there in a blank white V-neck T-shirt. I might've just had a hot flash. The only real symptom of pregnancy, I noticed, was that I was uncomfortable in any position, for no good reason. Also, things seemed to smell bad, and everything that wasn't ice cold tasted rotten. I had my shoes off and my arms wrapped around my knees. However I situated myself, it wasn't right. I wished I'd remembered my pillow.

Hundreds and thousands of cars were passing purposefully in the opposite direction: red cars, white cars, minivans, sport utility vehicles, cars with kids and personalized license plates, and trucks, massive trucks. Automobiles are the leading cause of death in this country, and still everyone wants a new car.

The highway felt like a river, winding and weaving along the Hudson, bouncing us along as if we were leaves. We passed gas stations and chain food restaurants, with their billboards advertising happiness. I know the images in magazines and on TV aren't true representations of the world; I mean, that's obvious. But I still get this sinking feeling of disappointment, as if it is the world I *should* see.

Every five minutes or so the man next to me would take a small, very calm sip of his beer and then rest his hands in his lap. You don't see that very often—someone sitting peacefully without any extra movement. His head was swaying lightly with the rocking of the bus. I stared at him. He still hadn't taken off his sunglasses or his knit cap or unzipped his jacket.

"Are you blind?" I asked.

"You didn't notice?" He grinned.

"No." I studied his face. I felt like somehow he'd tricked me.

"Are *you* blind?" he asked, and laughed a big cocky laugh.

"No, just self-involved," I said.

"Thank you!" He laughed again and slapped his hands hard, twice, against his knees. I put my legs down on the floor in their correct position. For some reason blind people make me self-conscious.

When I was thirteen my dad made me take this blind girl, Alison, from our church youth group, to Wet 'n' Wild. It was an amusement park full of water slides and wave pools and hundreds of half-naked teenagers running around with sodas. Not only could Alison not see, she was also extremely short. The two might have been connected— kidney problems, I think—but I was already tall and it added to how awkward I felt around her. I held her hand as we walked around the park, doing all the low-key slides in tandem. She was sweet but a pain in the ass; all she wanted to do was wade in the children's pool and place her vagina directly over a small bubbling fountain. "This feels *fantastic*," she would say loudly. "Oh, my goodness!" she'd exclaim. "*Wow*, you have to try this!"

All of a sudden, this businessman sitting in the row in front of me on the Trailways reclined his chair all the way back. I could see his beanie little balding scalp peeking up over the seat arrogantly. I was so uncomfortable I could've screamed. Taking my jacket and my sweater, I tried to position them under my legs and against the armrests. I tried to place any item I could to soften the space between me and the edges. Sitting all the way to Texas was never going to happen.

"Are you very beautiful?" asked the blind man.

"What do you mean?"

"I imagine that you are very beautiful."

"Why?" I asked. I couldn't tell if he was being lecherous. I wanted to like him.

He took a long pause and caressed his mustache with his whole hand. "I just have an image of you in my head, and you're attractive. I don't mean to offend you or make you uncomfortable," he said, in a removed tone, and took a sip from his beer.

"It's OK," I said, and adjusted myself away from him.

I missed Jimmy. I didn't want to go to freakin' Texas. Grandmother was so old now. She was the only one I wanted to see, but I knew it'd be depressing. When I'd speak to her over the phone, all she'd talk to me about was the time she met Eleanor Roosevelt.

Grandmother was a sixth-grade music teacher in Abilene, Texas, and Mrs. Roosevelt was rumored to be visiting her school as a part of some educational tour. Grandmother made herself a new dress and wore it every day religiously, waiting for the First Lady to arrive. After eleven days of wearing the same outfit, Eleanor did finally come, and she noticed Grandmother and actually commented on the dress, saying it looked like "desert flowers." As Grandmother has grown older, that experience has ballooned in its importance. It was her only contact with something she knew to be "real."

I felt my belly. I wasn't showing, but if you knew me well you could tell. My butt was expanding. If Jimmy had half a brain he would've noticed. I was averaging three ice creams a day.

I stared out the window, and my thoughts turned to my own mother, Mary. She left me with the neighbors when I was twelve months old and never returned. They called my dad, who rescued me and took me home to Grandmother's. I always thought there was no excuse for that kind of behavior. But now, with a baby of my own coming, I didn't feel confident enough to judge anyone.

My mother and I didn't meet again till I was fourteen, in Austin, at Woolworth's. The Woolworth's on Congress Avenue was gigantic, not small and dumpy like the ones they ended up having but really big, like a slightly upscale Kmart. Sometimes my dad would drop me off there, to occupy me for a while, if he had a business lunch or some other appointment. I liked it there; the hours passed quickly. When you first walked in, all you could smell was popcorn and candy. As you strolled up the hospital-clean floors, you got a different smell for each section: Makeup, hardware, clothes, they all had their own smell. I would glide around, looking at the magazines or just pacing the aisles enjoying the air-conditioning.

In back was a dumpy little restaurant that smelled like burgers and corn dogs. One Sunday I was sitting there, drinking a vanilla Coke, when a woman with auburn hair, pulled up tight in a bun, walked over and stood in front of me. She was tall. I looked up at her. She was wearing a deep-yellow, floor-length dress, with red flowers on it. I was wearing a tan skirt and a blue blouse, left over from church.

"You're Christy?" she asked.

I nodded.

"Hi, I'm Mary Larson. I'm your mother."

"Oh," I said. There was a long pause. I was instantaneously petrified. She might as well have been the Grim Reaper.

My mother was ravishing. Sweet blue eyes and a long voluptuous figure. She could've been a model, easy.

"What are you doing here?" I asked.

"Your father told me you'd be here."

He was sly like a fox, my father.

"You can sit down if you want," I said. "Is that what you want? I mean, do you want to sit down?"

"I'd like to, yes," she said. She had a strong southern accent. She smiled, smoothed her dress across her legs with her hand, and seated herself.

She brought out a small gift-wrapped box and handed it to me. I didn't open it. I hate opening a present in front of the person who is giving it to you. I poked it around the Formica table, feeling disoriented.

"Your daddy's getting to be a big shot these days, huh?" she asked, in an overly warm tone. My father had been elected to the Texas State Legislature.

"Why are you here?" I asked.

My mother's smile dropped. She began methodically running her hands over each other as if she were washing them. "I wanted to meet you."

"Oh."

"This must be very difficult for you," she said, picking at her bright red fingernail polish. "It's difficult for me." She looked familiar to me, not like I recognized her as my mother, but more like maybe I'd seen her on a TV show.

"Where have you been?" I asked. I was flicking my clogs off and on under the table.

"I live here in Austin."

"You do? Why?" I couldn't believe it.

"I don't know. This is my home."

"I thought you'd moved to California or something."

"I did. But I moved back," she said. She stopped fussing with her hands and appeared to try and force herself to be still.

"Oh. You look so familiar," I said.

"I'm your mother."

There was another pause. Mary reached over and gently caressed my arm. I wanted to swat her away.

"Do you play any sports?" she asked.

"What?"

"You look like such a big strong girl," she said, with her palm on top of the back of my hand.

"That's a stupid thing to say," I said.

"I'm sorry," she said, withdrawing her arm.

"It's just a stupid thing to say."

"I'm sorry," my mother said again. "You're right."

"I mean, no, I don't play any sports. Do you?" I continued, my own hostility surprising me.

"Do you have a boyfriend?" she asked.

I couldn't look at her. "No," I said.

"You will, you're very beautiful."

"Thanks, so are you," I said. That was true. Her skin shimmered in the light and her hands were long like mine but more feminine. Her teeth betrayed her; they were an off shade of yellow and had little black lines along the gums.

"Thank you," she said. There was a silence. "Do you like your stepmother?"

"Yes," I said, which wasn't true. "She's funny. She tells a lot of jokes." I decided to try and help out with the conversation. "You know, she'll say something silly, like a pun, and then say, 'No pun intended.' It's funny." I was rambling. "Do you know what I mean?" I asked.

"No. What do you mean?" Mary asked me.

My mother's stare scared me. She looked a little crazy. Her eyes moved too quickly. My mouth went dry. Then I recognized her. Oh, my God, she worked there. My mother worked in the makeup department at Woolworth's. I'd seen her half a dozen times. For a period of five months my father had been dropping me off while he "ran errands," so my mother could get a good look at me.

We spoke for a while that day, a pretty uneventful conversation. She was moving to Houston. She had a boyfriend. The gift she gave me was a locket with a picture of the two of us when I was about three months old. She offered up a few half-baked explanations about why she left me. She was a baby herself. She was an idiot. She was having a nervous breakdown. Whatever. She didn't offer an apology. I know for a fact she didn't, because that's what I was listening for.

"I know you think we don't know each other at all," Mary said to me, when we shook hands good-bye, "we've been apart so long, but I do know you. You're exactly like I thought you'd be. You were always such a terrific kid."

The second I walked out, I threw the locket away. I don't know why, I didn't even think about it. Right there on Congress Avenue, I jammed it down into an already full garbage can.

. . .

Through the spotty bus window I could see hundreds of brown trees against the gray of week-old snow. In front of a farmhouse off in the distance I saw a lonely coyote-type dog chained to a big red doghouse. The dirt in front of him was littered with pits and holes he must've dug. The animal himself was sitting tranquilly on the roof of the doghouse, staring at the passing traffic, his chain hanging slack from his neck.

A motorcycle drove right beside us, below my window. The guy on it looked miserable. He wasn't properly dressed.

"Do I sound like anything else?" I asked the blind man sitting next to me. I wasn't sure whether a second or an hour had passed. "I mean, other than pretty?"

"What do you mean?" He leaned his head down closer to me as if to hear better.

"People can look like a kind person or an honest person or they can look shifty." I was still facing the window, peering blankly out at the man on his motorcycle and the passing landscape.

"May I touch you?" he asked quietly. He was still peacefully seated, facing directly forward, with his hands wrapped around the beer can in his lap.

"Where?" Suddenly I was afraid. I react to any and every new situation with the exact same body-chemical result: adrenaline.

"Your face, your chest, your skin." He spoke in a perfectly normal tone of voice, not sly, not aggressive.

"My breasts?" I asked.

"Your heart," he replied.

"Are you flirting with me?" I couldn't help but grin.

"Are you flirting with me?" Now he was grinning.

"You can touch me if you want," I said, trying to sound casual. I thought maybe I should face more toward him, but I didn't want to come off slutty. For the first time in weeks my mood was lifting. This was a new experience. It felt exciting, like waking up.

He rubbed his hands together to heat them and blew a steady stream of warm moist breath into them. The skin on the underside of his hands was close to the same shade of pink as my own. First he reached up—he was on my left—and put his right hand on my left shoulder, as if to hold me still.

"Breathe," he said, and placed his left hand ever so gently across my face. He drew his finger around the sockets of my eyes and traced the bridge of my nose as if my face were a Braille poem. My skin rippled with goose pimples, like I'd never been touched before. It was all I could do to leave his hand there. Every fractional move of his fingertips tickled like a soft wind against a bare nerve.

"You have a prominent nose," he said.

"Obvious, even to a blind man." I laughed nervously. This takes the cake, I thought.

He held the flat of his palm against my cheek. I stared at him. I wanted to see his eyes, to make eye contact. I imagined his irises to be gray and dead—or perhaps they were clear and luminescent, like the eyes of a saint.

After Jimmy told me he didn't love me, I cried for eight straight days. I went to work, I was pleasant, but in the bathroom and in the back hospital stairway where we used to smoke, I cried. I was a hollow glass sculpture of myself. A loud noise would've broken me into a thousand shards.

I didn't know what I would live for. Jimmy, I had thought, would take me away from my selfishness. I longed for some kind of center, some starting place from which I could judge how I was doing. How long can you live, opening your eyes in the morning, going to the bathroom, listening to the birds chirping, the cars driving by, and thinking, How can I please *myself* today?

Not one person had touched me in the eight days since Jimmy and I'd broken up. His black hand was hot against the skin around my mouth. I'm sure my face was cherry red, and my neck was breaking out in hives.

He touched my lips. My stomach flipped up into my lungs.

"I'm pregnant," I announced.

"Congratulations," he answered softly.

"I'm all alone," I said.

This was so embarrassing. For a moment we both were perfectly still and silent together. Then he touched my eye again and then reached across my face and touched the other, wiping away the wetness.

"You're going to be fine," he said.

In some way this man was not real to me, not human, more like a ghost or a vision. I wondered if I could put my hand right through his chest. I felt if I took my eyes off him even for a second, the spell would break and a dove would fly up from his empty seat.

Mustering all the courage I had, I said, "I'm very afraid."

"No reason," he said, dropping his hand to my neck. I was sure he could feel the whamming thud of my heart. "No reason for fear at all."

He lowered his hand till it rested on the top of my chest, and his long fingers played along my throat. I worried people were looking at us. The sun was beginning to pull behind the mountains, creating gold streaks of light, shooting through the bus, hitting some people's hair and making it appear as if their heads were glowing with fire. Others were left cold in the shadow. Everyone was oblivious of us.

Outside, it was nasty cold.

He moved his hand now on top of my cotton T-shirt and placed himself right between both my breasts. His skin was heated and encompassing like an electric blanket.

We'd be in Kingston soon.

I could feel my pulse in my fingertips, and the blood swooshing through the ventricles of my heart. Taking a deep breath, I scraped my fingers across the nail of my thumb, wondering how many molecules, how many atoms, were inside of me that were once part of another person's body.

I could hear his breathing beside me. I felt good. I did. I was aware of a sleeping confidence within me. I was not dead, I was alive. There would be life after Jimmy, and it had begun now. I tried to slide away from his hand, but he kept it firmly placed and moved it across my chest, passing over my erect nipple and resting directly on top of my left breast over my heart.

"Would it bother you if I mentioned God?" he said in a whisper.

"Yes," I said. "It'd scare the shit out of me."

SMART WENT CRAZY

MAN, WHEN I FIRST MET CHRISTY, and this is no joke—a cliché, but no joke—it was like my heart was literally stuck on my esophagus. I couldn't fuckin' talk to her; I was mute. I remember the first thing I ever said to her. We were over at the Coach and Horses Tavern in downtown Albany. We'd been introduced maybe fifteen minutes before, and I leaned over to the guy who introduced us and said, "Does everybody fall in love with her?" She was sitting at this circular wooden table smoking cigarettes like some people eat grapes. I don't remember what she was talking about—something to do with the Apollo Theatre in New York. I was just hung up on her voice: the cadence and the confidence. She had *class,* man. No shit, not one person in a hundred has intrinsic class—not affectation or money, not some lamebrain in a million-dollar gown drinking a highball or a private school chippie sashaying around like her daddy owned the joint, but natural poise, grace, dignity. She had that. You could take her and rub her around in the mud and kick her in the head and she'd still have

it. Seated there in the green tavern light, with six or seven people listening to her every word, I lean over and say, "Does everybody fall in
love with her?" Why did I say that? I don't know. But still, I couldn't
talk to her 'cause I knew I'd just come off like another goomba trying
to score, so I played it cool and didn't say a peep till later. We were
standing in a hallway waiting for the bathroom right next to each
other in silence for like three or four minutes, and then I just blurted
out—and she'll back me up on this—I said, "I'm not afraid of you."
A bald-faced lie but gutsy; I'll give myself that. The men's-room door
opened and I walked in and closed it. In the mirror I could see
my reflection, and I looked good; I don't often say that about myself,
but that night it was true. I was clean-shaven, wearing a suit (there
had been some function earlier, a buddy of mine was graduating from
a Special Forces program, and I looked good). Later on, we all went
back to the apartment Christy shared with her roommate, Chance. We
all laughed and drank and Chance played the guitar, I remember that,
and slowly people started going home and then Chance and her
boyfriend, Bucky, went to bed. Somehow—I guess I'd been angling for
it all night long—Christy and I were left alone, sitting across from each
other on opposite couches, and she said, "So you're not afraid of me,
huh?"

I smiled, and she did the strangest thing—she just lifted up her
skirt and showed me her pussy.

About a year and a half later, out of fear and emotional necessity, I
broke it off with her. Eight days after that I'd arrived at an alternative
solution.

We were facing each other in the parking lot of the Kingston bus
station.

"I don't want to fuck around, so I'm just gonna do this." I had the
damn thing in my pocket, but my hands were freezing and I was having
trouble getting it out.

"Now, I got this from these very funky . . . artists—uh, jewelers, you know?—So I think you'll like it. It's handmade by some substantial craftsman, is what I'm saying."

Christy was in front of me poised like a wolf, long thin limbs balancing her weight, about to dart in four directions at once.

She'd stepped off the Trailways bus behind some poky old lady. Her blond hair was dyed and cut differently. I didn't say anything about it right off the bat, and I probably should have, but I'm bad with crap like that. She looked great, though, with her hair choppy, wild, and jet black. Her skin was all splotches of white and red from the cold and she was wrapped in a poofy black parka with her long blue-jeaned legs sticking out. She has a dynamite ass. If you look at her from the back you'd think she was a black chick. I could see breath steaming out from her cold blue lips as she stared down at me.

You have to work on your confidence when you're going with a girl like Christy. She's got a fireball for a brain, she's radiant—that's not an opinion or a compliment, that's just the way it *is*—and she's taller than me. It's easy to feel all bearlike and domineering when you got some kinda small-fry chippie to make your dick feel like it's ten miles long, but with a girl like Christy you gotta hang on tight to any sense of self you got. She's the best-looking girl I ever went out with, bar none.

Anyway, we were standing in the freezing cold of this bus station parking lot. The wind whipped fragments of garbage across the asphalt. Empty bags of chips and newspapers were swirling everywhere. Behind us was the on-ramp up to I-87. It was five-thirty in the afternoon, so rush-hour traffic was still stinking up the air and creating a dull spitting rumble of engines all around us. In half an hour it would be dark. Up above the highway you could see the Catskill Mountains. They're not grand or majestic; they seem more kind of tired and disappointed. They're old, though—noble, even. They deserve better than to be obscured by the billboards dotting the horizon. Oldest mountains in North America, the Catskills, that's a fact. There wasn't too much hustle-bustle there at the station, just a few commuters running to the bus trying to keep their hats on. I didn't have a hat on; neither did Christy. The point is we were both bitch cold, and my hands felt dead like clay. They didn't have any blood in them. I was dying to get this puny thing out of my pocket. Christy was already just one moment away from being pissed off. She hates being cold or out in the open. She's a very private person, and there's something vulnerable about a parking lot that I knew she wouldn't find appealing.

"You know, this screwball thing is fryin' a friggin' hole in my pocket," I said, as I finally dragged it out. My head was swimming. If you pushed me, I would've fallen on my butt. I'd been staring at this dinky bit of baggage since I got it. Something about the little thing made me dizzy. The longer she didn't know what I was doing there, the more irritated she'd get and the harder it would be to carry the whole thing off. I had to act quick.

"I got this made and everything so you'd know I wasn't fuckin' around and not being flaky. I would have spent more money on it, but I know you like things that are simple and elegant and classy—not, like, ostentatious. So it's classic, not cheap, OK?"

"Can we go inside, Jimmy?" Christy said, shivering. She had this expression like she was completely misinterpreting everything I was doing. She didn't comprehend what I was up to at all.

"Nah, nah, nah, we're not gonna go inside and do this whole business standing in front of some Coke machine. It's too important for that."

She was irritated I'd followed her down here, I could tell that, which I have to admit surprised me. I thought she'd be more romantic.

"This'll just take a second." I wanted to touch her, but her hands were in her pockets and she was being too still. Standoffish. I needed to do it; then she'd be in a good mood.

"All right, look, I'm just gonna do this, OK?"

She nodded. The extreme temperature was making her eyes sharp and fierce, and she was looking at me as if she half anticipated I'd change into a frog.

BAM. CABLOOEY. WHOOSH. My mind went blank.

"Uh. . . ." I was standing there dizzy, noticing the little bits of yellow sprinkled in her blue eyes. It wasn't that I was having doubts, it was like I was a whirlpool and had been for days. I was gradually gaining speed, spinning around faster and faster until here I was, only a blink away from blowing out the other side.

"I love you, and I don't ever want to be without you."

That was all I could remember to say.

I needed to kick it up a notch. Like I said, Christy's not dumb. She always knows exactly what everybody in a room is thinking. Push came to shove, I'd have to say she's the smartest person I know. She and my father.

Boy, she was looking at me hard. I felt like I was just a rib cage barely holding on to a collection of churning and gurgling organs.

"Here's the deal. If I imagine my life with you, I see all this light in my future, you understand? Like I picture it, and I can feel all kinds of good things, you know? Like growth and light and green things, and . . . and—"

Green things had thrown me off; I hadn't meant to say that. I was trying to be articulate.

"And without you, I just see, like, gray, like shit, you know? It's the same: nothin'."

In the middle of this parking lot, with the frozen February air blowing through our coats, I did it—I got down on my knees, both knees. My hands were so numb, it was difficult to unclench my fists. The ground was icy and uncomfortable. Little gravel stones of the pavement were grinding through my pants. I wasn't wearing anything special, and I really should have. I had on my dad's corduroy coat with the sheepskin lining and some junky green fatigues. I should've shaved. Christy's always moaning about my scratchy face. I could've dressed better and shaved—I'm sorry about that—but everything else I did the only way I knew how.

The truth is, I'd wanted to do this whole dance in her crummy house, with Willie Nelson and Merle Haggard's album *Pancho and*

Lefty playing on her old turntable. Things were working out differently from what I'd foreseen, but I was feeling good about how I was rolling with the punches: adjusting efficiently to an alternative action.

The little black box was out in my hand where Christy could see it. I remember the exact expression on her face when I got down on my knees. She was perplexed, definitely. She was also a little self-conscious that I might be making a spectacle of myself, but nobody on God's asphalt earth was looking at us. It was too cold.

"Christy Ann Walker"—I wanted to be formal, lend myself some gravity—"will you marry me?"

Fuck, I loved this girl so much. I don't know how she did it, but I felt like she *was* me. I think that was why I'd broken up with her: I was fighting for myself, for the old me who had lived before we'd ever met—but then there I was, all alone again, and I realized there *was* no old me anymore, only this one.

"I love you, and I bought you this ring to be a symbol that this is no joke. I had 'em make it a little extra big, 'cause they told me it was easier to get these things reduced than expanded. So don't take it as some kinda sign, or metaphor, or analogy, or something, if it doesn't fit right. It *will* fit right eventually, OK? I promise."

I opened up the case, revealing the ring. It was a beautiful delicate thing with two little diamonds centering a third larger diamond. I'd designed it to match this toy jobby I bought for her when we first met. She used to wear that toy ring even after two of the phony gems fell out.

She was flabbergasted.

Which, like I said, surprised me. It just goes to show you, how when two people spend time apart, they can be thinking in completely opposite directions and coming to radically different conclusions and forming geometrically opposed interpretations about the same events that transpired between them, and—all the while—feel they've arrived at some mutual understanding.

Christy had her hands in her pockets and was looking down at me and this diamond ring. She'd begun biting her upper lip. A terribly sober expression had taken over her face. I thought she'd be crying by now and covering me with kisses—which in hindsight was unrealistic.

"I've thought a lot about this. I'm not a rash man. You know that." I paused, waiting for her to meet my eyes.

She nodded her head slowly.

"I thought this through, and I want to be your husband. For real. No shit. Sometimes you gotta take a good look at your life and ask yourself, What kind of man do you want to be? And what steps are you willing to take to be that man? Do you understand what I'm saying?"

She was listening. I desperately wanted her to hear me, to witness the changes I'd been going through. I touched her leg. She bent down and crouched beside me. My eyes were tearing up.

"People are always talking about how much they *love* somebody, or how significant *love* is, you know? But what are they willing to *do* about it? Mostly nothing. But, you see, I love you *and* I'm willing to do something about it. I want to be there for you all the time. I want you to be able to count on me, and I want the chance to prove that I can be counted on. I want to stop fantasizing about some fictional *me* I hold in my head, that *could* live if 'this' happened or *would* live if 'that' happened, and I want to *be* somebody right now. Some fuckin' integrity, you know? Some beliefs. I believe in you and me and in what my dad taught me: There is no obstacle that enough love cannot move.

"And you and I know you're the best thing that ever happened to me, and, yes, that's an expression, something people *say*, that has no meaning, but what I mean is there isn't anybody in the whole world who has loved me the way you have, not my mother, not my old man, not my friends, and you're also so damn beautiful and"—now I whispered this part—"you make the best love I've ever known and your pussy is so sweet, I love the way it tastes and smells and I love that soft flesh around it, and you're so smart and you're funny and you're nice, and I whack myself in my dingy head, and I think, How could I let this girl go? What do I want? What am I hoping for? Nobody likes to talk about it, but we're all gonna die someday. Dead. Eyes closed. Right? Ashes to ashes, dust to dust. It's true, right?"

She nodded.

"There's nothing preventing me and you from loving each other and being some kinda world-class shining beacon of love except how bad do we want it and what are we willing to do for it?" I took a deep breath, long, even, into my guts. I let my head teeter back into balance. My knees were killing me, so I shifted my butt and sat right down on the pavement. "Now, I know I did you wrong, and I was freaking out and being stupid and I was mean to you. You know sometimes I get *all fuckin' confused*"—I raised my voice and pulled at the short hairs on my head—"and I can't see outside of my own asshole. I'm unhappy. I'm unhappy. Why am I unhappy? It's gotta be somebody's fault, right? It couldn't just be that I'm a self-centered fuck spinning around inside my own dank cloud of concerns. And look, let's face it, I haven't been doing anybody any favors with all the drugs I've been doing. But we don't even have to talk about that. I don't want to do drugs anymore." The ground was arctic. I sat up on top of my ankles now. I was looking down at this ring she still hadn't taken from my hand.

"There isn't anything I can think of that I really want, or that the best part of me wants, that marrying you won't start doing. I love you, Christy, I want to be your man. This is it. This is love in action. I've thought a lot; like I said, I'm not a rash man. You gotta know I'm serious. You're my girl. I love you, and if you'll marry me I'll never leave you. I'll take care of you till I die and beyond. I swear it."

"Jimmy."

She looked at me with a sad expression she gets sometimes, like she's twenty million years older than me, which—I gotta admit— agitates the hell out of me. Then she looked down at the diamond glimmering there in the cold winter light. She took it out of the box and placed it in her hand. Her long queenly fingers were trembling softly. She didn't put it on.

"Jimmy, I'm freezing, can we please go inside?" she asked sweetly.

"Yeah, yeah, sure," I said. What the hell else was I gonna say?

· · ·

We needed shelter from the blistering cold of that Kingston parking lot, and some privacy, so we went and hid inside my Nova. I had these '73 Pontiac Firebird bucket seats I'd recently put in the car, and they're sweet smooth cherry leather, but they did get stone-ass cold. They annoyed Christy—she thought I put them in too close to the floor and too far forward into the windshield but I didn't. That's the way they go.

I flipped the ignition, and thank God it started. It would've sucked if the engine gave me any problems. I cranked up the heat, which was a little disappointing. The thing let out a heinous death cry but wasn't giving off much warmth.

Christy sat Indian style. Most times she'd sit that way in the car, playing with her feet and biting her toenails. She was undoubtedly cute, at least most of the time. She looked over at me and took me in for a long beat, about to say something, but then didn't. Turning her head to the window, she rolled it down a crack and lit a cigarette that she'd pulled from a mashed-up package I had left on the dash. The strike of the match filled the car with the pungent smell of sulfur. She did her best to blow the smoke outside but it wasn't an effective technique.

I still couldn't believe she wasn't more psyched about me asking her to get married. Maybe she was in shock.

"How did you find me here?" she asked quietly, not looking at me.

"Fat Chance," I said.

"Don't call her that," Christy snapped.

Christy's old roommate's name was Chance, but she's fat like a hippo, so everybody calls her Fat Chance. Anyway, after blowing me a shitload of static, Chance told me that Christy was on the Adirondack Trailways bus departing at twelve o'clock. So I grabbed Grace, Christy's cat (I couldn't figure out why she'd abandoned her); I already had the ring in my pocket and shot like a rocket down to Kingston. There's always a long layover there, and I thought I could catch her and pull a Sir Lancelot, propose marriage, return the cat, and let her know that everything was good-to-go. The whole breakup had been a big fat mistake, and it was my job to right the situation. I'd never opened up the Nova like that on public roads before. The mother-fucker has a '97 6.2 liter Mustang engine. Some people piss and moan about the sacrilege of putting a Ford engine in a Chevy, and intellectu-ally I agree, but the shit hauls ass.

Now I was sitting there going nowhere and getting the runaround like a pudwhacker.

"What else did Chance say?" Christy said, still not looking at me.

"Nothin'."

"What else did she say, Jimmy?" Christy was angry. Of all the reac-tions I'd imagined to my marriage proposal, anger had never occurred to me.

An old woman all loaded down with scarves and mittens and a hat walked slowly by our window, and this is exactly the point at which I remembered that Grace the cat was still in the car, loose because she hated her carry case. Grace was a small gray and white seventeen-year-old tabby that Christy's dad gave her when she was eight. I couldn't remember why I'd brought her. The cat hid underneath the passenger seat swatting at my feet the whole way into Kingston. Christy was really gonna go ballistic when she found out Grace was in the car.

"What else did Chance tell you?" she asked again. It was obvious there was some accessory information I wasn't clued in to that Christy was afraid Chance had spilled.

"Chance told me you're going to Texas," I said. "That's all."

"Do you know *why* I'm going to Texas?" she asked, getting increasingly brittle.

"No. I don't want you to go to Texas. I don't want anybody to go to Texas. Texas is for derelicts. They should make it a jail, give it back to Zapata." I was being good, keeping things light, not getting angry. Christy didn't respond. Her hands were slipped inside the sleeves of her parka with just the cigarette poking out.

She didn't laugh or smile, but finally she did look me in the eye. "Would you mind pulling up a little bit, so I can make sure my bus doesn't leave without me?" she asked quietly.

"You still want to get on that bus?" I asked. She might as well have stubbed her cigarette out in my eye. It had never occurred to me that she wouldn't accept my proposal. Never. Not once.

"Yes," she said, ashing into the Nova ashtray on top of a pile of other lipstick-stained butts. I was glad I hadn't cleaned the thing out; it was a subtle sign, reminding her of how much time she'd spent in this car, how she belonged here.

"I've made a decision, Jimmy," she said, in a choked voice, her eyes darting around out the window, looking anywhere but at me. "I'm going home. I have no idea how you found me here. I love you; you know I love you, I've told you that a thousand times. But something's gotta give in me, you understand?" Her teeth were slightly chattering. " I haven't been home since I was seventeen. I felt so sure when I was a girl that—I don't know, that I was born into the wrong family or something. But I've been gone eight years now, and I haven't found anything else. At least not until you." She looked down at her knees and brushed at the wrinkles in her pants. "I believed in you, Jimmy. I thought it'd be wonderful if we had a baby. I told you that and you freaked."

Her eyes found mine and stayed there.

"Jimmy, I've been lost as long as I can remember, and I don't want to be anymore. I want to be found. I know it doesn't seem likely, but the only answer I can come up with is to go back to Houston." She started biting her lip and picking what was left of the nail polish from her fingernails. "There's like this glass wall between me and the world. I don't understand it but I got to get rid of it."

I tried to interrupt her but she stopped me.

"People don't like me; they don't. I know you do, but I have trouble connecting with people. I want to go see my grandmother and my father. They loved me so much when I was a kid, and I've done nothing since I was, like, twelve but spit in their faces." She pulled hard on her long skinny cigarette and then reached her lips up to the window and exhaled through the sliver of an opening, with 98 percent of the smoke blowing right back inside the car.

"I want you to marry me," I reiterated. The only response I could think of to what she was saying was to stand firm. Listening to the thumping whistle of the second hand on my watch, I knew I had to be strong right now. People don't realize it, but it's in all these clicks that you make or break your life. I had made my decision as well, and I was gonna go after it. Whole hog.

"Well, *I'm* going to Texas. What are *you* going to do?" She was being tight-lipped and serious. The car was filling with more stagnant clouds of smoke. It's strange to be inside a car but not moving. After a certain period of time it's unsettling.

Christy put out her cigarette right next to all the other ones and breathed into her hands to warm them up.

"Baby doll"—I was still being cool—"I'm in the army. We've talked about this. I can apply for a transfer or in about a year I can get an honorable discharge, but, come on, I can't just split—"

She interrupted me. "Do you remember what I said to you inside the hospital cafeteria, when you so courageously opened your heart to me to say you didn't love me anymore? Do you remember what I said?"

She waited so long for my response, I was forced to shake my head no.

"I said, What will I live for?"

"I don't remember that," I muttered. Of course I didn't remember. How could I? I hadn't listened to a word she said. I was too consumed with figuring out what *I* was gonna say.

"I had this idea that we could be a *home* for each other, but maybe that's not right. Maybe a person can't do that for someone else. But people need a center, and I don't have one. It was too much for me to ask you to give me that." Without the cigarette her breath was still fuming like a dragon's, it was that cold. "But I'm sick and tired of being kept at a safe distance. I can't take your waffly plans: Today we should get married and build our own house, and then tomorrow me having a set of your keys is *too* big a step. Or being told I love you *too* much. I don't deserve that." She sat on her hands. I wondered what she'd done with the ring.

"Did you hear anything I said out there today?" I asked, wanting to concentrate on the new, more positive me. I gestured to the parking lot but knocked my knuckles on the glass. My hand was so brittle and cold, it stung like a bitch.

"I heard you, but I don't believe you," she said simply. "I don't want your guilty kisses and I don't want this ring." She lifted up her hand with the ring right there smack in the center of her palm, her pale fingers all stretched out pointing at me.

"I'm not going to take that." I wanted to slap her hand.

"Be realistic, all right? Take it back," she said arrogantly, like a schoolteacher. "I'm sure it was expensive."

My whole game plan, the entire agenda I had envisioned and tried to enact this afternoon, had been shot to shit. Sometimes I couldn't even talk to her. The plates of my skull were so tightly pressed together I thought my whole head might crumble under the pressure.

"You're not serious, Jimmy. You've got some idea in your head but you're not serious. My bus is gonna leave. I'll call you from Texas and we can talk. Here, take the ring." She offered it up again. I had my eyes fixed on the cracks in my blue plastic dashboard in front of me.

"Fuck that," I said, turning toward her, my head cocked like a hammer.

"You really are a piece of work, you know that?"

"Stop telling me I'm not serious!" I boomed. The dice hanging from the rearview mirror shook back and forth. I tried to calm myself. Christy shuts down when I yell, so I immediately regretted doing it. "This totally blows. This is wrong. How can I change this situation?" I was pleading, really asking her. "Just stop being what you're being like." She was acting so removed. She gets like that, like she tries to will herself into this all-seeing, all-knowing person who isn't emotional, who's detached from all the menial human ugliness around her.

"I want you to be in a good mood," I whined. "I want you to marry me."

"I can't listen to you anymore." She grabbed the door handle, fighting to get out of the car like we were sinking into a lake. Finally, after struggling awkwardly with the lever, she got the door open. Cold air rushed in. I leaned over her quickly and pulled the cocksucker shut again.

"Stay in the car," I said.

"Don't touch me!" she hissed. I thought she was going to scratch my eyes out. She kicked the door wide open again.

"Shut the fuckin' door!" I yelled, straightening up in my seat.

"Don't you ever raise your voice at me. Are you crazy?" Still seated in the car, she glared at me, her finger in my face.

"I didn't raise my voice," I tried to say peacefully. "Just, please, shut the door."

"Jimmy"—she moved one leg out on the pavement—"I wanted to love you, to really give to you. I know what happened with your dad. I know about your mother. . . ."

Mentioning my folks disoriented me. What did they have to do with this?

"But it hurts like acid on my skin," she went on, "every time you change your mind or turn me away. So just let me go."

She found the black velvet box wedged between the cracks in her seat, stuck the ring back, and tossed it up on the dashboard. Then she slipped her other leg out of the car, threw the cigarette package on the floor mat, stood up out of the Nova, and swung the clunky heavy metal door closed.

I turned off the car, took the keys and the ring, jumped out, and hounded after her across the empty parking lot.

"You can say all that"—I was tailing her, the cold air waking me up like electrodes zapping my temples—"and think you understand me better than I do myself. *But how I feel—*" I had started to yell again.

Christy snapped around, pointing her long finger directly in my face. "Shut up," she spat out, in a barely audible voice. We were standing in the open, wind tearing at our clothes. "Do not raise your voice at me." She has an irrational reaction to being screamed at: Nobody likes it, but she *hates* it. Turning back toward the front door of the bus station, she accidentally tripped and dropped her purse.

"You can walk away"—I lowered my voice, but I was still on top of her, walking right behind her—"all smug, like you're so much smarter and so much older than me—"

"What are you talking about?" she said, not even looking at me. She was struggling with her purse, trying to get it back over her shoulder, as she moved forward in long quick strides.

I carried on. "I still know myself better than you do, and I'm telling you I love you and I want to marry you, but I'm not gonna bullshit you, I'm scared. The whole thing scares me."

We stepped up onto the sidewalk that borders the entrance of the bus station. She stopped, finally, and turned to me.

"I'm *not* scared, don't you understand? That's the fundamental difference between us. *My* love doesn't scare me. Yours does because it's a lie." The skin of her cheeks was getting red and chapped.

"That's not true!" I threw my arms up in the air.

Christy didn't speak, but she didn't turn away either.

"I'm not gonna talk to you ever again if you yell. OK? Am I being clear?"

I took a deep breath. "Just because I'm scared doesn't have any pertinence to us." I went on trying to defend myself, not sure I used the word *pertinence* correctly. I wanted to sound mature, in control, like a grown man. "When I was eighteen I was petrified that I was a homo, but I'm not." I was on a bad track there and I knew it immediately. "Just being scared of commitment doesn't mean I can't follow through."

We were standing smack in front of the dirty glass door to the bus station. There were advertisements, bulletins, and timetables pasted everywhere.

"I'm leaving, OK? Stop following me." She was pronouncing

every word deliberately. "I'll call you from Texas. We can talk some more then."

"Come home with me tonight and talk?" I asked, as straight-forwardly as I could. "You can leave tomorrow."

She shook her head no.

"I won't let you go," I said, digging my hands into my armpits to shield them from the wind.

"Yes, you will," she said. She went through the door to the grimy old brick building and I followed her. I didn't give a rat's ass what she said.

The inside of the station was filled with vending machines and ticket booths. The air smelled lightly of stale urine, but at least we were out of the wind. A few other people were in there milling idly around.

"If you think for a second that this is the last time you'll see me," I whispered from behind her, trailing her as she looked around for her departure sign, "you're wrong. While you sit on that bus you can meditate on the simple fact that you're the one who's quitting; you're giving up, not me. Say what you want, but I *am* here and you *are* leaving."

She beelined straight across the station, not looking at anyone, making herself small and unnoticeable. She passed the wooden rows of seats, like church pews, where people were seated waiting, reading papers, drinking coffee, and then she was off toward a door with a sign above it marked TO ALL BUSES. Only she didn't go out.

"Shit, shit, shit!" She pounded the glass door with the flat of her hand. "Oh, my God, Jimmy, you've ruined everything!" She wasn't yelling, but her voice struck a tone of true anguish that rattled and spun the nerves lining my stomach.

"What? What?" I was about four paces behind her.

She pressed her face against the glass. "My bus left."

Everybody in the bus station was staring at us, waiting for the next move. I couldn't see Christy's face. She stood there looking out the glass door, shivering. I laid my hand gently across her back. She turned around and whacked me five times across the top of my head. She socked my right ear hard. Her boot heel slipped and she fell to her knees. Immediately I knelt beside her. Without looking up she adjusted her position, shielding her face, seeming to realize we were becoming a spectacle.

She sniffled, rubbed her hand across her mouth, and got up and walked calmly into the ladies' room. I was left kneeling on the floor.

I stood up, only to sit back down on one of the empty benches. Eventually people stopped gawking.

I peaked too early. When I was twelve years old, I did sixty-seven one-armed pushups. No one could believe it. I won this scholastic fitness award. I was like a god in my sixth-grade class. Every girl had a crush on me. I was always first pick in gym. By my sophomore year in high school I was already varsity in two sports. Fat lotta good it did me.

Chaplain Sheppard was the one who initially turned me on to this idea of marriage. I went to him all bent out of shape and upset after I broke up with Christy. You couldn't knock him over; he was boxy like a football coach, a good mellow guy who was wonderful to talk to. He always spoke so softly you could barely hear him. Even Christy liked him.

He told me that the definition of grace is the ability to accept change. He said I needed to start calculating my masculinity not by the amount of pussy I could grab, or how many girls I could bang, but by how true I could be with one girl. How infrequently I could lie. How often I could show up when I was needed. How willing I was to love the life I had rather than covet the lives of others.

The point is, he got me all fired up, and now here I was, shot down, sitting alone on an old wooden bench in a decrepit bus station. To my left was a vending machine selling candy, gum, potato chips, cookies, toenail clippers, and whatever else you could fathom. All the air had squeaked out of me. Eight other people were waiting there as well. Oddly enough, they were all men. Nine of us altogether, waiting: for a bus to arrive, for a ride—or for a girl.

I looked down the hall at the closed ladies'-room door.

For the first four or five months of our relationship I'd say Christy and I barely talked at all. We probably spent five nights a week together, but we didn't go to the movies, we didn't go out to dinner, sometimes we'd watch TV, but mostly we just had sex. We had sex all the time, but I literally could not converse with the woman. It was comic. Our entire courtship was nonverbal. She'd tell me, "I know you're not stupid. Don't you have anything to say?" But really there was only one thing I could think of and it sounded too corny: I thought she was unspeakably beautiful. She has these big ears that would stick out through her hair, and I'd just go nuts. I couldn't stop looking at them. They jiggled when she talked and I wanted to bite them. What are you gonna say when that's what you're thinking?

It wasn't until Virginia Beach that we started to communicate, and that was a good five months into our affair. My colonel was making some kind of official trip to a base down there and I had been assigned as his attaché or liaison, more like a personal assistant. It was a lousy job, but I had a bunch of free time. Christy wanted to meet me down there for a romantic weekend. I thought it was awfully boyfriend-girlfriend behavior, but I got railroaded into it.

I remember standing outside in the warm beach night air in front of the motel in flip-flops and no shirt. It was so humid, taking a deep breath almost made me cough. The salty air shimmered in a red neon light from the bowling alley next door. As I watched the traffic pass, standing in the parking lot waiting for her to arrive, the whole world seemed still and serene except for the thundering drumbeat of my heart. It was like there was a Thoroughbred sprinting on a treadmill inside my chest. I couldn't wait to see her. Finally she eased into the motel parking lot driving a candy-red Camaro (the rental company had botched her reservation and this was the only car left, so they had to let her have it), and as soon as I saw her face I knew I was a full-blown schoolboy in love. But I still couldn't speak to her. She parked and got out and—no shit—we didn't even exchange greetings. I did say, "How'd you get such a sweet car?" but she just shrugged. We held hands and walked out onto the beach.

Stepping into the warm ocean water, we started making out and soon found ourselves waist deep in the waves. I pulled her shorts down, letting them float away, and we started to make love (crazy girl never wears any panties). We still hadn't said "hello" to each other, for chrissakes! With one hand holding the base of her spine and the other in between her shoulder blades I could feel her heart thumping its way through the muscles and bones of her back just like mine. The water splashed against our bodies, lighting up like fireflies. There was a sliver of a moon just above the horizon, and I looked at it and wondered what the fuck was happening inside me. Would I survive this? In the dark I could make out the shape of Christy's eyes, but the night was too black for any recognition of detail. Then I looked down and, as if the shell of her torso were made of crystal, I saw the four chambers of her heart constricting and relaxing. In the hollow of her chest cavity was a heart pumping furiously, all muscle and blood, glowing like a ruby in a dark cave. This girl had a friggin' fireball for a heart.

The rest of the weekend we spent talking. Once I began, there was no shutting me up. The words came like water running out of a tub till they all drained out, leaving me empty but clean. I told her how I'd joined the army on a whim after my father's suicide. I told her about my crying fits, about how I knew I needed to leave the military but didn't know what to try next. She'd ask a question and actually listen to the answer. There was a sensitivity to her that was both hopeful and heartbreaking. Every now and then you meet a human being and you might as well be a bomb.

From my bench in the Kingston bus station I looked out the window. There were three hawks circling in the sky about half a mile away.

I read somewhere that General Sam Houston believed he always knew he was exactly where God wanted him to be whenever hawks circled above him. He had lived with the Indians for a while, and the symbol came to him in a peyote vision. I couldn't be sure it was hawks I was looking at. They might've been buzzards.

There was an ice-cream shop across the street from the station with a big sign in the window:

CLOSED FOR SEASON.
REASON? FREEZIN'!

Two guys both wearing blaze-orange vests pulled into a gas station, with a sixteen-point stag dead and bloody in the back of their pick-up. He was a big boy, his feet hanging over the rail guard. I've never been hunting. No interest.

An eerie sensation washed over me as I sat on the wooden bench inside the Kingston bus station. I had goose pimples on my arms. I could no longer tell how long I'd been there; it could have been a second or an hour. I began imagining Christy in the bathroom committing suicide. It felt like a premonition. This would be my story: LOCAL WOMAN TAKES OWN LIFE AFTER MARRIAGE PROPOSAL FROM LOSER BOYFRIEND. I could hear the gentle prodding tick of my watch, the volume of which seemed to vary mysteriously.

When I was twenty-three years old, my father jumped from the nineteenth floor of the George Taft Memorial Hospital in Cincinnati, Ohio, on the nineteenth of December and died from head injuries. I'd visited him in the psychiatric ward the day before. The last thing he said to me as I stepped in the down elevator was "These doctors don't know anything. Just get me a puppy, Jimbo." He said, "I need something to take care of. I miss you being a little boy. Not a Labrador or any pedigree bullshit, just some kind of mutt." And the elevator doors shut.

Grace: the ability to accept change.

I stood up. At first I wasn't sure if I should go find Christy or leave.

But I went toward the ladies' room, my boots making a loud thump with every footstep, and opened the door, hoping there were no other women in there.

"Hey, Bean Dog," I said quietly. "You doing OK?"

The bathroom was surprisingly clean: brightly lit, warm, with alternating black and white tiles on the floor that scaled halfway up the walls, three real glass mirrors, big heavy black wood stall doors, and high ceilings, circa 1940. Not like they build things now, when they throw up a sheet of aluminum for a mirror, and the commode and the sink are plastic dipped in piss. This room was like its own universe. For one, it was the only place in the building where you didn't see your breath. The radiator was conking and letting out a steady release of steam. Of course, people had scribbled on the walls and scratched the wood doors with names, sloppy-ass drawings, and other teenage vandalism, but still, everything about this room was substantial. I didn't even mind the bright light. It was the kind of halogen overhead light that unfortunately makes every pimple on your face twice as red.

Christy was standing at the sink, which was a thick heavy porcelain with old metal faucets. She was rifling through her purse, reapplying makeup. She'd been crying, which I was glad to see. Anything was preferable to the I-don't-give-a-shit, I'm-so-removed attitude she'd been assuming. Her face was swollen and puffy. Her black parka lay on the floor. Her wallet was slipping halfway out of the front pocket, which was classic Christy. I'm always barking about her lack of organization, never hanging things up or keeping track of her glasses, careless stuff like that. She was wearing my old hooded gray sweatshirt over a white long-underwear top. She has great big tits, and ARMY was spelled out bold across them.

I sat up on top of a wooden box that covered the radiator. My rear end started warming up. We were both silent.

"Let me drive you on to New York," I said finally. "We'll pick up your luggage and shit, talk some more, and see if you still don't want to marry me." I was speaking extremely softly but, with the high ceilings and the tile of the bathroom, sound moved well. I hadn't thought of that plan before I said it aloud.

There was another long stillness, both of us calm now. Christy looked away from me to herself in the mirror, then to the sink. She began biting one of her pinkie nails.

"What are you going to do about work?" she asked, so sweetly I wanted to grab her face and smooch all over her red cheeks. It blows my mind how much Christy's face can change from instant to instant: one moment hard, crisp, and angular, the next vulnerable, shy, and soft.

"I'll blow it off," I said. "I'll call Ed and tell him to make something up. I can get away with maybe three days."

Christy started crying, not frantic or sobbing; she was simply staring at me and her eyes filled with tears. Be a man, I said to myself. Let her cry. Take a giant breath and fill that body. You're not an idiot.

"I know you think everything has some secret hidden underground meaning that only you can interpret," I said, still sitting high up on the radiator. "But you don't understand everything about me; neither do I. Some things are mysteries, right?" I was speaking calmly, avoiding the echo of my voice. "You're smart, smarter than me, but you still can't see everything."

Her eyes were trained on me, peaceful and unmoving. There was a window in the back of the bathroom, and the wind outside was blowing the leaves of a bush against the glass.

"You think you make a decision, and then you gotta go forward two hundred percent on it, even if it doesn't make any sense. It's all or nothing. But see, you were missing the late-breaking update: that I love the shit out of you, I can change, and I'm not leaving you. You should process that and then if you want you can alter your coordinates."

I was in armory for about six months, tank division. We talked mucho about coordinates.

"I'm sorry I hurt your feelings, but I love you," I repeated. I wanted her to accept my apology and then we could kiss and get married.

"You love me now?" she asked, straight-faced, turning so she was flat toward me, her hands tucked into the armpits of her sweatshirt.

"I love you now." I tried to be clear, unafraid, unconflicted.

"Tomorrow?"

"I want to marry you," I said.

There was a giant pause. We looked at each other.

She tried to speak, but her voice broke. Biting her upper lip, she continued. "Why didn't you call me?" She cried like her body could disassemble. She shook softly, rhythmically, with her arms now flat at her sides; she had no more energy. I didn't move toward her, I let her cry. I knew she wouldn't want me to patronize her by cuddling her in some fake way. Some things suck; they hurt bad. The question is, Do you have the courage to let them?

This may sound insipid, but it's honest: Until that moment I hadn't really considered how Christy had been feeling. I realized how egocentric I'd been.

"I'm sorry," I said again. "I was trying to get myself in order."

"You're forgiven," she said, and tried to smile. She clenched her jaw and wiped away her tears, frustrated with herself for crying. "But forgiveness is . . . overrated. Actions have repercussions—like a science experiment, a chemical reaction." She moved back to the sink, turned both faucets on, and let the water swirl together. She looked worn out. I perceived in her eyes and in her gestures that, yes, she cared about me, she would cry about me, but in the end she could and would get over me. Somehow, I hadn't realized that.

"The truth," she said, talking almost to herself, "doesn't need us to protect it. All we have to do is live inside it and it will protect us, right?"

I nodded, I don't know why; I didn't understand what she was going on about. She reached into her purse and pulled out a handful of three-by-two-inch pieces of paper and held them out for me. I slid myself off the radiator and took them. They felt thin and slippery like

facsimile paper, with black-and-white images of what looked like con-
stellations: Orion's belt, the Big Dipper. Each image was different. On
the left side of each slip was a line drawing of a naked woman's body
with an arrow pointing directly above the belly button. There were a
ton of numbers and letters along the top and bottom. I'd never seen
anything like these images before. I had no idea what they were supposed to signify.

"That's our daughter at seventeen weeks," Christy said.

My stomach, my hands, my knees all shook with a sensation of fear
I hadn't known since I was twelve.

"How come you didn't tell me?" I struggled to ask.

"I don't know. I tried, but the more I tried the more distant you
seemed. And—I don't know—I got scared."

"It's a girl?" I asked. I couldn't breathe. I was gonna cry. I held my
gut tight. I tried not to breathe, not to blink my eyes. My fists clenched,
I bit the inside of my cheeks to stop my mouth from quivering.

I was surprised Christy was pregnant, but somewhere I'd known.
My father had said that. "There are no secrets, just things people pretend they don't know."

"They can't be sure," Christy continued, "but the woman said, 'If
I had to say, I'd guess it was a girl.'" Christy was looking at me intently.
I tried to inhale, to take a quick little breath, but as soon as I did I had
to sit down. Christy knelt beside me and hid my face in her sweatshirt.
There was no one else in the bathroom, but she covered my face
nonetheless, and I felt my cheeks swell hot and my eyes sting.

"You don't have to do anything," she whispered in my ear. "This
was my choice. I will take care of everything. I couldn't ever tell you
because I couldn't find a way where it wouldn't seem like I was trap-
ping you into a life you expressly hadn't chosen. I do love you, Jimmy,
and there's no regrets. This will be one beautiful child. I've been thinking about all the options now, but none of them will require anything
from you." She said this holding me in her arms. I uncovered my face.

"What options?" I asked.

Christy looked deep into my eyes, kissed me once, and then kissed me again and again and again. Our faces were sopping wet. Her mouth was sweet like cherry candy. I unbuttoned the top of her jeans and dove my head straight between her legs. Christy has a fantastic pussy. I'm not saying that to be vulgar. I'm saying it because it's true.

"Not here," she whispered. "Not here."

Inside the Nova, with the windows blotted out from the fog of our breathing, Christy was naked from the waist down, sitting on my lap, her black parka zipped up her chest, and that little diamond on her ring finger. The sun had set on the Kingston bus station parking lot and we were making love, her vagina soft, silklike, encompassing, while I warmed up her feet by massaging them with my hands. Grace, the cat, was still sitting undisclosed beneath the passenger seat of the car.

There's something about the feeling of snorting cocaine till your brain freezes and you weep 'cause you can't fall asleep that I enjoy—it's a fear of death or an awareness of life—and there was something about being near Christy, kissing her, feeling her wetness, that touched the same pulse, only with her it was the opposite of poison. It was more like some ancient healing elixir.

"Can you say all that stuff again?" Christy breathed above me.

"What stuff?"

"About how you want to get married?"

"I'm not sure I can remember it."

Christy snarled, stopped moving, and tightened her vaginal muscles around me.

"I'm never gonna love anybody more than I love you," I said. "So the question is: Do I believe in love?"

"Yes, you do," she answered for me, excited. "You do." She moved her hips again and continued to fuck my lights out.

I thought of Franklin Delano Roosevelt, who, the story goes, knew the instant he heard the name Adolf Hitler that he had brushed up against the reason he was born. He had been living his whole life with this nagging sensation that he was waiting for something, and the moment he heard that name the feeling subsided into nothingness. He had arrived.

Now it's different, and to me it was shockingly humble, but there with my girl in my arms and our child in her belly I knew I had reached the moment my life had been waiting for. I was going to be a father and a husband.

I spanked her bottom and cranked up the tunes.

ISAIAH

JIMMY WAS SITTING in the driver's seat. I was on top of him, naked from the waist down, looking at his face. In the position we were in, Jimmy was almost uncomfortably deep inside me. The windows were steamed over from our breathing. I could barely see the empty bus station parking lot outside. The sky was midnight black. Every winter it surprises me just how dark it can be by five-thirty. What I could see outside was balmy and serene, like a restful ocean. As I moved my hips, our car would gently rock as if we were drifting.

Looking away from his face, I saw two yellow eyes floating in darkness in the backseat, like some cryptic dream. I said a prayer for Jimmy and me, asking a blessing on our love. I didn't ask anyone in particular; I was just dreaming in my head, reaching out through the glass and metal of our car hoping for some compassion. I knew I shouldn't have put on the engagement ring. I didn't want to be misleading.

. . .

The first time I remember praying was in the third grade, sitting Indian style on my bed, the moonlight turning my white sheets blue like magic. There was a chance of snow. They were talking about it all over the TV and radio. Snow in Texas is momentous. I asked God, If I matter at all, please let tomorrow be a snow day. I hated school. I had a test on the states: capitals, flowers, rivers, junk like that. I remember staring at the streetlamp outside my window, impatiently waiting for it to illuminate the first flakes. I remember the sound of cars, their headlights moving across my ceiling. I remember my room; there was an American flag with forty-eight stars hanging against the wall. It had been on my grandpa's casket. I remember the aqua shag carpeting and the phony wood paneling on the walls. I even remember my prayer. I was on my knees, speaking out loud, directly to the moon. I imagined God simply as two sweeping large arms and strong masculine hands like my father's.

"Dear God, my name is Christy Ann, and I promise that I will believe in you forever, and I will be good always, if you can find it in your heart to let it snow tomorrow, enough so I don't have to go to school. Thank you very much, and I say an extra prayer for all the lonely people who don't have any friends. Thank you. Amen."

I was very concerned about lonely people when I was a little girl.

I remember all that, but I can't remember if it snowed or not.

I looked down at Jimmy's lips. Sloppy sounds of lovemaking accompanied our every movement. The interior of the car was heavy with our scent. Sometimes when we made love it seemed our sexual organs didn't belong to either one of us. They were a link, or a bridge, for the two of us to meet. Jimmy and I had such trouble talking sometimes. Making love, everything softened; my head would open up and miles of space would enter in. Our sex was what I imagine it to be like after you've run a great distance and all your anxiety has been hammered away and you aren't even able to think; there is only your breath, coming easily in and out.

Two yellow unblinking eyes appeared to me again, still floating in the darkness of the backseat. I wondered from which dream these eyes erupted or what symbol was being revealed to me in this vision.

I hadn't said good-bye to Gordon, the blind man on the bus. He must've been concerned about me, disappearing like that. We would never see each other again for the rest of our lives, of that much I was sure.

"All that matters is grace," Gordon had said to me.

"I have a cat named Grace," I mumbled.

"Grace is living with an awake heart, open to the knowledge that your every gesture is the will of Allah." He paused. We were only minutes outside of Kingston.

"Is Allah a man?" I asked. I couldn't help it but whenever people mention Allah, in my brain I picture medieval horsemen with scimitars chopping off Christian limbs.

"You cannot think of God as a thing, a person, a man, or a woman. Allah is not an object. God isn't over there or up here." He made several almost spastic gestures with his hand. "God is the root of me." He brought his hand into a fist and moved it in toward his chest. "He is not me, but he is my root. Allah is revealed in his creatures, but Allah is not his creatures. Tashbe: Allah is manifest in everything. Tanze: Allah is beyond knowledge, completely invisible. The unity of both is reality. To know God is to know how he makes himself visible."

Looking around the bus, I noticed there were a lot of old people. I always imagine old people are Ku Klux Klan or former Nazi officers or else just really really *nice*—like they make dinner for disabled people all the time and sit around praying and counting pennies, making up for the sin and meanness in the world. I think both those things simultaneously. Each young man is either a rapist in waiting or my future husband. Maybe everyone sees the world like that: Everything's true, all the time.

"The world is spinning, right?" Gordon asked. There was a long pause. I was worried; I knew it was a leading question. I wanted a sip of his beer.

"Go on," I said simply.

"Well, I'm not the same person I was yesterday, so how could you know me? How could I know you? I'm trying still to figure out who I was ten years ago."

He laughed. I did too.

"Thank you." He smiled big.

There have been a few times, when Jimmy has been very far inside me, that neither one of us would move. I would hold him there, staring into his eyes, and after a damp mystical time we would both simultaneously orgasm. Only by accident would it occur. We could never try and make it happen.

Outside the Nova it had begun to snow. I could hear the soft patter of snowflakes melting on the heat of the automobile and see thousands of crystals falling on the parking lot where Jimmy had just asked me to marry him. It was a brave act, but I knew we would never get married. I understood and had come to terms with the fact that our destiny was to break each other's hearts, to destroy each other. Making love was only delay. Wearing his ring was only delay. Jimmy's great problem was that he wanted to be liked so badly—by me, by anyone—that he couldn't hear his own mind. This deafness made him unpredictable. You never knew when his own voice would find him.

But we could make love. I was sweating under my parka now.

"Every one of us has a 'charge,'" Gordon had said. "Simply by being born we've asked for something to do. The child in your belly has already asked to participate. Is there anything in your life that in some way you haven't asked for? Life does not crash down on us. Isaiah said, 'Here I am, send me.'" I remember Gordon blindly thumped his breast with his fist like a boxer asking for a fight. "Here I am. Send me."

I'd had sex with Jimmy on our first date. My friend Chance had practically dared me. I knew I shouldn't have, because immediately I really liked him. I remember exactly the moment he first entered me, because he took my breath away: literally. It was like being a little girl falling off the merry-go-round; for a couple seconds I couldn't for the life of me remember how to breathe. From that moment forward I was just waiting to be pregnant.

"Do you control whether this bus arrives safely at its destination?" Gordon had asked. "Whether or not the fan belt was correctly fastened? Do you control the water supply? the grain harvest? the manufacturing of gasoline? the tides? the moon? Yet all these so-called extraneous events manipulate your every breathing moment. Freedom is grace. Living with the knowledge that you are a manifestation of God, that all your actions are the working musculature of heaven, that is grace."

When I stepped into an abortion clinic in Albany, I knew I was in breach of an unverbalized agreement I'd already made. There in the waiting room while I was reading a magazine, a woman I barely recognized from my high school back in Texas came up to me.

"Christy, is that you?" She was Mexican, with curly black hair. Her name was Cruz Alvarez. "Christy Walker! Oh, my God, it's good to see you!" I looked in her pale brown eyes and knew I wasn't going to be able to go through with the abortion. This was the last place in the world I wanted to be recognized. I knew I was old enough to handle a child. Even a year earlier an abortion could have been justified, but I couldn't pretend I hadn't asked for this baby, because I had.

"Creation didn't happen. It's happening. Grace will come as you acknowledge how much of every instant is beyond your control." Gordon's voice moved inside me like a reed instrument. "That is freedom. People in this country believe freedom is the ability to choose—I choose a Cadillac over a Buick; I am a Cadillac man; our only avenue toward more choice is more money—but choice and money are not freedom." He adjusted his sunglasses and raised his head. "There is a right kind of dissatisfaction. There's a void within us that cannot be filled. This void is our need for God. You must search for and stay with that longing."

The snow on the rear window was melting into small streams and pouring slowly down the glass. Still those unblinking cat eyes were staring at me, drifting in the blackness. They reminded me of my own cat, the cat I left behind. Looking down on Jimmy I wanted to kiss his face, bite his cheek, make it bleed, drink the blood up, kiss it better, put a Band-Aid on it, heal him, and do it all again. I wanted to suffer. There was no way out, only through.

The eyes came forward into the perimeter of the dashboard lights. I couldn't believe it.

"Oh, my God, Jimmy," I said, breathless and dizzy. "Is that Grace?"

"WHO'S IN THE DOG?"

AFTER A NIGHT at the Kingston Skytop Inn and Steak House, a motel with a banner view of Interstate 87, we drove into Manhattan, picked up Christy's bags from the Port Authority Bus Terminal, and opted for lunch.

The Howard Johnson's in Times Square felt like the crossroads of the universe. A good portion of the planet passes through this restaurant at some point in their lifetime. It was about twelve-thirty in the afternoon. I couldn't get Christy to eat anything of substance; she was curled up across from me practically making out with a root beer float. It was seedy as all hell, but to me the HoJo's was like heaven. The place was walled with giant filthy glass windows that let in a peculiar funky gray filtered light. It was right on the corner of 45th and Broadway, and outside looked like Tokyo or some futuristic dream: a madness of blinking lights and billboards all selling different variations of sex. It was like sitting in the dim calm of an aquarium as schools of manic fish flashed by in explosions of color and energy.

Christy's bags were laid up against our red plastic booth. This waitress kept hustling by, accidentally tripping on them and giving me a nasty look each time. She was pretty sexy, actually—she was in her early forties but she wore her little black-and-white waitress outfit like a stripper might, real tight and slutty—but that's a look that works on me. Christy was in a great mood. It's easy to love her when she's in one of these moods. Her eyes were bright green; her root beer float had the effect heroin has on a junkie. She kept turning her long skinny spoon upside down in her mouth, closing her eyes, and meticulously licking off the ice cream.

We were trying to figure out what to do, and it was starting to become clear to me that I didn't have any options, not really—not if I truly wanted to marry her. I'd been maneuvering in different ways to get her to consider returning to Albany as an option, but it was a no-go. The only real question was what I was going to do about my lieutenant. But that was my problem. I'd figure it out. This was where the rubber met the road.

The noise in the HoJo's was pretty deafening. The place was buzzing with lunching tourists, and everybody was chattering away full steam. Christy herself was yakking a blue streak.

"It's funny, isn't it? When you look at this many people all in one place"—she was pointing with her spoon at the crowds of people scurrying by outside—"it's easy to imagine us all like water: like waves on top of the ocean. Don't you think?"

"I guess," I said. Maybe I should just resign, I thought, and let the chips fall. In truth, I never should've joined. I went to college for two years for chrissakes; I'm not an idiot. I've made so many mistakes in my life, wasted so much time.

There was a little blond girl maybe three years old sitting at the table across from us with her father, who was probably just a year or two older than me. His beard was thicker than mine, but otherwise we could've passed for brothers. I was having a tough time not eavesdropping on their conversation. They had tickets to *The Lion King* laid out on the table. The girl had bright Irish red cheeks. She leaned forward, sticking out her clean tiny tongue, and said in a high voice, "Dadda, what does my tongue smell like?"

"I don't know, darling," the father answered. His voice sounded startlingly like my own.

"Where do we go when we die?" Christy asked, forcing me to look back at her.

"What?" I asked.

"Or, more to the point, where did I go? The first time I came to New York City I was with my father on a business trip. I was probably only ten. That girl isn't alive anymore. You can't go talk to her. You can't find her walking around out there." Sometimes when Christy speaks, it's like there's a tiny hole on top of her head and light is just pouring out of it. She relaxes and lets go so rarely that when she does, it feels like a great rain of light.

"I look at you and think of the evening I first met you, and you're not that person anymore. I mean, the elements are the same, but you're different. Look at me right now." Christy lifted her long arms up in the air, still holding the dripping spoon, asking me to take in all of her. "I will never be this person again. When we walk out of here today— when tomorrow morning comes—I will be somebody else, not exactly the same as I am right now. Maybe that's all that dying is."

"What are you talking about?" I asked. The sun had come out from behind a cloud, and I still couldn't take my eyes from the child across from us. The girl was silhouetted against a now-bright window; her father had on a smokin' cool leather jacket. It'd be fun to take your kid to see *The Lion King,* I thought. I don't know, maybe it'd be boring. I've never really spent any time with children, and I had no idea how I was going to handle the whole up-and-coming situation.

"I haven't been home to Texas in eight years," Christy continued. "How did that much time go by? I'm a woman now; when did that happen? I'm gonna be a mother." She was holding her hand to her chest, giving me an expression of disbelief.

"You sure you don't want any of this?" I asked, holding my burger. More than halfway done with the monstrous thing, I could say with authority that it was excellent. Probably the best burger I ever ate: fresh tomatoes, fresh onions, a gargantuan crisp deli pickle.

She shook her head no and went on talking. "I mean, let me tell you this. You hear people talk about whether or not 'you' are your body or if 'you' are your mind. What your spirit is, right?"

She paused and I nodded.

"Well, let me tell you what you're not. You are not your body, no way. I mean, my body right now is a carnival and I am not in control of it. You should feel what's going on inside of me; I'm vibrating like . . . I don't know, like the fuselage of a crashing plane. OK?" She smiled at me, set down her spoon, and cradled her belly with both hands. "This body that you see is not me. I'm not doing any of this. Feel my elbow." She held out her bent arm for me to touch and, laying my hands on her milk-soft skin, I felt her whole joint popping with electricity.

"Sometimes I wonder if our personality—or what we think of as *ourselves*—isn't just more like a radar device on a plane. You know, this consciousness, or whatever, is just there to keep our bodies out of trouble, to keep us from bumping into one another." She leaned over and, without using her hands, sipped up some root beer from the straw. "We get so hung up on things like our names, where we were born, our country, our religion. All this information that was just handed down to us—I mean, even our genetic codes, right?" She held out her almost misshapen long fingers for me to observe. "These hands are my grandmother's hands, OK? They're not mine. Even what a person is good at: he can run fast, he's good at math"—she was randomly pointing, selecting from the people sitting around us—"I mean, none of that is *us*."

"All right, Christy, none of that's us," I said, taking another big bite of my cheeseburger. It was greasy, I'm not saying it wasn't, but man, oh, man, it was scrumptious. No shit. This restaurant was giving me a buzz. Maybe it was just Christy talking, but for the first time in maybe years I felt myself blowing up with air. Christy seemed lighter too. I like it when she talks to me—whatever she wants to say, I don't care; I just like it that she wants to tell me things. If the way we were feeling was any kind of indication, I knew we were doing the right thing in getting out of Albany. Just being miles away from the military made my shoulders fall back into position and my breath come looser and deeper. The juxtaposition of Times Square outside with the warmth and the relative calmness of all of us inside made me feel like we were dining in the center of the earth.

The little girl across from us spoke loudly to her father. "Dadda, when you were a little boy and I was your mommy, I took you to see a play once. Did you know that?" I couldn't hear his reply.

"Do you know how hard I worked to get out of Texas?" Christy went on, her ideas falling one on top of the next. I don't think she even registered the little girl, the father, or the scowling waitress passing us by. Right then it was all about me. She wanted to communicate. "All I ever wanted was to go to New York City. I went to summer school and took extra classes just to graduate a year and a half early, and then what did I do? I came here, got married to some alcoholic kid from back home, and took care of him for three years. Was that what I was in such a hurry to do? It didn't make any sense. It's like I broke my own leg, you know?"

I've always thought that way about Christy, that she was like a cypress tree who for some hidden reason refused to turn its branches all the way toward the sun.

"And I never wanted to go back home until I was somebody strong. A person with authority who could speak with experience and intelligence to justify why I left so suddenly. But I haven't become that person. I was a seventeen-year-old girl and I walked right by these windows in a leopard-skin jacket, and now eight years have gone by and I don't feel anything important has happened."

"What about the baby?" I asked.

The question interrupted her momentum.

"Until now, I guess. Until now." She looked down and dug with her spoon into the last giant ball of ice cream at the bottom of her fountain soda glass.

I was feeling more in love with Christy right then inside this

Howard Johnson's than I knew I was capable of; I wanted to be her, to be inside of her, to have her own me to use as she wished, to protect her, to read her to sleep at night, to be that root beer float sliding down her throat.

"Yes, I was your mommy," the girl beside us announced, nodding triumphantly to her father. "Your name was Sofie, and I took you to the park and I gave you chocolate and juice. Do you remember?"

"No," he answered simply.

Christy and I looked over at the father and daughter across from us and then back at each other.

"Can I tell you something really corny," Christy asked me. "Promise not to bring it up later and hold it against me and make fun of me? 'Cause sometimes you do that."

"Sure." I nodded.

"Promise," she insisted, smiling.

"Promise."

"When I was a little girl, do you know what I secretly wanted to be when I grew up?"

"What?"

"A saint." She smiled, her red lips wide and wet with foamy ice cream. "And if I had to say—I mean, if I could actually choose—I still do. I'd like to be the saint of all the people who don't have any beliefs at all and don't want them."

The sound of her voice was beautiful; air seemed to move right through her.

"Is there any way I can talk you into getting something to eat?" I asked her.

"I'm really not hungry," she said simply. "Seriously."

"Yeah, but you didn't have any breakfast either." I was starting to worry with this news of the pregnancy that Christy had better start taking care of herself. She was still sneaking cigarettes and she hadn't eaten anything but candy bars and this ice-cream float since I'd picked her up the night before. She's never been good at the whole self-maintenance bit. She could drink like a hound dog. I've held her head over the toilet countless times. I don't think I've ever seen her do any exercise.

"Don't get all cocky about this, but being with you is the closest I've ever come to a sensation that I was someplace authentic. But how are we supposed to carry that with us? How do we build a house with that? Can you? Or is that just a feeling, like the feeling that I love this root beer float.

"What am I besides what I *think*?" Christy moved on. "'Cause what I *think* is always revolving. I know, I know"—she cut herself off—"that's why people have beliefs. They lock things down in their mind and put up some fence posts and decide what to believe in, but that doesn't mean the fence is real. It's all pretty arbitrary, isn't it? Honestly, it can't be that all the Hindus are going to heaven and the rest of us are screwed to the wall, can it? Whatever is happening is going to happen to all of us whether we like it or not, don't you think?"

She pushed away the ice cream and ran long fingers through her hair.

"I have to go to the bathroom," she announced, but she didn't move.

"Why don't you go?" I asked.

"Oh, I'm OK." She shrugged.

"Do you want to see my angry faces?" the high voice of the child by the window called out. "I have two." Then she proceeded to demonstrate two comic presentations of ferocious anger. One with arms crossed and a furrowed brow, the other with her fists clenched in the air and her teeth menacingly exposed like a tiger.

"I mean, let me ask you something." Christy started up again, smiling, amused by the little girl's antics. "Here we are right in the center of Times Square surrounded by everybody and their mother, right? I mean, there's a giant world outside, right?" She glanced out the windows beyond the little blond girl. "Look outside, you can see the passage of time."

She was right. At least a hundred years were represented out there—some sad scraggly tree trying its best to grow in its designated patch of dirt, a pigeon-stained crumbling statue of a once-famous actress, an old tired dog tied to the metal grating of a forlorn tailor shop that looked like it'd been closed since Jimmy Carter was president, a Day Glo–bright billboard of a naked woman holding a microwave oven—anything you were looking for could be found there.

"Do you honestly think that we two, here alone at this table, can make each other happy for the rest of our lives?" Christy asked. She waited for an answer.

There was a silence between us that seemed to occupy the whole restaurant.

"Obviously no, right? I mean, let's face that. Let's look that in the eyes." She bent her head forward and stared intensely at me, then shook her head lightly as if to break her own spell. "But happiness is over-rated. Nobody who's gonna live for more than, like, a couple of days is gonna be happy for the rest of their life. So let's forget happiness. The more interesting question is can we build a home together? Is it possible? And what is home? Is there a place we can live that is permanent? This little baby in my belly is more at home right now than it will be for the entirety of its breathing life, and it isn't even born. It will spend vir-tually every evening, for hopefully the next ninety years, trying to feel as safe and warm in bed as it does right now inside its mama's belly. And this mama is no saint." She pointed both her long fingers at herself accusingly. "I love to drink, and I don't think saints do that. I can't even quit smoking. You don't see many paintings of saints with a Marlboro hanging from their lips, you know what I'm saying? But if I had my choice that's what I'd be—a person who does the right thing all the time, not because I'm trying to but by instinct. I want to be one of those girls who says, 'Oh, from the minute I got pregnant, cigarettes tasted like an ashtray.' But they don't. They taste great. And I've got this free-floating anxiety that lives in me and transports itself from one worry to the next; it's powerful and it's lurking, trying to find anything at all to give me cause for a nervous attack, you know?"

I did. To say Christy struggles with her nerves is an understate-ment.

"This feeling twists me up through all the minutes of every day, and smoking calms it. It does."

"What are you talking about, Christy? I feel like you're trying to tell me something but you're not saying what it is." I felt like that most of the time we spoke.

"I'm just telling you that if you want to try and drive me *home,* it's a long way."

"I wanna take you home, Bean Dog."

"You do? Do you really?" she asked, biting her nails.

I nodded.

"Well, I want to take you home too."

"Cool."

"No, I mean it. What are we gonna do about the army?" Christy asked.

"I don't know. I'm gonna quit, I think." I was uncomfortable now that the conversation's focus had turned to me.

"Is that what you want?" she asked.

"I know I don't want to go back there," I said softly. That was the truth. I needed to move on; it was as obvious as the sun. At that moment I wasn't even scared. I had a friend and that was all I needed. If I went ahead and left this restaurant, it seemed I'd come out somebody new. My only fear, still buried in my guts, was, Who would that person be?

"I love you as you are, Jimmy, I don't need anything about you to change. But you're gonna change," Christy said, seeming to answer my thoughts. "Things will happen to both of us. I only want what you feel is right, but if we're ever gonna get married, if I'm gonna have a baby, there's certain things we probably should do to get ready. Like, I'm gonna need to meet your mom, see where you come from, visit your father's grave. I think that's important."

"Let's not do that," I said, as naturally and as instinctively as I've ever spoken.

"We should, Jimmy," Christy said, crossing her legs in the Howard Johnson's red booth. "Let's go tell your mom about the baby, deal with the military, take care of business, you know? Then head out to Texas. We need to begin this right. My whole life I feel I've been continually starting from a standing-still position. I never *build* on anything. It's always move on and"—she snapped her fingers—"start from scratch."

"We don't need to go to Ohio," I reiterated.

"I think we do," she said peacefully.

I looked down and picked up one of my remaining French fries. My mom, I thought. What a drag.

The little girl across from us was pointing at that old tired dog leashed to the grating of the tailor shop. My eyes followed her small finger. The animal looked to be a black Labrador patiently waiting for its master.

"Dadda," she called out, "who's in the dog?"

MY ACTIONS MAKE ME BEAUTIFUL

JIMMY'S FATHER WAS A HELICOPTER PILOT in Vietnam. He personally never killed anyone, or so Jimmy claimed. When he returned home from the service he worked in landscaping and construction during the warm months, and in the winter he harvested and sold Christmas trees. Jimmy was eight when his father suffered his first severe manic episode. After breakfast one morning, a twenty-nine-year-old Mr. Heartsock called his wife, Jimmy's mom, out onto their front porch, took off his wedding ring, and threw it down their suburban street. He stepped up onto his motorcycle and roared away. Several weeks later he was institutionalized for the first time, after he was found sleeping naked and half frozen in a snowy local high school football field.

On his release he moved to a neighboring town, became a tree surgeon, and maintained a decent stability as a weekend dad until Jimmy's high school graduation. After that his mental condition vacillated. He killed himself about a year before Jimmy and I met. Jimmy spoke about his father in great detail sometimes, but it was always at peculiar moments, like while we were in the grocery store or on the way to a party where the topic would have to be abruptly abandoned on arrival.

On the drive from New York City to Cincinnati, Jimmy finally told me the whole story.

In the summer after Jimmy's first year at college, he arrived at his father's apartment for a visit. His dad was standing in the doorway with half his face clean-shaven and the other half still lathered in shaving cream. He was a beautiful man with movie-star good looks: smoldering deep blue eyes and red hair. There was a homemade banner hanging from the ceiling that said WELCOME HOME in childlike watercolors. On the table a Duncan Hines birthday cake was piled high with icing and about six or seven unlit candles. Two men sat at the table staring at Jimmy blank-faced. One man was nineteen or twenty, only slightly older than Jimmy and clearly mentally retarded. The other was elderly with the bright spark of lunacy in his eyes. Jimmy'd known this second man by sight since childhood but had never spoken with him. He was the town weirdo, Bill. You could smell him from fifteen feet. Local kids were all afraid of him. He would loiter outside the grocery store talking to himself, and weekdays at rush hour he would direct traffic. Cars driving by paid no attention to his fanatically waving hands. And now here was Bill, sitting in Jimmy's father's living room, anxiously waiting for the cake to be cut.

The walls of the apartment had been scribbled on with Magic Marker and other kinds of ink and paint, phrases like DON'T BE ANXIOUS, ONLY CONNECT, and CHECK YOUR EGO HERE, with an arrow drawn to the door. In giant beautiful red and yellow calligraphy, over a Steinway grand piano that took up most of the apartment, was written MY ACTIONS MAKE ME BEAUTIFUL and just underneath in black ballpoint ink, SO DON'T BE AN ASSHOLE. But the single oddest change in his father was that, despite having been born in Buffalo, New York, he was speaking in an Irish brogue.

"I met these two blokes at the train station and told 'em about your impending arrival, so we decided to have a wee party," his father said, his razor still in his hand. "But you fucked it all up, lad, you poxy *bastard.*"

Earlier in the day, while visiting his mother, Jimmy had asked if she'd seen his dad and she promptly burst into tears, so he expected the worst, but his father had become unrecognizable. The party lasted only about ten minutes before Mr. Heartsock began to weep, and Jimmy politely asked the two guests to go home.

For three days, Jimmy and his father left the apartment as little as possible. Jimmy got his dad to give him the car keys and to agree not to go out in public. Mr. Heartsock was unsure what was happening to him and would waver between a feeling of what he called crystallizing elation that he was just being born, seeing and feeling the molecules of the universe for the first time, and a black depression where he admitted fears of hurting someone or himself. He asked Jimmy to remove from the house all the knives, a hatchet, and several saws and spikes he used for tree work. Jimmy tried to rent simple clean straightforward movies, but his father would read wild tragic meanings into the lightest comic fare. There were tirades about the fall of America and the failure of the great democratic experiment. How the identity of America had become solely rooted in capitalism, and how our power as consumers surpassed our power as voters. How government itself had become a simple mediator between big business and the public. Mr. Heartsock referred to the Bible as the Truly Tasteless Joke Book Numero Uno. Then he would bring himself to tears as he described the humiliation Christ must have suffered as he was being crucified. They would perform the holy Eucharist twice daily. There was a candlelight memorial service for puppeteer Jim Henson, whom Mr. Heartsock dubbed the most significant artist of the twentieth century. Listening to the sound track of *The Muppet Movie* three times in a row, Jimmy's father talked about feeling like he'd stepped into a candy store he'd been told his whole life he wasn't allowed to enter, and now—once inside—he realized everything was free. People were consumed by fear, he said, and now they'd fear him because he had learned the secret that everything was there for the taking.

He was coy and unrevealing about some conversations that had taken place with Jesus, and, as crazy as his father had become, Jimmy believed that his old man had indeed talked to Jesus. In some way, perhaps, if you let yourself slip into the stratosphere, you might meet the Blessed Savior. That certainly didn't mean you'd be able to handle it. Mr. Heartsock would play beautiful piano compositions he'd written and weep for an hour at a time. He then would make Jimmy play the only five songs his son could poke out from the lost memory wells of childhood. After days of no sleep, Jimmy couldn't tell which one of them was nuts anymore. They would watch TV, and Mr. Heartsock would rant brilliantly about how technology is eroding all our mental faculties and how there should be a worldwide Chinese fire drill and all the people from China should march to America and all the Americans should march to China—reversing the earth's rotation and altering our understanding of time.

On the morning of the fourth day, Jimmy woke to realize he'd slept for thirteen hours straight and his father was missing with the car keys and the hidden tree equipment.

He spent the next two days back with his mother and stepfather, anxiety swarming in his blood. Every time the phone rang he would stare at it, wondering if this would be the call telling him his father was dead or that he'd killed someone else. Deep in his bones he believed his father was not alive. On the second evening, Jimmy and his mother sat out on the front porch (the same front porch where Mr. Heartsock had taken off his wedding ring years before). It was a hot summer night, and the air was thick with insects and humidity. They smoked several cigarettes in a row and sipped ice-cold beer. Jimmy commented on a sturdy tree house the neighbors had built out in the woods behind their house, saying he wondered what it was like inside. His mother said it was comfortable, with a thick brown carpet.

"You've been inside it?" Jimmy asked. His mother turned bright red and buried her face in her hands.

"Your father's manic episodes have their up sides." She blushed.

"You mean, he comes by here?"

"Sometimes," his mother whispered, putting her finger to her lips to show she didn't want her present husband to hear them.

"You're too much, Mom," he said. His mother had been Miss Teen Ohio when she was a kid and was still very beautiful. She explained that his father had been coming over all summer, asking her out on walks through neighboring farms, and they'd had some of the best times they'd ever had. She confided in Jimmy that his father would always be her greatest love; she just couldn't spend her life as his nurse. She was worried that their recent affair had exacerbated his illness. Although he said nothing, Jimmy thought she was probably right.

At that moment, the lights from Mr. Heartsock's silver Dodge pickup truck lit up the porch. Jimmy put out his cigarette as his dad walked up the drive, carrying two long coils of rope, several handsaws, one long pole saw, a pair of spikes, and his hatchet. Mr. Heartsock continued behind the house without acknowledging either Jimmy or his mother and dropped all the equipment with a loud crash. Jimmy could sense his mother's back tightening. He stood up and walked behind the house after his dad.

"Where you been?" he asked.

"These are for you," his father said, staring down at the ropes and saws.

"Thanks, but I can get my own."

"You're a good kid, Jim, you glow inside," he said quietly. "You were wondrously created, and you don't need anything; you're perfect. You are exactly the way you are supposed to be." His father reached forward, grabbed Jimmy's face, and kissed him on the lips, something he had never done before. His beard was sharp and abrasive. "I love you with all my heart," he continued. "You're the only thing that ever kept me here. But you're a man now. Take care of your mother."

He began to walk away. Jimmy grabbed hold of his sleeve.

"Don't fuckin' touch me, Jimmy!" Mr. Heartsock shouted, and

threw his pointed finger in Jimmy's face. "God help me, I love you, but if you fuck with me I'll kill you." His eyes blazed like someone off to the moon on drugs. "I'm not afraid. Do you understand that? Can your pea brain comprehend a true liberation from fear? Eternity exists. Do you understand? Death is an illusion." He paused, trying to read Jimmy's expression. "There's nothing to fear," he said, and turned and walked back toward his small pickup. A neighboring couple was peeking out of their windows.

"Where you going, Dad?" Jimmy asked. "Don't be a crazy person, OK?"

"James, where are you going?" Jimmy's mom said in a high nervous voice, as her ex-husband walked past her in heavy deliberate strides.

"Dad, I'm not going to let you drive off in that car. I'm worried about you, OK?" Jimmy spoke as if he were addressing someone hard of hearing.

Mr. Heartsock opened the thin metal truck door but dropped his keys. As he bent over to pick them up, Jimmy laid his hand gently on his father's back. Cringing as if he'd been burned, Mr. Heartsock snapped up and took a wild roundhouse swing at his son, barely missing the tip of Jimmy's nose. Jimmy was slightly bigger than his father, and he wrapped his arms around his dad, holding him from behind in a tight bear hug.

"Calm down, Dad," he whispered in his father's ear. "You're not going anywhere tonight, you're scaring me too much."

"We have to call the police, Jimmy, we have to!" his mom shouted, from about ten feet away.

Mr. Heartsock started yelling and kicking his legs wildly, trying to strike Jimmy's shin. He threw two more hard punches directed at Jimmy's head, and Jimmy let him go.

"Fuck, Dad, stop it!" he shouted, putting his arms up over his face.

Several more neighbors gathered.

"Someone please call the police!" Jimmy's mom shouted out.

"Take care of your mother, Jimmy." With a final curse, Mr. Heartsock jumped into his pickup and took off. Jimmy felt sure those would be the last words his father ever spoke to him.

They weren't. The cops called the next morning to tell Jimmy his father was being held at the George Taft Memorial Hospital in Cincinnati. When Jimmy arrived, his father was strapped to a bed, being interviewed by a young girl in an all-white nurse's outfit, including one of those white paper hats. She had a clipboard in her hands and was listening with an expression of martyred patience.

"Let's cut to the chase, why don't we?" Jimmy's father was maniacally haranguing the nurse. "You want to know if I'm crazy, and you think you can check your little boxes there to determine the line between sanity and insanity: 'Hmmm, has trouble sleeping,' *check;* 'Hmmm, currently unemployed,' *check*! But if you were able to take a step back and objectively assess this situation, you would see one person dressed entirely in a white outfit with the look in her eyes of a young girl who has stared at a television for about four years too long and there next to her you'd see a man strapped to a sheet of metal unable to move being forced to take drugs against his will. You would see this and think, Why is that woman dressed in that silly outfit, and why is she making that man take drugs? He did nothing to her. Why is she so sure that *she's* the one who's normal? Is it not possible that perhaps the woman who dresses the same every day should be given drugs to enhance her freedom of thought, give her a teensy little energy boost, perhaps stimulate her into wearing some more-exciting clothing? I mean, isn't it at least *as* likely that you're too slow as it is that I'm too fast? Maybe we should be giving you some amphetamines instead of having me swallow all these downers."

"That's one way of looking at it," the nurse said in a subdued tone.

"Well, then, there we have it. Everything is perspective. *I* say what you need is to have your pussy licked so feverishly you can't remember your own name, and *you* say I need a lobotomy."

"Nobody says you need a lobotomy, Mr. Heartsock," she said, without visible reaction.

"But somebody did mention your pussy," he said, smirking. "Does that make you uncomfortable?" At that point Mr. Heartsock spotted Jimmy in the doorway. "You gotta get me out of here, Jimbo. Did you hear what I did last night? We gotta get the papers. I'm sure it's in the papers. Last night was unbelievable."

"Are you the next of kin?" the woman asked. Her eyes were a deep warm brown, understanding and kind. Her hair was brown and her skin was magnolia white.

"The next of kin?" Jimmy asked.

His father jumped in. "Yeah, he's the next of kin. Do you have my release? Let's get the fuck out of here, Jimbo. Let's go buy the news-papers. I freaked 'em out last night, boy. The cops, man, they love me."

"Yeah, I'm the next of kin, I guess," Jimmy said.

"Would you come with me?" she asked politely.

"Don't listen to them, Jimmy! Just get me out of here."

Jimmy looked at his dad and was frightened. He didn't recognize him at all. The normal green color and warm smile in his eyes were completely gone. His father looked scary, menacing, evil.

"Get me outa here, Jimbo, you're my boy. I can't take these drugs; they're trying to kill me. This should be illegal, all of you should be in jail." His father started crying. "Don't leave me here, boy. I cleaned your diapers."

A cloud seemed to pass from the room. Jimmy could recognize his father simply as the man he had known since birth, strapped to a bed, in terrible pain. The nurse led him to the chief psychiatrist, who informed Jimmy that Mr. Heartsock had given away his car and his bank card and PIN number and led a small group of vagrants and pros-titutes into the Cincinnati Hyatt Regency Hotel, demanding rooms for everyone. When they refused he stood up on a balcony and begged everyone present to rip up their credit cards in protest against a money-obsessed culture and the erosion of the American mind.

When the cops tried to arrest him he screamed that he was dying of AIDS and if they touched him he would spit in their mouths. The doctor recommended that Jimmy, as the next of kin, sign the required papers for his father to be admitted into the high-security mental facility. Jimmy could hear his father screaming as he signed the papers, but he didn't know what else to do.

A few weeks later Mr. Heartsock was released, but over the next two years no one could find a drug combination he would stay on: The inevitable side effects of impotence, shaking hands, and lack of productivity were too debilitating. He was hospitalized at least once a year and sometimes twice. In his suicide note he claimed the fear of recurring insanity had left him incapable of any enjoyment.

Jimmy told me all this, looking straight ahead, his eyes on the road. I didn't say a word.

MISS TEEN OHIO

THE HOUSES IN HUNTING GLEN where I grew up came in four models: Adams, Beauford, Caroline, and Denver, but they were only variations on the same theme—one had the garage on the left, one had it on the right; one was a split level, the other had the master bedroom on the ground floor. There were sixteen colors to choose from. The whole development looked like it was built in a single afternoon. My old man used to say, "If the big bad wolf comes, open the door." His nickname for the development was Identity Hell, and driving through the streets with all the neatly groomed lawns, right on Walnut, left to Chestnut, right on Pecan, it was easy to get lost.

As soon as I saw the house again I stopped the car. From a hundred yards away we could see tables laid out across our front lawn and most of our belongings being rummaged through by neighbors. Then I saw my mom, bebopping around the grass and chatting with everyone. My mother was having a yard sale. Hot blistering rage scraped through my veins. I sat there unmoving in my car as I watched some pudgy brainless suburban dad ask questions about our old chain saw.

My mom was Miss Teen Ohio; that's all you need to know about her. She takes the Easter Bunny seriously and gets pissed off if you try to imply she hid the eggs or attempt in any way to dampen her enthusiasm. At Christmas, she gift-wraps presents for her little white Maltese doggie and everyone has to sit around the tree and watch him claw them open. She was dancing around the yard, basking in all the neighborhood attention. Her light-brown hair was washed and sparkling like an ad for conditioner. Another thing I should mention about my mom is that she's probably slept with a quarter of the men in our town. She just can't help herself; she's self-proclaimed boy-crazy. It used to bother me, but now I'm over it. Sitting in the Nova watching the yard sale, I felt like I was being robbed. About twenty years of frustration was about to go off like a grenade in my skull. I couldn't move. I just watched her dart around like a squirrel, her still pinup-quality figure sashaying from table to table. My stepbrother and sister were flitting between people with wads of bills in their hands. Audrey and Julian, sixteen and twelve respectively, are handsome kids and were dressed in perfect Top Forty hip-hop clothing. Audrey wore a store-bought pressed tie-dye, and Julian had on a bullshit outfit with embroidered dragons on his pants—some kind of pseudo-eastern Buddhist look.

I couldn't bring myself to turn the car off or pull up closer. I just watched. Christy was staring at me. I could feel her concern hot on the side of my face.

Julian was in the process of selling my father's old Martin guitar. The lower half of the instrument was scorched black. I could still vividly remember the night my dad set it on fire. Until I grew older and could compare him to other people, I never realized the level of eccentricity my old man had reached. When I was five he was all I knew, and his chaotic antics were the norm. We were sitting on the basement floor by a dim little table lamp painting miniature plastic cowboys and Indians that we'd bought at this upscale toy store. Not your ordinary fare, each guy was unique, made with precise detail and with individual and specific belts and guns. It was late at night and we'd been painting with my model paint, watching sports for hours. I don't remember where my mother was but she was out. Eventually my dad got bored, busted out his guitar, took some paint thinner, and poured it over the bottom half of the body. He said he wanted it to look like Willie Nelson's. Apparently Willie has a Martin that's mangled, and my dad wanted his to be like that. With paper matches he lit the guitar on fire. Right away he started waving it around, trying to put the flames out before it got too badly damaged. Well, of course the more he waved the damn thing the more it flared up. Finally he ran out the back door with it and rubbed it around on the grass. The fire burned a small hole through the bottom of the base, but basically the idea worked. The guitar now looked wicked cool, and it even had a unique bass lilt in the sound that was appealing.

I shifted in my seat as that pipsqueak Julian with his dragon pants sold the instrument to a middle-aged housewife for what looked like fifteen bucks.

"That's my dad's Martin," I said out loud.

"Let it go," Christy said. "Do you think you can?"

I watched items I recognized and things I didn't get passed around and sold. I took several long deep breaths and realized how profoundly fuckin' pissed off I was at all these people. I missed my father, but the one question I probably most wanted to ask him was one he wasn't the right person to answer: What am I supposed to do with all this anger? What's the right way for it to manifest? God knows I was getting sick and tired of tripping all over it.

I pressed the gas, revved the engine about three times, and pulled the Nova around sharp in a quick U-turn. Walking down the middle of the street was that oafy woman with my father's Martin. She carried it from the neck like a dead chicken.

Three quick rights and I was back on the interstate. And I'll tell you something about that afternoon. I've seen my mom lots of times since, but that was the last time I ever tried to go home.

CRAZY HORSE

I WAS SITTING all bundled up on top of an old weatherbeaten wood picnic table watching Jimmy shoot a basketball. He hadn't brought any sneakers, so his feet in their clumsy black military boots clomped on the cracked asphalt court. Clouds were thick, heavy, and low above us. The air was cool and wet and smelled like evergreen. There were scattered patches of snow spread around, but the grass was mostly visible, steaming slightly like a warm lake on a cold morning. To our right was an empty children's playground. The seesaws, swings, and jungle gyms looked lonely and abandoned in the afternoon mist. Miniature metal horses, unicorns, and mermaids were standing, erect and unused, on thick metal springs. With my baby's cells multiplying exponentially inside my womb, these toys looked different to me now.

This was Jimmy's community rec center, where he first learned to swim over in the pool directly adjacent to the parking lot. The pool was closed; a giant plastic blue tarp covered the whole concrete area to protect it from the cold. There was a changing house painted barn red with a door on either end, the left marked BOYS and the right GIRLS, in white hand-painted letters. Jimmy fingered Heather Moore over on the grass behind that pool house. I don't know why he told me that. It was his first time "getting to third." His father's grave was in the cemetery just over the fence, which we did visit, briefly. Jimmy sat in front of the tombstone for about three or four quiet minutes. The wind made my throat cold as I stood behind him. A tiny American flag by the headstone marked his father's service in the Vietnam War.

After those few moments of quiet in the cold cemetery grass, Jimmy said, "You know how Crazy Horse got his name?"

"The Indian?" I asked.

"Yeah."

"No," I said, trying to maintain a respectful air.

"You'd think it was because he tamed some wild stallion, right? Or maybe 'cause he was fearless like a deranged horse might be." He didn't look at me, and I didn't answer. It was a peculiar trait of Jimmy's; he was a fanatic about history.

"But it was just his dad's name. That's all." He paused. "He was actually Crazy Horse Junior."

The wind blew through the short bristles of his hair.

"I'm sorry about all this, baby," Jimmy said to me, still sitting in the damp earth around his father's headstone.

"What do you mean?" I asked. I was cold. I wanted to go back to the car and get my coat.

"This must be a downer for you, you know?"

"It's OK," I said, slightly bewildered. "I want to be here."

"This is my baggage. I hate to make it yours, you know?"

When Jimmy's nervous or uncomfortable, he talks a little too loud and he always says, "You know?" We sat there another couple of minutes, and then Jimmy abruptly stood up and said he wanted to go shoot some baskets. He keeps a basketball in his trunk, along with a tent, some blankets, and other miscellaneous emergency junk. Now, only fifteen minutes later, he was dancing around the pavement and tossing the ball, trying to impress me the way you imagine Tom Sawyer might, pretending he was some famous athlete. He'd ask me to count down the final seconds of some fictional game so he could let fly a buzzer winning shot and then jump and cheer for himself like a stadium of frenzied fans. Enjoying it all only because I was watching, he clomped around on his boots, talking quickly, his breath steaming from his nose and mouth like a teakettle. I sat there, bundled up in my jacket, watching him.

"I think Michael Jordan sucks," Jimmy said, as he ran and jumped toward the basket, spreading his legs wide in a spastic imitation of a sensational move. "He's not my hero. I don't relate to him."

"Who *is* your hero?" I asked. I wasn't really listening to him. I was fiddling with my engagement ring, spinning it in circles around my finger. The wind was blowing wet and clean, gently brushing my hair out of my face. I was glad to be out of the car. We'd been driving for sixteen hours. Jimmy hadn't slept at all. I didn't understand why, but he almost always found a way not to let me drive.

"John Starks, baby, that's my hero." Jimmy is a tireless New York Knicks fan. Shooting a long jump shot, he shouted, *"Glass, boom!"* The ball bounced off the shimmering sheet-metal backboard and dropped through the hoop and into the chain netting.

The Nova was parked right up on the grass; he'd left the car on and the doors open so we could hear the music. The Rolling Stones' "Exile on Main Street" echoed out into the Ohio plains.

Two kids, maybe thirteen and fifteen, were shooting on the other half of the court. I could tell they were irritated by the music and by Jimmy's boisterous shouts, exclamations, and general demeanor. They were sniggering and throwing scowling looks back at us.

"Don't you want to talk more about your father, Jim?" I asked, patting the picnic table and motioning for him to step over and sit by me. It was important, I thought, that we try to communicate more deeply with each other.

"I don't have anything more to say about the subject. I told you everything last night."

"Are you angry at him?" I asked.

"No," he said calmly.

"Are you angry at me?" I tried to smile.

"No," he said, dribbling the ball. He was wearing a navy blue base-ball jersey with his name printed on the back over a gray hooded sweatshirt; he always wore the two together. It's funny, the absurd teenage quality of every outfit he owned. He and his intramural base-ball teammates each paid an extra fifty bucks for those jerseys. They wanted their names printed on the back. HEARTSOCK was on his in white letters above the number 34; he said it was important. The jer-sey couldn't help but remind me of his father's headstone.

"I'm just worried about your not really addressing it," I said, and I was.

"I have addressed it," he said, bending down and tightening his bootlaces. Immediately after the suicide he'd seen a psychiatrist for four months, but it didn't have much impact. I'm sure Jimmy just entertained the shrink with BS.

"I know you pretty well," I added, trying to maintain a friendly tone, "and I don't think you have. I'm sitting here watching you, won-dering when the other shoe is gonna drop."

"If you're worried I'm gonna go nuts, you can stop." Now he was irritated. He stopped dribbling the ball and held it tight under his arm. "Don't start backseat analyzing me, Christy, it makes me feel like a rat in a test cage or something." Fear of insanity is the only reason Jimmy joined the military, I'm sure of it. He needed the structure.

Trying to stop myself from neurotically spinning the engagement ring, I started rubbing my knees. My joints are horrendous, and the long car trip hadn't done them any favors. All my cartilage had begun popping and cracking with every shift of my weight. "What do you want to talk about then?" I asked.

"The 1994 NBA finals," Jimmy said, dribbling the basketball again. "Coach Pat Riley calls the Knicks out for the season's opening day of practice at exactly one minute after midnight."

"Spare me, buddy," I pleaded. He knows I really couldn't care less about the finer details of professional sports.

"He tells them Michael Jordan has retired and gone to play baseball. 'This is our year,' he says. 'We're first in the NBA to step out on the court, and we will be the last to leave. When we do, we will be champions.'"

Jimmy spoke with an intensity about basketball that was almost never present when he talked about his own life.

"And they did it. The Knicks made the finals. They were playing Houston. Each team won three games before the deciding game seven. Starks played phenomenally. You gotta understand, John Starks was a Kansas boy who two years earlier had been stacking cans at the fuckin' Piggly Wiggly. He was no first-round draft pick, no fancy-pants little Nike mascot." Jimmy's dad had loathed Nike. Apparently they don't make any shoes in the United States and employ all sorts of underage Third World children. His father had taught him that to be wealthy was intrinsically evil, and that to hold on to so much when so many had so little should be a jailable offense.

"Let me make one thing clear. Starks wasn't a basketball player," Jimmy went on. "He was an artist. He played with feeling, like Mozart. You understand?"

I nodded, teasing him with a phony doe-eyed look of rapturous attention. It was my favorite kind of moody day, air so thick you felt you could see it. Pregnancy had given me an uncanny ability to space out, like being mildly stoned all the time. I was quick to cry, quick to laugh, and I must say I had a larger sexual appetite than at any other time in my life. A natural incentive to draw and keep a man close for birth, I figured.

"You mock," Jimmy continued, "but at times he looked shabby, like he belonged in junior high summer leagues, and at other times the intensity level in his eyes would get so ice hot that opposing coaches in the league quaked with dread." He said all this while dribbling the ball between his legs. "One minute the Knicks would be trailing by twelve points; the next thing you know—*whoosh!*—John Starks drops thirty points and the game is over. *Bam!* Knicks are on top." Jimmy ran toward the basket and laid the ball in the net, his heavy boots all of an inch and a half off the ground as he leapt. In his mind he looked glorious.

The two younger boys across the court had stopped playing and were looking over at us. Maybe I project it, but I always see something dark and foreboding in the eyes of teenage boys. They all look like they're capable of bashing your head in.

Above us on the hill, over the fence, the graveyard was still visible. The picnic bench was beginning to make my butt hurt. I stuck my hand under my jacket and under my shirt and felt the soft skin below my belly button. There was a thin dark line slowly forming on the skin of my abdomen, every day creeping up toward my belly button, the external measure of my growing uterus.

"Just so you know," I told him, "you're not playing into my fantasy right now."

"So there he is, this grocery clerk from Kansas, John Starks." Jimmy was so enjoying telling this story it would've been cruel to stop him. "The little train that could, Mr. I-Think-I-Can, starting in the greatest basketball game in the world: *Game Seven of the NBA finals*! And you gotta understand how deeply Starks loves to play. You can see it in the way he snaps off his sweats, like Clark Kent seeing a little girl in danger. And here he is, living the dream. The series was tied at three apiece, but the Houston Rockets were favored to win. They were playing on their home court, and no team in NBA history ever won Game Seven on the road."

"No way, Jimmy, really, no team in *history*," I teased. He was so enthusiastic I had to jerk his chain. "Unbelievable. But you and John Starks did it, huh?"

"I'm not done telling the story," he said, holding his finger up like a history professor.

"Sweet Jesus," I said.

"Hey, why don't you shut your fucking trap!" shouted a thin young voice from a distance, shocking both of us. It was the younger of the two schoolboys. His buddy was behind him, choking, trying to hold in

his laughter. "It's bad enough the music you've got playing, but to have to listen to your diarrhea of the mouth is torture." The kid was probably five-seven and obviously still growing. His arms and hands were much too large for his body. His face was scatter-shot with pimples, but you could tell he'd be handsome someday; he had high cheekbones, a sharp nose, and the physique of an athlete. He was wearing expensive purple sneakers, and his sweat pants were stuffed into his socks to show them off. MICHIGAN STATE was written across his chest, gold lettering on blue cotton, and a wild look of adolescent discomfort and anger smoldered in his eyes.

"What did you just say to me?" Jimmy stopped dribbling and turned around. His entire demeanor changed instantly.

"Jimmy, he's just a kid," I said quietly, drawing him back toward me. "Watch your language!" I shouted to the boy, thinking that as a girl I could somehow disarm any male posturing.

"Hey, pipsqueak," Jimmy said, walking toward the two kids, "why don't you go home and let your mom rub some lotion on your dick for you?"

"Jimmy, leave him alone," I said.

"I'm not afraid of you, faggot," shouted the kid, throwing his head back like he had antlers on top of his head.

"Can you believe this?" Jimmy turned around back toward me.

"Fuck you, dirtweed," said the kid, and started walking toward Jim. But then he turned around instead, saying something inaudible to his crony. They both sniggered with their backs turned.

"What did you say?" Jimmy asked, exasperated, turning back toward them.

"Nothin', faggot." The kid scowled at the ground.

"That's right you said nothing," Jimmy continued. "Get out of my sight."

"You wanna run one right now?" The kid was walking toward us again, his basketball under his arm.

"What, play basketball with you?" Jimmy laughed. "Are you nuts? I'm not gonna play some kid with a smart mouth."

"I would destroy you," the boy stated, now uncomfortably close.

This is where I first became aware that something terrible might happen.

"You have shit for manners, all right. Go home and play some video games," Jimmy said. "Get lost. Scram!" he added.

"You chicken?" the boy asked.

Jimmy started laughing. "You got a hundred bucks? I'll play you for that," he challenged.

"You ain't got a hundred bucks. Your fuckin' car ain't worth a hundred bucks." The kid pointed to Jimmy's Nova and motioned to the bumper sticker on the back. "What, you really in the army?"

"Yeah, I'm really in the army."

"Nice job. What, no openings at the gas station?" The boy's buddy busted a deep hardy laugh on that quip. The whole dialogue was obviously going nowhere constructive.

"My father was in the army," Jimmy said, "and he's dead up on that hill, so watch your mouth."

"Your dad doesn't need to be dead for me to feel sorry for you." The kid was feeling confident now, hearing his friend's laughter rolling across the basketball court.

"Go home, kid," Jimmy said firmly. I was proud of him for not biting.

"I'm coming back with a hundred bucks, and you better have it," the kid pronounced.

"What, you gonna steal it?" Only Jimmy's back was visible to me, but I could hear a tightness in his voice.

"I'm gonna kick your ass," the kid stated officially, grabbing his buddy's shirtsleeve. They both pranced off across the rec field.

"I can't believe that punk," Jimmy said, turning back to me casually, but his lips were tight and angry.

"Let's go, Jimmy, I don't like this place anymore." I began getting up from the picnic bench.

"No way," Jimmy said, dribbling again. "Let's stay right here."

"You're not gonna play that kid."

"Nope, but I was telling you about John Starks."

"You know, I don't care, right, Jimmy? I mean, do you realize that this conversation is of absolutely zero interest to me?"

"No, no, no," he said. "Don't be mean. You do care, I know you do." The look in his eyes was earnest and sincere. That boy had upset him, but he was going to go on simply to prove otherwise. He was also convinced that deep down these ramblings held some level of interest for me.

"I woke up on the morning of Game Seven—*blink!*—my body stinging with electricity. I went outside and shot some baskets to try and calm down. I felt if *I* could compose myself then *they* could."

"They?" I asked.

"The team, the Knicks. I had this . . . uh . . . foreshadowing ritual where if I could make my first seven baskets in a row, the Knicks never lost. And that morning—*ding, ding, ding*—I drained 'em all. I couldn't believe it."

"How old were you?" I sat back down.

"I was twenty-four, but you have to understand that I'm not telling you about some random game, I'm telling you a fable, a parable, all right?" He looked at me hard from underneath his dark black eyebrows. "These sonsabitches taught me about empathy, compassion, integrity, and the real meaning of dignity. I'm telling you the truth now; this was only a little while after the death of my old man, OK? And this game taught me more about the real nature of prayer than anybody in the church ever could. I was so amped up, with my head spinning around in delirium about this game, that I ended up going to church to calm down. No shit. I got down on my knees and prayed."

"But then I thought, What the fuck am I praying for?"

"For the Knicks to win, right?" I asked, listening to him, trying to understand what he was really telling me.

"Yeah, but I'm smart enough to know that some other shmuck must be praying for Houston to win, right? There's a lot of people in Houston. Why should God choose me over this guy?"

"Jimmy, you're nuts. You realize that?" I was still anxious that the kid would come back with his money.

"I'm kind of kidding and I'm kind of serious," he said with a wink, looking like himself again. "I should just pray for the best man to win, or for everyone to do the best that they can, or for no one to get hurt. But I want *my* guys to win so badly I can't even think straight, so I say, 'Holy Mary, Mother of God, please watch over the New York Knicks. Let them blast those fuckin' bastard Houston Rockets to hell! Let John Starks rain in three-pointers for forty days and forty nights. Let the common folk of America sit around their dinner tables and know deep in their hearts that sometimes the ordinary man can rise above the sludge of his environment and kiss the greatness set aside for kings. Let him win so the rest of us, every motherfucker stackin' cans in the Piggly Wiggly, can dream. O sweet Mary, hear my prayer.'" Jimmy was standing in the middle of the court like a TV evangelist.

I couldn't help asking. "Did they win?"

"At the start of the game, the Houston crowd was so raucous they were already wearing their HOUSTON ROCKETS WORLD CHAMPIONS T-shirts." He started dribbling again, and I knew it had been a mistake to show any interest.

"Please don't give me a play-by-play coverage of the game," I said.

Jimmy unveiled a giant toothy, gummy grin. "Houston jumped out to an early lead, but the boys hung tight—not letting the game slip away."

One thing I've noticed in young couples is that the boys often seem to do the majority of the talking, rambling on, wanting everyone to listen to them, to hear them, to acknowledge them; and then in older couples the gentleman often sits silent with a distant look in his eyes as the woman chatters on like rain falling. At what age, I wondered, does the switch take place?

"The team needed Starks to step it up and find his groove. At one point he missed three shots in a row: *clang, clang, clang.*" Jimmy shot up a ball that hit the front of the rim hard, bounced off the court, and went into the grass. Chasing after it, he kept right on speaking. "The ball kept going to him as the team waited for him to rekindle that spark that'd lit the way all season. He would find his shot: he had to."

I looked down at my engagement ring, trying to see only the intent behind it, but it was challenging not to focus on how ugly it was. My man had zero taste. He should've asked me to go pick it out with him. He'd said it was hand-crafted by a local artist, but it looked more like it was made by a teenager in metal shop. I tried it on different fingers, imagining my hand old, bony, spotted, and frail with this ring still drooping off it. I wished it was prettier; it didn't fit perfectly on any finger.

"Again and again Starks would carefully place his toes on the three-point line, as he always does, and let the ball fly, looking for that magic *shazam*." Jimmy tossed another shot up from almost the middle of the court. "And still, brick." The ball missed the basket, banging hard against the backboard. Jimmy sprinted over and caught it before it touched the ground. "Still, his teammates and the coach believed in him, long after everyone else had stopped. They knew the heart of John Starks would not fail."

I watched the father of my child chattering away at me and wondered which of us would outlive the other. I would, of course. I wondered if we would be buried together. The thought stopped my blood: I pictured our two names on one headstone. I didn't want to get married, no way. I wanted my own headstone.

"Starks's eyes burned red. You could see how bright they were from the top of the stadium. *I think I can, I think I can* . . . he was saying to himself, looking for that miracle play that'd turn the tide of defeat, the moment that would live on forever in highlight reels and little boys' minds. Grandpa would see a picture of Starks come on the television as they hung his number up in the rafters of Madison Square Garden and as John Starks was inducted into the Hall of Fame, and Gramps would say, 'There's a winner! See, kids, the meek shall inherit the earth.'"

I couldn't help it, a part of me viewed marriage as putting blinders on a horse and racing toward the finish line of death. Also, I was wondering what happens when the sex life goes. I decided I'd demand we make love once a day whether we wanted to or not.

"But that's not what happened." Jimmy paused dramatically and went on in a subdued voice. "At the end of the night John Starks slunk away into a jubilant Houston crowd completely unnoticed, his eyes blood-red and blurry with agony, looking up to heaven. The Knicks lost, and he finished the night having made only two shots and missing fifteen."

I was staring at Jimmy talking. He was very handsome, with a well-shaped head that looks good with the short military haircut. I imagined I could feel his DNA regenerating inside me. I was getting so fat. My tits were swelling. Goddamn, I hoped my tits wouldn't be ruined. I don't like aging. The skin around my fingers wasn't as good and tight as it used to be. I have the same problem around my toes. My nails used to be difficult to cut they were so thick and hard; now they're verging on wispy. Aging gracefully is such a big goal. When I was little I didn't think I was vain, but now I can see how hard it's going to be when I lose my looks. Already I can see the pores on my face and the start of a giant crease between my eyes.

"Random guy, comes up to me the next day, says, 'Did you hear? John Starks tried to shoot himself?' I'm like, No fuckin' way! 'Yeah,' the guys says, 'only he *missed*. Ha-ha-ha!'

"So I go back to the church, to Mother Mary, and I ask, Why is there no justice? Why is life unfair? Why does Michael Jordan get to win so much and others not at all? I understand that a basketball game is not as crushingly complex as, say, an issue like disease or starvation, but I also understand that things are not as different as they seem, and inside a fully examined game of basketball is the answer to how you fix a combustion engine; you know what I'm saying?" His eyes were seeking affirmation. "Sitting there, in that church, looking up at that same image of Mary that I'd gazed at so full of hope only the day before, I realized that prayers are left unanswered for a reason. And that reason is: We have no inkling of what is good for us."

Sometimes it's so obvious Jimmy is an only child. When he goes off talking like this I imagine his mother just gooing and gaahing, encouraging him. I asked him once if I reminded him of his mother. I know I do. I've seen her pictures and I must, but he got all uptight, like admitting it would be some kind of taboo sexual thing. He definitely reminds me of my dad. They both have big oversized hands and a space between their two front teeth. Also, the way they both kind of half run, half walk, when they're in a hurry; their shoulders wriggle the same.

"Hakeem 'the Dream' Olajuwon is the big superstar for the Houston Rockets, right?" he continued. I nodded my head as if I understood what he was talking about.

"Winning that championship might be the worst thing that ever happened to him. It's possible. If he doesn't handle it right, gets a swollen head, starts screwing around, his wife takes the kids back to fuckin' Kenya or wherever he's from. He develops a twenty-thousand-dollar-a-day coke habit that leaves him dead in a whorehouse outside of Philadelphia with his precious championship ring being melted down by some local pawnshop owner."

I was trying to listen, but I wasn't sure I wanted to get married. Making vows about tomorrow seemed to be uselessly tempting fate. You could make vows of intent, but promising anything further about an unknown variable like the future seemed arrogant. The world has its ways, its nasty tricksy ways, to bring you to your knees and spin everything you hold true into a bald-faced lie.

"John Starks might have become a great man that day of his seeming humiliation. He could have realized that grace, integrity, and hard work are their own reward. It's easy to be gracious, tolerant, and accepting and say *Everyone is equal* and *I wish everybody well* when you get everything you want. But the real challenge is to still be this way when you *don't* get what you want. Gratitude in the face of loss or suffering—now, that's a man or a woman who knows the courage of their convictions. Is Michael Jordan a great basketball player? Yes. Is he my hero? No. I don't want to idolize somebody because he wins. I don't win. Look at me, man, I'm how you spell *disappointment*. I thought I was gonna be great like Jack Kennedy, you know? Somebody in cool important places doin' all kinds of fantabulous things. Mr. Merrill Lynch. Instead I'm, like, Mr. Mediocrity."

I shook my head at him. I wasn't thinking about basketball.

If we could just love each other and live in truth as much as possible and not act out some idea of what a relationship is supposed to be. To not lie—at all. To be able to sit down, look each other in the eye, and speak our minds freely. To maintain a perspective on the other and not wholly judge him in context to yourself. I don't want somebody to stay with me just 'cause he promised to do so eighteen years ago or whatever. He should stay with me because he wants to, because he loves me and believes that being with me is what he needs most deeply. An awake, conscious life, that's all I really desired.

"Somebody like that kid"—Jimmy was still talking, pointing across the field toward the housing development the young punk had disappeared into—"might look at me and think, What a nobody, but then they'll see you and they'll see our love and our soon-to-be scoobie baby crawling around, and if they got a brain in their noggin they'll say, 'That Heartsock, he's got something on the ball.' And who knows, maybe the worst thing that ever happened to me—you know, my dad's death . . . my dad's suicide"—he corrected himself—"made me available to show up and love you, or maybe it kindled or woke something inside me that makes me attractive to you in some way."

"You think I find you attractive?" I asked. I'd started listening. His breath was steaming out of his mouth.

"I'm just saying we don't know what's good for us. I prayed my everlivin' guts out in the church right over that hill for Shannon Macquarrie and I to be together forever. Shannon had her foot amputated recently because her circulation was so demolished from years of heroin abuse—you get it?"

"So John Starks taught you acceptance?" I said, still watching Jimmy. I love the way he moves through space, languid, like a boxer warming up.

"Yeah, I guess," he said. "You know what Starks said when they traded him away a couple years later? Some reporter guy asked him if he regretted anything, and he said, 'Yeah, I regret not winning New York a championship. I regret going two of seventeen that Game Seven, but I hope if I can give the fans anything it would be the joy of the unexpected, and if they ever believe they can't sink any lower they'll think of me and know it's possible to go on.'"

"I want to talk about our wedding, Jim," I said, inching my way toward a different conversation.

"You do wanna marry me, don't you, Christy?"

Out from behind the pool house, tramping aggressively over the grass, came that little twerp and his buddy. This time with two more friends, the four of them all moving toward us at a quick clip. We could hear them cackling and cursing.

"Let's go," I said. "I hate that kid. He creeps me out."

"No, no, no, hold on a second," Jimmy mumbled, looking out.

The kid shouted over the barren damp field, still wearing his Michigan State T-shirt, "You said you want to play me for a hundred bucks!" His voice sounded as if it had changed two days ago. "Maybe you should take out a loan," he added, as he arrived at the playground, throwing down a pile of five twenties at the center of the court, like he thought he was an action hero.

"What the fuck is your hang-up, kid? Is your dad the Pop Warner coach or something?"

"Jimmy, let's get out of here." I stood up.

"You ain't got the money, just say so." The kid was standing cock-eyed, one shoulder much higher than the other.

"I can't take money off a child." Jim turned back to me, shaking his head.

"Fuck you. I'll beat you straight up."

"You gotta be careful with that word." Jim snapped around and walked deliberately over to the boy. "*Fuck you* is a big word." He stood only a few inches taller than the kid.

"*Fuck you* is two words," the boy said, staring straight up into Jimmy's eyes while his friends tittered with nervous pleasure.

"Jim, this kid obviously has a problem. Please drive me out of here," I said, trying to give him an out.

"You're lucky I got better things to do, shmuckface." Jimmy dismissed the boy and turned to walk away.

"Fuck you! You said you'd play me for a hundred bucks; now you're gonna chicken out?" The kid was so aggressive it made my stomach hurt. It amazed me how a day could be going one direction and the wind could just blow everything backward.

"When I win I'm gonna take your money, wipe my ass with it, and flush it down the toilet, you understand that?" Jimmy said, standing dead still in the middle of the court.

"Jimmy, let's go," I called out impatiently.

"You keep talking, but I don't see you laying down the cash."

"You're a fuckin' arrogant little twerp, you know that?"

"Jimmy, don't do this," I said again.

"Let's see the jack. Or maybe you want to borrow it from her?" The kid's eyes were blue like an exploding constellation.

"Twenty, forty, sixty, eighty, one hundred." Jimmy flipped out his wallet and threw the money on the ground. "Come on, wiseass, let's run it." He picked up both piles of money and set them on the picnic table beside me with a rock on top to weight them down.

"Don't do this," I whispered.

"I have to, now," he said.

"I'm gonna get in the car."

"Baby, please stay."

"I'm not going to watch you get goaded into some ridiculous game."

"I can't tell you why, but this is important," he said.

"No, Jimmy, that's the thing; it's *not* important."

"I'm gonna win," he muttered, tying the laces of his boots tight.

"I don't care if you win, I care if you're an idiot." I tried to get him to look at me. "In what way is this going to turn out well? Use your head. He's a child."

"Please stay and watch; it *is* important," he repeated. He looked at me, his eyes cold and faraway, and then turned around and walked onto the court. "Come on, motherfucker, shoot for ball, you little faggot."

"Kick his ass, Jamie!" His friends were standing at the edge of the court cheering him on. Jamie, I thought. This kid's name is Jamie.

"Twos and threes to twenty-one," Jamie said.

"Fuck that, homo, ones to eleven or no deal." Jimmy has a temper—I've seen it before—and this kid had lit it.

"You scared?" the punk said, trying to rile Jimmy even more.

"Of what?" Jimmy said, throwing the ball far too hard at the kid's head. "Shoot for ball, faggot."

I could see what bothered Jimmy most was that this kid wasn't afraid of him.

"By two?" the kid asked, catching the ball a fraction of a second before it shattered his nose. He wasn't even slightly disoriented by Jimmy's incredibly aggressive stance.

"Straight up," Jimmy said.

The kid stepped back and shot the ball. It went high up in the air and fell cleanly through the basket, barely moving the chain mesh netting. In that moment I felt Jimmy would lose, and I was both petrified and angry at how miserable the rest of the day would be.

"Your ball," Jimmy said, throwing it back at the kid. "Check it up."

"I'm not going to watch, this is so stupid," I said loudly, and turned around without looking back. As I stepped into the car I heard the kid's friends cheer as he scored the first basket. I slammed the door, turned the radio up to a deafening roar, and switched all the old levers, trying to muster something from the heat. I couldn't watch. I directed my eyes in the opposite direction over the graveyard and up into the large gray expanse of sky. On a telephone wire, two blackbirds tucked their necks into the warmth of their own feathered chests and looked off in my direction. With the music cranked up, I couldn't hear any of the game shenanigans. Jimmy was still such a child. I could never marry him. What was I thinking? I stared at the two birds, thinking of Jimmy's ninth-grade school photo, which I'd found once in his apartment. He had freshly washed sparkling-clean hair down to his shoulders, parted in the middle and feathered back out of his face; on his chest was a Black Sabbath T-shirt; and on his face was the sweetest smile. He was then about the age of this kid Jamie. The blackbirds flew away. I couldn't see where they went.

I turned and looked at my fiancé. He was frantically defending against this teenager, sweat dampening his hair, his boots moving around clumsily, his face all splotchy, Irish, and red. The pipsqueak bystanders were looking concerned now, so the game must be close. Jimmy kept shaking his head, tossing it up in the air like a horse, gasping for more oxygen. He stole the ball and quickly put it in the basket. His eyes looked for me and met my gaze. I wanted to smile but he'd looked away before I could. I've never been very good at sports. I was tall so girls were always trying to drag me out for baseball or basketball, but whenever people started getting super enthusiastic, I just wanted to go home. Jimmy was huffing and puffing while this kid was dancing around him in three-hundred-dollar sneakers. If he didn't win this game, the rest of my week was gonna suck.

I couldn't help it. Before I knew what I was doing I'd reached up onto the dashboard and taken a mutilated cigarette from Jimmy's pack: my fifth one in the last two days. He'd been giving me grief about smoking, yet *he* wasn't quitting. My mother smoked when she was pregnant with me, and I turned out all right. I mean, I'm tall, at least.

Then I realized, sitting there on the cracked leather seat, that I could not under any circumstances smoke. It was one of those times in a person's life where they either show up or don't, a moment that determines your mettle, defines your character. You couldn't smoke through a pregnancy and pretend to yourself in any way that you deserved to be a mother.

The bass of the car radio was thumping away at my insides. No outside noise could penetrate the bass line.

I wanted my grandmother's arms around me. I thought of how much I loved to hear her play the piano and sing silly songs. There was one about a fish that I loved best: "Sing a Tune of Tuna Fish."

I put the cigarette in my mouth. It was a little crooked but I straightened it out.

I wanted this cigarette more than I wanted anything. I told myself again that I couldn't have one. I shouldn't. I thought if you were pregnant you would be able to feel the soul, but I didn't feel anything.

I touched the skin above my womb. Was there someone there?

I flashed on a memory of my father, in the Broadway Diner on 54th Street in New York City eight years earlier. I had asked him to sign my emancipation papers so I could work and get married. He was asking me to come home, but I needed him to stop me and not let me go. But he did it; he signed the papers. I was wearing my leopard-skin zip-up jacket that day, and I could tell he was scared of me. It repulsed me, that he could let his seventeen-year-old daughter walk out alone into that city.

I remember him asking, "What makes you think you can hate me so much, and I'll just keep on loving you? Huh? What makes you think that?"

Pretty soon I was gonna start crying. Maybe it was the progesterone, but I seemed to be crying a lot.

What had I done? I was going to be a mother. Everything was getting so *serious*. I felt like the real me was sitting in a bar somewhere doing shots. I wanted this baby, Jimmy's and my child, but there was so much responsibility. I hoped I didn't have to have an episiotomy.

What if it *is* a girl child? The thought filled me with hope.

I tried to breathe.

Now was a perfect time to quit smoking. As good a time as any.

With the cigarette still in my mouth, I took out my little pink lighter.

I've been smoking since I was twelve. My girlfriend Danielle and I put on a pile of makeup one Sunday, walked over to the Crystal Diner and put our quarters in the cigarette machine, ignored the frightening glances from the big cashier woman, pulled the squeaky metal lever on a pack of unfiltered cigarettes, and snuck out back to smoke them. Unfiltered cigarettes were a must for us, we'd both just read a biography of our idol, James Dean, and that's what he'd smoked. In fact, a few nights earlier the Ouija board had told us that Danielle was James Dean in her last life. We stood out back by the Dumpsters and smoked two in a row, both getting dizzy, and then all of a sudden Danielle bent over and vomited. I've never forgotten that moment, because when I heard Danielle had died at twenty-three the first time she ever did a speedball, I immediately thought of her puking that day. Her chemical makeup or something just couldn't hack abuse. I thought of her, sparked up the little pink lighter, and drew the smoke deep into my lungs.

I apologized to my baby.

I said, I can do better than this.

I said, I'm sorry, but sometimes I'm weak.

I took another drag and rolled down the window.

"Out on you, motherfucker, out on you!" I heard Jimmy bellow across the Ohio valley.

All along the horizon you could see the beginnings of little spring redbuds hidden in the gray mass of bristling trees outlining the park and the cemetery around us.

"My ball," Jimmy said, mostly to himself, exhausted and out of breath. "What are we looking at?" he asked. The cropped hair on his head was dripping wet with perspiration, and his cheeks were cherry red. I'm sure his feet were bleeding, and his eyes were wicked intense.

"Seven–six, me," the kid said, passing the ball in to Jimmy. I wished the game were over. "Ball's in." The kid was serious and nervous, always twitching some part of his body.

Jimmy quickly grabbed the ball and without hesitation jumped up and shot. It rattled in. "What's the score now?"

The kid didn't answer but threw the ball back in to Jim.

"Ball's in, Buster Brown, seven–seven."

Jimmy quickly shot the ball up again, making his second shot in a row.

"Oh, gosh darn, Scooter, I didn't mean to make two in a row like that. I know how badly you want to win." Jimmy was grinning a contemptuous smile.

"Just play," the kid said, under his breath.

"You wanna put a little extra money on whether I make that same jumper again? Huh? Thirty bucks says I can't make that shot three times in a row. Not a pathetic dirtweed like me, huh? Isn't that what you called me, a dirtweed? Whatcha say, Scooter?"

"Just play."

"Okay, Your Highness. I'm sorry. Am I talking too much? I'm sorry," Jimmy said again, faintly, out of breath as he dribbled easily around the perimeter of the court. "You see, the good Lord didn't give me no rich daddy to buy me fancy sweatpants like yours. The good Lord didn't give me no rich papa to buy me them sweet purple sneakers you got on your feet," he taunted. "The good Lord didn't give me no sweet mommy to give me a hundred bucks to go out and play. But do you know what the good Lord did give me? Huh, Scooter? Do you know what the good Lord did give me?"

"Just play," said the kid, keeping his eyes on the dribbling basketball.

"The good Lord gave me *a jump shot*," Jimmy said quickly, leaping up way far back from the basket and shooting the ball. It swished in again for the third time. I felt like this was the closest I would get to meeting Jimmy's father.

Watching Jim play basketball, I wished so much I could free him from his past.

"What's the score now, big shot?" I heard Jimmy ask the boy as he passed the ball back in.

"Nine to seven, you," the kid muttered.

The boy was barely out of breath, whereas Jimmy was obviously fighting for every gasp.

I threw my cigarette out the window, opened the car door, stepped into the damp air, and sat up on the hood of the car. Jimmy looked over and smiled. His victory could now be complete. It wouldn't have been good enough for him to win, I needed to watch.

Never again would I smoke, I vowed. It was a firm decision, a moment of clarity. The guilt of smoking had become so unbearable that the only relief I'd been able to find was to smoke. I thought of Antonia, a client of mine back at the hospital. She was an attractive twenty-three-year-old woman from Guatemala addicted to crack cocaine and in her first trimester of pregnancy. I was fairly sure she was a prostitute. She'd already lost one child to foster care. I pleaded with her to enter a rehab program so she could maintain custody of this new baby.

"Drugs are the only thing keeping me alive," she'd told me. "If I got clean and took a good hard look at what kind of person I am and the things I've done and left undone, I'd have to blow my brains out."

I talked her into coming to the hospital for a check on her pregnancy. She wore a long red evening gown, her only presentable outfit, she'd said. The nurses left her in the waiting room for six hours, refusing to address a crackhead. Finally she left. I never saw her again.

I sat on the hood of the Nova. The one great thing about these old muscle cars is that they don't dent every time you touch them. The dusty taste of smoke was still present like a dry film inside my mouth. I cursed it: no more coffee. I would eat broccoli and start taking those horse-sized prenatal vitamins. If only my stomach wasn't always so nervous and edgy.

Jimmy scored again. This time he said nothing. The silence was his most menacing and intimidating approach yet. There was only one point to go.

"Come on, beat 'im, Jamie," the boy's friends encouraged him. You could see clearly the fear in the boy's face. I wasn't sure but I thought he was trembling. Jimmy didn't notice him at all; he simply lunged toward the basket and then spontaneously jumped back and shot the ball up one last time. Nothing but net, as he would say. Then, without speaking, he walked over to the picnic table, lifted up the stone, grabbed the money, divided it in half, walked back to the boy, and slapped a hundred bucks on the boy's chest.

"Don't say shit about a man's dead father, OK? Don't make fun of someone older than you. You have no idea what it's taken for me to become the lame-ass dirtweed I am. You understand? You have no idea."

The boy's lip was now shaking uncontrollably, and fat tears were welling up in his eyes.

"Success isn't measured by what you achieve, it's measured by the obstacles you overcome," Jimmy added, with his hand holding the money still firmly fixed on the boy's chest. I wanted the boy to say, Euphemisms are the tool of the feebleminded, but he didn't say anything; he was simply staring at the ground trying to will his tears away.

Jimmy went to step back, but the boy wouldn't take the money and let the twenties fall and scatter on the pavement. There was no breeze, so the bills lay motionless where they fell. Turning back to look at the kid, I could see his face begin to contort.

"Let's get the fuck out of here. Fuck that guy," his friends called out, but the boy still kept his back turned on his peers.

"Hey, what are you crying about?" Jimmy said softly, walking back in front of him, trying to bend low so he could see up into the kid's eyes.

"Fuck you," Jamie said, through a buildup of snot.

"Watch your language, OK?" Jimmy was trying to get the kid to look at him. "How old are you?"

"Twelve," he said simply, looking up.

"Oh, my God, you're only twelve? You look seventeen." Jimmy turned and looked back at me. "Jesus, where'd you get a hundred bucks?"

"I borrowed it from my brother." He inhaled deeply. "He's gonna fuckin' kill me." The kid looked up to the sky, trying to keep the tears from dribbling down his face.

"Here, don't be a creep, take the money back." Jimmy had an exasperated expression on his face as he picked up the bills and put them in the boy's hand, but still the boy wouldn't take the money, refusing to close his fingers.

"You kicked my ass," the kid said, shaking his head furiously.

"Do you realize I'm almost thirty years old? I didn't kick your ass, I barely beat you. You kicked *my* ass. Let me tell you something. When you're thirty I pray you won't be playing little kids for money, OK? In two years you're gonna be out of my league. I'm the loser. I'm gonna have to go get in my car and explain to my girl why I behaved like a teenager, and I'm gonna have to look at that question myself. You're still a child, you got that going for you, but trust me you'll do yourself a lot of favors if you stop being such an arrogant prick."

"Fuck you," he said, sniveling.

Jimmy looked down at the ground and shook his head. "See? That's unacceptable. You can't say that to me."

"Why not?"

"Because first off I could shove your head up your rectum. But that's just the obvious reason." Jimmy paused. "What's your name?"

"James." The kid sniffled and wiped his nose.

"Your name is James? So's mine." Jimmy ran his tongue across his teeth, taking in the irony. "OK, the real reason, *James,* you don't say that to me is you don't talk that way to anybody. 'Cause if you don't respect other people it becomes real hard to respect yourself. You hear me?"

The kid nodded his head.

"Trust me."

Jimmy looked so much like a father. He was getting a few little lines around his eyes, and his chest and arms were beginning to look thick and substantial. It occurred to me then that there was a plus side to aging. Staring across the playground at Jim's sweaty head and his HEARTSOCK baseball jersey, I understood that in attempting anything you position yourself for almost certain humiliation, but I would bet on love. Beats the hell out of the alternative. I loved Jimmy and would marry him as soon as possible, tomorrow if we could. Hopefully the gods would witness my humility and feel my willingness to accept whatever fate befell us, but they would also see my effort. In less than six months I would give birth to our child. I was ready to get married. I wanted it. Jimmy was the father, a member of my family, and my next of kin.

THE SAD LAMENT OF JAMES AND CHRISTY HEARTSOCK ON THE EVE OF THEIR REBIRTH

CITY HALL ★

ON OUR SECOND DAY in Ohio we went to apply for a marriage license. My knees felt all buzzy like it was the first day of school. Standing there in city hall checking out all the pale, twitchy couples, I noticed that the waiting area was done entirely in shades of brown: tan walls, wood paneling, beige linoleum floors, faded gold ropes sectioning us off. There were no paintings or designs on the walls, only red placards reading MARRIAGE LICENSE $30 and lists of rules and required items of identification. It looked like a line for tickets in a train station just after Christmas—depressed faces, bits of garbage on the floor, and a peculiar funky human odor. The other couples didn't look nearly as excited as we were—well, as I was, anyway. Christy was rather subdued. I couldn't stop moving and cracking jokes, smiling at everybody, pinching Christy's fanny. The whole process struck me as comic. I like doin' ordinary shit, waiting in line, asking someone where the john is, ordering a cup of joe, talking about sports or the weather. I don't think those conversations are banal; I like them.

Behind us in line was another couple our age. They were Hispanic, and the guy had on a John Deere baseball cap. I wondered if his girl was pregnant as well.

"I'll meet you here in fifty years," I said, "and whichever one of us doesn't bring a wife has to buy the other a twelve-pack."

The dude smiled at me, but Chris turned away in a mixture of embarrassment and irritation. Everyone in the place was so sober, like it was a library or something. There were two armed security guards with disapproving expressions standing around, not helping the mood. I wondered why they were positioned there. Did fights break out a lot or what? Nothing was gonna slow me down, though. I was fuckin' elated. Getting a marriage license made me feel very "normal," positive, upstanding, legit. Sign the papers, give 'em your information, document your actions: I like that. Put your love on the books.

It was strange how glum everybody else was, especially the Chinese guy behind the bulletproof registrar glass. When I gave him the thirty bucks, I said, "Now, when we get divorced, do I get this back?"

He just looked at me expressionless, like a tree. Christy pinched and twisted the skin on my back. Whenever people get *über* serious I can't help but get all twitchy and goosey. In high school during a big football game, the coach would huddle us up and be cranking himself up into a zealous reverie about the work ethic and fighting through the pain, the regular "heart of a champion" speech, and I'd start humming "The Star-Spangled Banner." I got kicked off the team for that kind of horseplay—well, that, and I got busted for doing a couple rails of coke in the back of Deke Hammerle's Oldsmobile in the gym parking lot. It sucked for Deke worse than me; he'd been stoked with a football scholarship to Ohio State, but that flew right out the window. He never spoke to me again; I don't know why. It was his blow.

Anyway, standing in line waiting for our license I couldn't keep my legs still. I was literally bouncing. I kept thinking about Jackie Robinson and Branch Rickey. Branch Rickey was the manager for the Brooklyn Dodgers and he was searching for the perfect man to break the color barrier. He knew he needed not only a Hall of Fame ballplayer but a real man: a man who could play with death threats; a man who could handle some nationally famous second baseman whispering heinous racial slurs in his ear; a man who could face the world's spotlight, smile, stand tall, be mocked, ridiculed, and still get a base hit. Rickey immediately passed over the single men. A single man wouldn't know about sacrifice. A single man wouldn't intimately understand "the greater good," delayed gratification, the end, not the immediate result. The family man understood these values. The family man had specific personal reasons why he didn't kick the living shit out of that second baseman; he had a son and a wife and was accountable to them before baseball. A family man "with a quiet faith" would be the only man strong enough to withstand the heat.

And now that was gonna be me. I couldn't believe it. How could I stand still? I filled out my form with all my dates and info, and then I watched Christy fill out hers.

She was leaning over a counter against the far wall, scribbling. Her butt looked even better now that she was putting on a little weight. Her skin was too pale, though, and her eyes had been looking tired. All this traveling had been taking its toll on her. She sensed me staring at her and turned around, looking up. She had a little pimple on the corner of her chin that was cherry red, and I watched her try to hide it by bringing her hand up.

And then *boom*, as if I'd been hit in the gut with a baseball bat, I thought I'd be sick to my stomach. The air deflated out of me. There on her page right underneath my name was that cocksucker's name, Alexander Shelberger: her first husband.

Motherfucker.

"Oh, shit, why you gotta write his name there?" I asked, scowling. Literally all the electrons and neutrons or whatever in my limbs had stopped dead.

"What do you mean?" She looked at me, nervous and scared. As a pregnant person she had become exceedingly emotional.

"I mean, that sucks." I was trying not to be mean. "That does somethin' bad to the air, you know? I don't like that." In some ways I'm very possessive, and the thought of him, combined with the idea that she might've stood in a line just like this with someone else, made me hold my stomach like I would literally regurgitate. I knew about this guy; he was a rich kid from Christy's hometown named Alex but everyone called him Tripp (because he was Alexander Shelberger the Third), but denial seemed to be the best way to deal with his presence. He was the main reason Christy refused to have a civil wedding, because that's what they had done. He was also the root, I figured, of her reluctance to get married in the first place.

"What are you talking about?" she asked again, her face totally devoid of color.

"I forgot you were married before." I paused, suddenly unsure about how big a deal I should make out of this. "It's just a real bummer, you know?"

"Yeah, I know," she said, still as a stone. There was a long silence before she spoke again. "I never loved him, you know that. It wasn't a marriage; I was trying to get him to go to rehab. I wish I hadn't done it; he was a mean disgusting human being. But it's my past, OK?"

Once when I helped Christy move apartments we found all these photos of her and Tripp, grainy arty pictures that he'd taken. She got so depressed, a black cloud covered the air around her and her limbs looked as if they weighed ten million pounds.

"Old pictures of people not in your life anymore . . . it's just so sad," I remember her saying. "Times that were important to you, that you were invested in, and now you feel nothing." She had looked at me hollowly. "It makes you wonder if the moment you are living now will be any different." Then she dumped a shoe box full of photos into a big green plastic garbage bag.

"What are you gonna say about me in ten years?" I asked her now, quietly and sincerely, staring at my bootlaces as I shuffled across the brown city-hall-linoleum floor. "That you were pregnant and out of your mind?"

"I hope not," she said simply, not averting her eyes. Her short hair was held back in a silver barrette. "I don't want to get married, Jimmy. It's not something I'm dying to do. It's not interesting to me to be married. I want a family, I believe in the two of us, I would like to marry *you,* but if you don't want to, then screw it."

She was going on the offensive. She's good at that. When she gets mad at me I always start apologizing, but when I get mad at her she's like *boom boom*—two straight to the jaw. She doesn't take any shit.

"I married Tripp"—she whispered his name—"because the douche bag told me he'd kill himself if I didn't, and I was so young and stupid I believed him. I was divorced before I was twenty, OK? Every time he said the word *wife* it was like someone jabbed a fork into my shoulder, but if it does something bad to the air"—she scowled—"well, there's nothing I can do about that."

"I know, I know, it's just a buzz kill," I offered, shrugging my shoulders.

"Well, grow up. What do you want me to do?" she asked, exasperated.

"Don't ever do this with anyone else again," I said, giving a fake smile.

"Jimmy. . . ." You could see how tense she was in the sad tight way she was holding her mouth. "That's the idea."

When I'd walked into city hall I'd felt thirty feet high, godlike, large, and thundering, but now I was disoriented, small, whiny, and fragile. The idea hit me so ferociously, and perhaps for the first time: What if she doesn't love me the way I love her? Oh, my God. What if she isn't sincere? I looked around at the collection of sullen betrothed faces milling around us. Of course, nothing is forever.

We sat down at a small desk on these beige swivel chairs in front of a young overweight female government employee who started processing our material. Christy didn't have her divorce documents, so there were these ridiculous calls to the New York State record board for verification. It was kind of like being in the checkout lane at the supermarket and having the clerk get on the PA asking for the price of herpes ointment.

"And you're taking your husband's name?" the woman asked Chris, in a flat midwestern accent.

I didn't say anything. I couldn't.

"Yes," she answered, and spelled it out: "H-E-A-R-T-S-O-C-K. I'll keep Walker as a middle name."

I know it's not important, and if I make too big a deal out of it you'll think I'm some kind of macho asshole, but pride swelled in my heart, man; I won't deny it. Christy Heartsock. I loved the sound.

"We're gonna be a family," she said, without looking at me. "Don't be a prick about me having been married before. Unfortunately, the past doesn't go anywhere. I'm willing to do whatever it takes to get us on firm ground. You understand me?"

I nodded, trying to be cool.

"Nobody's making us do this; it's something I want. Do you want it?"

"Yes," I said simply.

"Now just one more thing." The heavy woman leaned over her desk and spoke quietly. "It's just a formality. Y'all aren't related, are you?"

I was back, ten feet tall and smiling.

INVITATIONS ∽

From the bed inside the Millstream Motor Inn, I did it: I invited my father to my wedding. Bright hot sun was bleeding through the natty brown curtains, it was only eight-thirty in the morning, but it was now or never. I'd been thinking about calling him ever since the faint blue line appeared on my pregnancy test two months earlier, and finally right then and there I reached into my bag, took out my little red date book, looked under D for Dad, and called him. My hands shake whenever I call my father. I could barely punch in all the buttons on the motel phone. "Good morning, fear," I said to myself. "You are my oldest friend."

Inside my date book, along with receipts and other odds and ends and folded up eight times into a small square, was a note my father gave me when I was ten years old.

Seven Rules for a Princess
on the tenth anniversary of the birth of my daughter
Christy "Beetle Bomper" Walker

1. Never announce to anyone that you are a princess. You know it and, if you behave as one, in time they will know it.
2. Never pretend you are not a princess in an attempt to lessen yourself because you deem it will make others more comfortable. You show others the most respect by offering the best of yourself.
3. A princess knows that success is most easily measured by how one handles disappointments.
4. A princess is never so arrogant as to think she has nothing left to learn. As much as you like to be heard and understood, so does everyone else. The more you learn, the more intelligent you are. It's that simple.
5. There is no such thing as a once-in-a-lifetime opportunity in regard to anything significant. Make time your ally. A princess understands the value of patience.
6. A princess is not frivolous. She seeks the just, the compassionate, and the wise. When she finds it she protects it. It is never a bad idea to be your own hero.
7. Above all a princess cherishes honesty. Hiding, shading,

manipulating, or controlling the truth is a waste of everyone's time. The truth exists with or without our acknowledgment. If the truth is unclear, silence is often a useful tool.

What always bothered me about this letter my father wrote was that these princess principles were based on the assumption that he was a king. If you knew my father, it would annoy you too.

Frank Steven Walker had two passions: politics and baseball. As a young man he played minor league ball for five years and then managed the Fort Worth Cats for three years, which led him into local politics. He won his first election to the State House of Representatives easily and served for eighteen years before moving on to become a deputy mayor. People loved my father, especially the ladies. He's tall, with big broad shoulders and a large gap between his front two teeth, but more than anything else he's disarmingly confident. He never touched alcohol or smoked a cigarette in his life; his only vice, he would say, was crazy women. He knew LBJ, he shook hands with John Kennedy the day he was shot, and in my limited experience as a child he seemed like one of the most important people in the world.

The phone rang three times before my father answered.

"Hi, Daddy," I said, holding the phone so tight against my head I was hurting my ear, "it's me."

I could almost see my father sit down.

"Something big is happening, Daddy," I whispered. "Something wonderful."

FATHER MATTHEW ★

The door was open, but I knocked anyway. You gotta knock.

My intended course of action was to have Father Matthew marry us. He was the priest who'd confirmed me and definitely the holiest guy I'd ever come across. The last time I saw him was when he buried my old man, which everyone appreciated. Suicide makes a lot of folks uneasy. He had a stern serious face, but you could make him laugh, no problem—make a fart noise in your armpit and he'd bust a gut. He was our youth group leader, and he let us get away with smoking and all kinds of nutsy behavior as long as we were respectful of one another. Christy wasn't Catholic but she was OK with the idea of him marrying us. Her only condition was we had to have the service at night, with lighted candles, but I figured Father Matthew would be hip to that.

I went to visit the old priest in the church offices, which were directly underneath the main chapel. The cold, wet-stone smell of that church basement brought back ten thousand memories. I stood in the hallway outside his office, noticing how little had changed. His room was open and airy, with sunlight pouring in the one small high window. It was the kind of room where you can see lint and junk sprinkling the shafts of light like stardust. You felt awkward or clumsy if you moved too quickly. There were books everywhere, books stacked on top of books, ledgers piled in one corner you could tell were forty or fifty years old. Old mail was piled here and there, and Father Matthew was sitting at his heavy wooden desk staring up into space.

He was still as big as I remembered. Some things get smaller as you get older, like the hill on Pecan Avenue where I grew up. I remember struggling to ride my bike up to the top, but now when I drive by it's hardly a hill at all, more like an incline. But the old priest sat there, twisting his head around like he was looking for something on the ceiling, and his shoulders and arms were just as mammoth as I had remembered. Father Matthew Allen was probably six feet six inches tall. The palms of his hands were bigger than my face. I'm not joking, he was, like, a first-growth human being.

"Come on in," he said loudly, in a raspy Boston accent. We were in southern Ohio, and I bet this guy hadn't been back to Massachusetts for fifty years, but he still sounded like Robert Kennedy.

I went in. There was a thick oval rug in the center of the floor that was coiled in ropelike spirals going down smaller and smaller to the middle. That rug was older than anybody living in my family. It was gnarly and covered with foreign-looking hairs. I stepped on it and stood in front of him. When I was thirteen I thought he was ninety, so I had no idea what his age was now, but he was damn old.

The word on him was he had been on intimate terms with several famous people—famous religious people, I should say, not celebrities. His eyes were the gigantic pale-blue eyes of death. When I was little I had this drippy idea that God used Father Matthew's eyes as kind of a peephole, or outpost, like maybe God picked a few people every hundred or so miles to use for visual reconnaissance. Anyway, he confirmed me. Deacon Smith led our confirmation class and everything, but Father did the actual confirmation. I was stoned when it happened; it was a point of pride for me and my buddy Deke. We got it into our heads that we'd be baked for our confirmation and we were. We did our SATs baked too. Another shining moment in my history. When you're reciting the Apostle's Creed stoned and you peer into Father Matthew's pale baby blues, you can sense that old guy manhandling every impure thought that ever embarrassed its way across your mind.

"I'm sorry to trouble you," I said, holding my hands behind my back so as not to appear uncentered.

"Are you?" he said, extremely loud. He must've gotten hard of hearing.

"No, I guess not that sorry." I smiled. Christy was outside in the car with the cat. They were listening to the radio and waiting for me.

"Introduce yourself!" he shouted.

"You want to know my name?" I asked, kind of devastated that he didn't recognize me. You like to think you're memorable.

"Where are you from?" His voice was so loud I'm sure everyone in the adjacent church offices could hear us.

"Originally? Or like where am I coming from recently?" I asked quietly, hoping our conversation would assume a more private tone.

"Both!" he barked, rattling the panes of old glass in the window.

"Well, originally I'm from here."

"That's why I'm supposed to remember you."

"I thought you might."

"Hmm." He paused and fiddled at a dangling fold of skin hanging off his wrist. "And where are you coming from *recently*?"

"I arrived from Albany a couple days ago."

"How did you get here?"

"Pardon?" I said. My gut was sinking. I understood how old he was now. He probably wouldn't remember me even after I told him. Saint Patrick's Holy Trinity Church of Cincinnati was a large congregation.

"How did you transport yourself from Albany, New York, to Cincinnati, Ohio?"

"I drove."

"You drove?" he responded, with a quickness that was unsettling. "What kind of car?"

"A Chevy Nova."

"What year?

"Nineteen sixty-nine."

"What year were you born?"

"Nineteen sixty-nine."

"Uh-huh," he said, smacking his lips together, as if there were a peculiar significance to the symmetry of this information. I couldn't be sure if he was looking at me or not. He had a walleye that made him look slightly confused. On his desk was a paperweight of a horse, a large galloping stallion. Father Matthew leaned over awkwardly, picked up the heavy paperweight, and moved it across his desk childishly, as if the horse were trotting over papers and pens onto his books.

"And what do you do with yourself?" he asked, looking down at the paperweight.

"For employment?" I couldn't stop staring at the horse myself.

He nodded.

"I'm a sergeant in the U.S. Armed Forces."

"Marines?" His eyes peeked up hopefully.

"No, the army."

"Uh-huh." He looked back down and set the horse aside. "It's a difficult profession, the Armed Forces."

"Oh, well, I'm doing pretty good," I said, shifting my weight, wishing he would ask me to sit but not wanting to presume I could.

"You are?" he asked, tilting his head with suspicion. "You're doin' pretty good, huh?"

"Yes," I said.

"Well, then, God be praised," he said calmly, but with an intensity that made me want to apologize.

"So"—he cleared his throat—"your name is Jimmy Heartsock Junior, you're almost thirty years old, you're in the army, you're doing great, but still you find it necessary to drive a 1969 Chevy Nova all the way home to come and visit the priest who confirmed you."

"You recognized me!" I was touched. This guy was probably the most legitimate person in my life. I vividly remember listening to his sermons, watching him break the bread during communion. He was powerful, commanding, and regal. On the downside, though, he was a shitty chanter. There's that part in the mass where the officiate has to sing all the Latin creeds and prayers. Some of the deacons and other guys could do it so it sounded formal and reverent, but Father Matthew with his Boston accent was atrocious. It took him ages to get through one little passage.

"Yes, I recognize you; you always smelled like smoke. You still smell like smoke. *You should quit smoking!*" he shouted, in a deep gravelly rattle.

"I know I should, sir. " I laughed. It felt so good to be recognized.

"It's a habit. If you're not careful, ninety-eight percent of your life will be habit. These young priests go around crossing themselves and thanking God twenty-four hours a day out of habit. They'd be better off doing it once, if they really contemplated gratitude."

"You're right about that, sir. Habit'll kill you."

"Sit down," he said, gesturing to an old wooden chair in the corner. As I picked up the chair and moved it closer to his desk I accidentally knocked over a calendar hanging on the wall. It was a cheap jobby, like it came free with the purchase of something else. Each month had a photograph of a different kind of flower. I put it back to February. I didn't know the name of the flower pictured, but it was a pretty yellow one.

"So, why are you here, to check on me?" he continued sarcastically. "To make sure I'm still hangin' in there?"

"No. Well"—I smiled—"I mean, that's part of it."

"I'm sure." He grinned to himself.

"I want to get married," I said clearly, looking him straight in what I was pretty sure was his good eye.

"Do you believe in God?" he asked immediately, in a resonant throaty voice.

I didn't answer him. I couldn't. The question was so unexpected.

"I mean, why do you want to get married in church? Is your faith part of your life? Is it part of your relationship with each other?"

"Not in any kind of spoken way, but she's pregnant—you know?" I don't know why I phrased it like that; it made us sound more pathetic than we were.

"No, I didn't know, but it is interesting nonetheless. Go on."

"Well, we want to start a family together and we want a blessing, you know? And we thought some kind of ceremony to mark it might give us courage, you know?"

"Would you please stop saying *you know*? It bothers me. Assume I *don't* know and proceed with the information." He let out a giant cough. He was still intimidating. "If the blessing isn't rooted in some kind of belief system," he went on, "I don't know how much courage it'll give you, son."

"We haven't figured out the whole God thing yet, but that doesn't mean that in some part of us we don't want to." I was stammering. It was horrible to think he might turn us down. "What I mean is, the best part of me thinks about that—about God, I mean—but I'm not gonna lie to you and tell you I'm a practicing devout Catholic, 'cause I'm not."

"I understand that you are not a practicing Catholic. I understand that both you and your girlfriend are not practicing Catholics." He said this with a real twinkle in his eye, as if the fact that I was constantly botching up my life amused him. I smiled back.

"Do you ever pray?" he asked.

"I usually don't, not unless I want something real bad, you know?" I said it as a joke, but it came out making me sound like a blockhead. "The last time I prayed it was for the Knicks." I smiled.

"Who?"

"The New York Knickerbockers—the basketball team." I squirmed. My toes were still raw from playing ball in my boots a couple of days earlier. Blisters on your feet take a long time to heal.

"Uh-huh," he said, real slow and deliberate, as if I were all of a sudden even less intelligent than he'd assumed I was.

"I'm joking, really." I smiled again, but I could tell he wasn't buying any bullshit. "Here's the problem, sir," I went on , shuffling my feet, unsure where I was going. "In many ways—in many of the most important ways I'm disappointed in myself. My life has never been in the service of anything except chasing after my own thrills, you know?" I looked at him for a sign of approval.

"No, I didn't know." He shook his head.

"Which has led me absolutely nowhere," I said, and right then I started getting those rumbling twinges like I might cry. "I haven't amounted to much, and to be candid with you I did intend to—it wasn't from lack of desire or ambition. I think it's lack of skill, really, or talent. You know?" I bit my lip. "I just don't seem good enough at any one thing. And I struggle with that. But I know 'It ain't what you do, it's how you do it.' Right?" That was a phrase my dad would lean on all the time. "And I really love this girl and I see her as an opportunity, a window, you know?" I bit my lip again. "A chance to show up for something. Even if it's a terribly humble goal, it's one I might be able to achieve."

"How long has it been since you've been to confession?" he asked quietly.

"Oh, Christ!" I accidentally said it out loud. I didn't want our conversation to go there. All of a sudden I felt sure this meeting was gonna drag on for way too long. Christy was still waiting for me out in the parking lot.

"A pretty long while," I answered, trying to laugh as I said it. I wanted to get out of this room now. Coming here in the first place was just a sentimental idea. Sometimes I can be a real harebrain.

"People think ceremonies like marriage, confession, confirmation, baptism"—he shifted his weight, uncrossing one leg while crossing the other, his bones making painful noises—"are just tradition and ritual, and certainly they can be. Indeed, they most often are. But"—and here he brought his fist up to his face, his eyes watery and intense—"they are meant to be something richer: an orientation, a return to center, a refocusing, a cleansing. And confession is the most misunderstood. Sin itself is not something you should feel guilty about; there is no punishment for, or disapproval of, sin. The sin itself is punishment. Are you following me?" He forced me to meet his eyes. "You turn away from the light, and darkness is the punishment."

He shrugged his shoulders like a little kid and then jammed his forefinger into his loafers, trying to get at an itch.

"If you lie," he continued, scratching, "you live life in deceit, and if you do that long enough you'll come to see that there need be no penalties other than the ones you've created for yourself. Confession is not designed to alleviate guilt; confession merely indicates the desire for realignment. You understand?"

I nodded dumbly.

"To acknowledge the desire for light and honesty, that's the point. It's helpful sometimes to articulate things to yourself. You understand?" He said *You understand?* quickly, as if it were one word. I wondered what the big difference between that and *You know?* was.

"You want me to confess stuff right now, is that what you're saying?" I asked, my skin all goose-pimply and nervous.

"I want to go to lunch," he said, sarcastic, "but I am happy to sit here for a moment and discuss your spiritual life. Which is why I believe you came to me."

There was a long silence. Was that why I was here? I looked down at my feet. The Band-Aids I'd put on my blisters were all twisted and undone. I could feel them wadded up inside my boots.

"I would love to be the celebrant at your wedding, James," he said at last. "It would be my honor. But I want to know who I'm talking to now. I knew the boy you were, and I liked him very much, but I don't know you as a man."

"I've gotten three girls pregnant in my life and had the—you know, subsequent abortions," I said quickly, more as a challenge than a confession.

"Uh-huh," he mumbled. It seemed awfully bright in the room for this kind of conversation. I preferred those little dark booths. "What were their names?" he asked.

"Um—ah, Lisa, Juliet, and um—ah, you know?"

He shook his head.

"Susan Morse," I added quickly.

"That's pretty irresponsible of you," Father Matthew noted simply. He hadn't said it to be mean, I could tell.

"I know," I said. "I've slept with a shitload of prostitutes as well," I added, surprising myself.

"How many?" he asked plainly.

I've slept with strippers, prostitutes, married women, divorced women, a fuckin' seventeen-year-old girl, two and three girls at once, mothers with their kids in the next room. I mean, seriously, I've been in some rooms where if you saw me there you wouldn't like me at all. Sticking my fingers where they shouldn't go. That's the truth, and I feel like shit about it. The trouble is, you just follow one day to the next, and sometimes when you're doing something it doesn't seem as bad as it does later if you have to tell somebody you did it.

"Five or ten," I said calmly; of course, I could remember exactly. "Twelve," I added, "but I don't know their names." I tried to smile.

"And you regret that?" He paused, adjusting himself in his seat.

I thought about whether I regretted it but I couldn't pretend I didn't have a ball while I was doing it. Calling the hookers and waiting for them to arrive was the most exciting part. I remember laughing hysterically with my friends as we'd recap our exploits.

"I don't know," I said. "Looking at you and saying it out loud makes me feel kind of ashamed."

"You feel you *should* be sorry."

I nodded and looked down at the floor. I remembered my first time with a hooker. She was from Virginia and worked as a dental assistant in the daytime. I don't know if that was true, but it's what she told me. I couldn't meet her stare after we were finished; I stood around in my boxers with my eyes glued to the hotel carpet as I handed her a hundred dollars. She put on her tiny items of clothing, went to the bathroom, called somebody, snorted a line of coke, and opened the front door, and I watched her shoes walk out. We didn't say a word to each other. Immediately I went to the mirror and stared at my face to see if there was anything different about it. I felt lousy about the whole experience, but as soon as my buddy came in I started laughing. We did it again the next night.

"I've done a lot of drugs, too," I said spontaneously. "Snorted up a great deal of cocaine, taken methamphetamines, smoked heroin a couple times. . . . Just recently I was high on duty when I had to inform a mom that her son was dead. I felt bad about that."

"What was her name?" Father asked, looking away now, lightly breathing into his hands.

"Anderson. Something Anderson," I said, remembering.

"It's important to think about people's names. You understand me, Jimmy?"

I nodded, but I was pretty sure I didn't.

"Are you angry, James?"

"What?" I asked. "No."

"Because I imagined that someday you might come to me, and I thought that when you did you would be very angry."

"What would I be angry about?" I asked, genuinely curious.

"Your father and mother. You were a great kid, but you didn't have it easy."

"I didn't?" I asked. My eyes started burning like a scorpion had stung them.

"If *my* father killed himself I would be very angry," he said quietly.

"I love my dad," I said, shaking my head no. My chest started to swell, and I knew if I took another breath I was gonna cry. "Why's everybody always so mean to my dad?" I was getting a little pissed off. Whenever anybody asks me about my old man they've got this pitying glint in their eye, like I don't understand something.

"I liked your father too, Jimmy." There was a long silence as the priest decided how to move the conversation forward. He was still sitting across from me at his old desk while I nervously patted my mustache. I tried to master my feelings, collect myself, and look up to meet his gaze. As our eyes met, I risked taking a breath and immediately I began to cry. At least two or three minutes passed as I heaved and sobbed in his uncomfortable wooden chair. Like a four-year-old, stooped over in my seat, I cried so hard I lost my breath. Father Matthew never moved or reached out a hand to comfort me. He just sat there patiently.

"Can you tell me why you're crying, son?" he asked finally.

I had no idea. All I could remember thinking was how fucking exhausted I was with all my own bullshit. My life story held no interest for me any longer. I wanted to get married, to start clean, but memories hung on me with the weight of large sprawling dead branches.

"It's just . . . it's just—" I had no idea what I was trying to say until I said it. "I'm so vain, you know? I can't tell you . . . but I am. Incredibly vain. I look at myself in the mirror all the time and it makes me sick." I cried some more, placing both my hands over my face. I didn't know I could sob so hard.

"What do you see?" Father Matthew asked. "Describe it to me."

"Weakness," I said, covering my burning eyes with both hands.

"I see a strong young man sitting before me. Everybody's vain, Jim. Give yourself permission to like yourself."

He crossed his arms while we sat in silence for another moment. My head was still in my hands.

"It's all right to cry, son, it doesn't mean anything important; it's just natural." Again for a moment he was quiet. "People think when they cry that something monumental is happening. But it isn't. Emotion doesn't mean much of anything."

I wiped my eyes, looked up, and took a long deep breath.

"If you hear one thing I say to you today," he went on, "I hope it will be this: It's all right to be angry; you have permission. It takes an awful lot of energy to keep pretending you're not."

After I got myself together, Father Matthew asked me to bring Christy in for an introduction. She could tell I was upset, it was obvious, but she didn't say anything. Her hair was all frumpy from my knit hat, and her eyes were puffy, probably from napping. She spoke briefly to Father, with poise and dignity. Concerned she might say something offensive, I was extremely uptight, but of course he was more smitten with her in three minutes than he had ever been with me.

"If you're asking me why I want to get married, my answer is: Jimmy." She spoke lightly, brushing her hair down behind her ears and straightening the buttons of her top. "Every time he opens his mouth I have absolutely no idea what he's gonna say. He's the most honest person I've ever met. He's a quick study and rarely needs to make the same mistake twice." She said all this without ever glancing over at me. "He really tries to learn, and does, and he makes me laugh, and the world's generally a lighter place when he's in my sight."

She crossed her legs. "I should tell you that when we first got together it only happened because my girlfriend Chance talked me into trying to loosen up and experience life a little more. I made a decision to have a one-night stand, and that night in a bar I met Jimmy. What can I say? He got under my skin." Placing her hands on her chair and gripping the seat tightly, she added, "He's the most emotionally strong person I've ever met. You can hang on him. He faces problems head on. He challenges me and listens to me. I've known him for a year and a half and I feel like I met him on Tuesday. Either that or maybe I've known him for ten thousand years, I can't tell which."

Finally, she looked over at me, shrugged her shoulders, and

brought her eyes back to Father Matthew. "And besides all that, he loves me. And when I feel his love I realize that I'm not sure if I've ever been loved before."

She smiled and continued with barely a pause. "When I got my wisdom teeth taken out I had a fever for like six days and could barely eat. And this lunkhead over here took care of me. He rented videos for me, he made me soup and fed it to me, he took off from work, he wouldn't let me smoke, he read me the paper and rubbed my feet. I didn't know he had that kind of behavior in him. It was like—I can't explain it—I watched him put a banana in the blender to make me a shake—I'd been with him for nine months at this point—and it was like finding out your best friend knows how to fly and for some reason never got around to telling you. And I thought then, If I have a brain in my head I'll hold on to him, and that's what I'm trying to do."

For a moment there was silence. Father Matthew held his gaze directly on Christy, expressionless.

"I've told Jimmy this, but my whole life I've been looking for a still point. And I hope that Jimmy and I can be that point for each other." She took a breath for what seemed like the first time since she walked in the room. "You know?"

"Yes, I understand," he said. He didn't bust *her* chops about saying *you know* too much. Christy knows how to make an impression. She glanced around the room, taking in the piles of books and the general sloppiness. Her eyes were bright and green and I could tell she was enjoying this whole experience. In some way she felt she was defending me, and she liked doing it.

"To be completely frank," she added, looking over at me to gauge how far she could go, "as far as the church thing goes, I really wouldn't care if it was a Jewish, Hindu, or Islamic wedding, but since Jimmy was raised Catholic, this seems as . . ."—she stumbled, looking for the right word—"elegant a place to start as anywhere else."

"You got yourself somebody here," Father Matthew said to me. "The way she talks, I'm starting to like you."

I smiled insecurely.

"When do you want to get married?"

"Friday, is what we were thinking," I said, my voice still a little froggy.

"This Friday?"

"We've got a baby coming," Christy added.

My head was still kind of blurry and thumping from the crying I'd done earlier, but I was proud of my girl and pleasantly embarrassed about all the complimentary things she'd said about me. I'd never heard her talk like that. Life ran hard in her; you could feel her pulse from ten paces. Fifteen people seemed to live inside that body.

The old priest sent us out with a small Episcopal red cloth-bound book of common prayer. We were to study the various services, work on one suited specifically for ourselves, and call him the next day. He would check on the chapel availability. Then he gave us each a hug, which kind of made me laugh, and shuffled down the cathedral corridor.

BREAKING BREAD ⌘

He arrived in Ohio two days later. My father was like that, dramatic. I had called back to tell him we were planning a small wedding at Saint Patrick's cathedral in Cincinnati. "I wouldn't miss it for the world," he'd said, firmly and immediately. Chance and my father were the only people I invited. Jimmy invited his mom, his stepfather—and some army friends from Albany, none of whom could come because they were on some field training exercise. He wasn't too disappointed. He said he didn't want a best man anyway. He wanted to stand alone.

We met my father and his new wife, BJ, at the restaurant inside the Ramada Inn where they were staying. Jimmy was on his best behavior; he can really be winning when he sets his mind to it. He spoke intelligently when addressed but for the most part he was quiet, standing beside me, watching my back.

My father and Jimmy had met once before back in Albany when I turned twenty-five. I'd only just started dating Jimmy a week earlier, but he stopped by this little party I was having and left early. I remember walking him down my driveway and kissing him good-bye on the hood of his car. "You know what I like about you?" I said, kissing him on the mouth. "You treat me like the piece of ass I am."

I went back to the party and continued dancing with my dad. Jimmy told me later he'd found the party "depressing" because he didn't feel anybody there knew me at all, including my father.

I could never explain to Jimmy the strange thing that happens to me whenever I see my father. Spontaneously, I seem to experience some kind of internal personality revolution. There are usually such time gaps between our meetings that I somehow revert to an idealized version of the person I was when we were last close. Essentially I become an adult manifestation of an eight-year-old. Each time we meet I try not to do it, but I always do. As a visit with my father approaches, I begin to dislike the person I've become and start wanting desperately to be that eight-year-old girl. The way I've done my hair will irritate me, and I'll wind up with a ponytail. No earrings seem exactly right, so I go with none at all. My father has no idea who I am, and under the burden of his stare I don't want him to know. I want his love and approval so badly it makes me hate him. And I don't want to hate him, I want to love him. I need to tell him he's gorgeous and I'm proud of him, and that need creates a thunder so loud I can't hear anything else.

From the moment my father walked into the restaurant in Ohio I was reminded of what I dislike about him most: the way he dresses. He arrived wearing a suit that looked like he bought it at J. C. Penney's in 1983. The man is not poor. He's managed to save up quite a bit of money during the course of his public service life. He insists, however, on never buying new clothes. It's easier to get him to give you ten thousand bucks than lend you a five-dollar bill.

You can smell Frank Walker's masculinity from twenty paces. His shoulders, his jaw, his slightly receding hairline, are as male as the horns on the head of a ram. This man appears to be able to handle any-thing, from the subtlest emotional crisis to a barroom brawl.

Charging up through the restaurant, he gave me a great big hug and rubbed his hand across the bump in my belly. Instinctively I jerked away. We hadn't seen each other for almost two years, but he always just moves ahead, oblivious to our estrangement.

"So you've elected to get married again, huh?" was the first thing he said to me.

The tension was obvious to Jimmy, BJ, and anyone else paying attention, but not to my father. Once we all sat down he launched in telling BJ an old boring anecdote about me.

"When Christy was seven years old, seven, I tell you"—like all politicians, he loves anecdotes—"she saunters up to me in my office and says, 'Daddy, I been thinkin' about it, and I just can't decide whether I want to get married once or a whole bunch of times.'" He laughed. He neglected to mention the preface to that story, which was that I had come downstairs the night before and caught him sleeping with my baby-sitter, Janice.

His new wife, BJ, was as sweet as could be. My father claimed to be experimenting at marriage with a sane person. He'd been married four times before and dated numerous other women, but there was only one sane one in the bunch: my first stepmother, Estella. She was the best, twenty years old and a preschool teacher. I loved her. One time she sewed me an all-leather cowboy outfit complete with jacket, vest, and chaps—all with turquoise beaded dangling fringe.

Their marriage only lasted eight months. The day she left us she walked into our ranch-style house over on Norwood Avenue with both arms full of groceries. I was right behind her, carrying an azalea bush we'd just purchased. We came in to find my father whispering into the telephone. Immediately he hung up and turned around with a guilty look on his face.

"Who were you just talking to?" Estella asked.

"Iris Harding," he blurted.

"Who is she?" Estella asked.

"Oh, uh, you know, she works over at Montgomery Ward."

"Why were you talking to her?"

"Well, that's a good question," my father said, trying to stifle a smirk. Estella dropped the groceries to the floor and walked out the door, leaving me confused—but not my father. She returned six or seven weeks later with divorce papers in hand. It was not her intent to split up, however. She told him either to sign the papers or to promise never to sleep with another woman. She said she knew God could give him a clean slate, and she would try to do the same. My father said, "I truly do want to stay married to you—you are the best woman I've ever known—but in all candor if you're adamant about the fidelity aspect of marriage then I am going to make you one miserable human being." He always spoke that way, very formally, using the largest vocabulary possible.

I remember all this because I was sitting right there in between them on the blue sofa. Estella burst out crying, and my father signed the papers on top of the kitchen table. She was married to another man not a year later and had three sons, all of them blind. My father still insists she is the best woman he's ever known. "She's a saint," he'd say, even in front of a new wife or girlfriend, "raisin' those three blind boys. If I wasn't such a child myself I coulda had a great life with her."

BJ smiled politely. She was a few years younger than my father, maybe forty-eight, but attractive in a dignified fashion in her gray suit. The women in my father's life all seemed interchangeable. I don't know how, but even in his later years he managed to land tremendously fetching wives. BJ was no dummy either; she worked as head of marketing at the Alley, Houston's largest theater.

"So what's up, Beetle Bomper?" my father asked, still standing awkwardly in the center of the dining area.

He never did know how to talk to me. When I was a girl, he would ask me the most ridiculous questions in an attempt to communicate. "How do you feel about the hostages in Iran?" "Any opinions on Carter?" One time when we were backing out of the driveway, he ran over the neighbor's kitten and didn't even stop; he was too preoccupied. He also had this peculiar habit when I was little of putting out his hand for me to kiss. I don't know where he got that; I've never seen any other man do it. He was only interested in a life of the mind, that and women and baseball. Manual labor reminded him of the town he was born in, Sawkill, Texas, and he hated Sawkill. "I have no patience for people uninterested or unwilling to learn. That whole goddamn town is full of people intolerant of tolerance," he often said. His hands are almost disfiguringly large. They're like Popeye's forearms. Once you notice them you can't stop staring. He seems old not because he's fragile or sickly but more as a last remnant cut from an older, stronger, more intricate fabric than my generation. Inside of him lurks an explosive temper. He ripped the door off a refrigerator and even hit me on occasion, but more than anything else he simply frightened me.

But I will give Frank Walker this: He has been completely engrossed in life and did take custody of me at a time in Texas when single fathers were even more uncommon than they are now. Granted, Grandmother put in a lot of time too.

"Thanks for inviting me," he said across the table, after we sat down. His stare was like a punch in the face. The earnestness in his yellowing brown eyes was terrifying.

"Thanks for coming," I mumbled uncomfortably, my own eyes immediately darting around the restaurant. At that moment I couldn't remember why I'd asked him, but it had something to do with the idea that to start my new family I needed to be at peace with the old.

"You got your hands full with this one," my father told Jimmy. "We were shopping in Neiman Marcus one time, and Christy—she couldn't have been more than five—walks into the women's department, runs over to the most expensive section, and starts rifling through dresses on the rack, swinging them over one at a time. Finally she finds one— she can barely lift the damn thing up—and says to me, 'Daddy, this one. I *need* it.' It had to be the most expensive goddamn dress in the whole mall, and it took her all of three minutes to find it."

"Did you buy it for me, Daddy?" I asked rhetorically.

"Hell, no!" my father exclaimed. "Listen, Jimmy, this girl thought I could do anything. I remember one summer I got her a job working as a page in the capitol building over in Austin. We spent the whole summer living together in the Omni. That was a great summer, wasn't it, Chris?"

"It was a Marriott," I said, fastidiously refolding my napkin. All I remember of that summer was how hot it was and all the lonely hours I spent tooling around the halls of the air-conditioned hotel.

"Well, whatever. September's rolling around and we're each lying on our beds there in the room watching television, and she tells me she wants to be a page again next year. So I tell her, which of course she knew already, that children of congressmen only get one summer apiece. And she says, 'Oh, Daddy, you and I both know that if you really wanted—I mean, if you *really* wanted—you'd find a way.' " He paused for dramatic effect. "She refused to believe I was a nobody."

I'd heard my dad tell this story before and always found it peculiar that he loved it so much. I guess he thought it reflected well on him in some way, but I could never figure out how.

He kept asking Jimmy cliché questions like what did he think he was going to do with his life and how was he going to apply himself after the military? If I looked down at the salt and pepper shakers I could handle it; my father's voice was even pleasant. Just the cadence of his speech brought back so many memories, letting me know the world doesn't change that much. The sound of him made me want to sit in his lap but his eyes made me want to excuse myself and go to the bathroom.

"I brought you this book. I figured you'd remember it." He lifted up an old worn green book I'd carried with me from ages eleven to fifteen almost without fail. "Emily Dickinson. You were a fanatic for Emily Dickinson. You remember that?"

"Of course," I said, holding the weight of the book. Inside he'd written *Just to let you know some things are always here. Love, Daddy*. He always tried so hard to love me, I know he did, but even with that knowledge I'd find it almost impossible to reciprocate. Many people grow up without a father, but growing up without a mother is like being assigned a dunce cap. No matter how my father tried to compensate for that hollowness, he couldn't.

"You're very sweet, Daddy," I said.

"Hell, I'm just glad to be invited *this* time." He smiled, revealing that giant space between his teeth. Immediately he'd pissed me off again. I gave Jimmy an apologetic glance.

Part of why I'd hated him so much my whole life was somewhere deep down I did truly believe he could do anything he set his mind to, and it made me angry that there was so much with regard to me that he left undone. After a car accident that occurred while I was fifteen in a Trans-Am with some drunken older boys, I needed a blood transfusion. I believed one hundred percent that if he wanted to he could have healed me. I didn't need to be in this doctor's office getting hooked up to machines and heart monitors. He could've taken care of it, but for some reason he wouldn't. On some core level I felt any misfortune I experienced was the direct result of his lack of attention.

As a girl I never felt outright anger, toward him or anyone. Mostly if things became uncomfortable I just wanted to be alone. Even when I left Texas, I didn't leave feeling mad. I left feeling elated that there was finally some quiet around me. From the time I was seven I hated Texas and most of the people I met there. I would go to sleep early so I could dream more. My father would drive us along those interstates, and it seemed to me that all there was in Houston were highways and car dealerships. I wanted to run away, from the first time I heard of the concept, not because anything so dreadful was happening but because I craved solitude. My childhood was spent looking and waiting for a proper reason to run away, and when my father married Marilyn I found it. She told me I was the root cause of my father's philandering, that a lot of men become sexually frustrated around a teenage daughter, so we'd all be better off if I left. Suited me fine. I'd saved up three thousand bucks scooping ice cream, and I took a plane to NYC. Of course, Tripp followed me, and I never got off to the start I wanted.

Unable to look my father in the eye as we all broke bread together there in the Ramada Inn restaurant, I realized I needed to develop some new coping skills. The tools I'd used to get through my childhood were advantageous and useful then but not anymore. Almost all my true enjoyment of people could take place only from a distance. Appreciating people was easy as long as they weren't close: my father, especially. I'd learned to love him through separation, but I didn't know how to communicate with him when he was right in front of me. It felt too dangerous. Being alone was the only time my breathing would come easy. In some ways I'd felt allergic to my own life. With people talking to me and wanting reactions from me, my head would swell and my skin would break out. Would that happen with my own child? Would I love my daughter when she was off at school but feel distant from her when she was in my arms? All my favorite memories didn't seem to involve anybody else. Reading, walking down the street, taking the bus, washing my clothes—inside that kind of quiet peace I could feel and enjoy my life. After Jimmy and I broke up it was almost a relief. This way I would be able to love him forever; it would be easier. The habits I'd learned about how to survive all seemed to involve moving and solitude.

"Are you ever going to learn to sit still?" my father asked.

"What do you mean?" I asked.

"You're a little fussbudget over there, squirming around."

"You should talk," I snapped.

"She's excited and nervous, Frank," BJ said warmly. "Leave her alone."

"This one can't sit still, Jimmy," my dad said, pointing at me. "You'd better hold on tight to whatever handle you got, 'cause this one's always on the move. I've been trying for years to keep up with her, but it seems like she doesn't want to be caught up with—least not by me."

"That's not true," I said, motioning for the waiter.

"You're not an alcoholic, are you, Jimmy?" my father asked. Immediately my blood froze. I knew exactly where he was headed.

"No, man," Jimmy said, smiling. "I don't want to mislead you, I'm sure I have plenty of unflattering attributes, but I'm not a drunk."

"You know about Tripp, though, right?" my father asked innocently.

I could have vomited right there on the table. Since the moment we'd arrived I could tell my father was hell bent on shoving my past into my face for me to smell.

"I know Christy's been married before," Jimmy said, his face taking on a more serious expression.

"Well, you never heard it from my point of view." My dad grinned. "This guy was an L-O-S-E-R. I can say that, right, Chris?"

"You can say whatever you want." I bit my lip and braced myself. *Look him in the eye,* I told myself. *Look him in the eye and tell him the truth doesn't scare you. Tell him you are loved and you are not afraid.*

If I could just bring my gaze to his and hold his stare, I thought, I could change the future. Someday, scientists will discover that our DNA is not some absolute unalterable code. There will be one link near the bottom of the ladder that twists or unwinds as our life proceeds. If I could reveal my core and look my father in the eye unashamed, it would thunder through the membranes of my body and his, leaving some microscopic genetic fragment permanently altered. My fear would be dissipated and courage would take its place. This shift, the result of one small action, could change my programming and even affect the hard-wiring of my child. I knew the only achievement I'd ever accomplish that would ever be worth a damn was the subtle growth or deterioration of my instinct. Like, can I look my father in the eye as he insists on telling my fiancé, my betrothed, the love of my life, what a loser I am?

"She wanted permission to marry this creep, OK? She was only seventeen, living with him in NYC—I mean, can you imagine? I come up to New York and visit them, OK? They're living in the Algonquin Hotel 'cause they both have some fruity idea that they're gonna be famous writers—" He stumbled. "Who was it who lived there?"

"Dorothy Parker," I answered curtly. I never even liked Dorothy Parker.

"Now, Christy has some natural skills. This girl, one look at her even at the age of five, you could tell there was nothing she couldn't achieve. She was a winner. She succeeded in everything she set out to do, but she didn't think it was *cool* to be a winner. She thought it was cool to piss her life away. And this creep Tripp was like the champion urinator. You following me?"

I just held Jimmy's hand under the table and studied the skin of his face. He had a slew of red whiskers, even though the hair of his head was black. For him, looking my father in the eye seemed to present no challenge.

"I go up to their hotel room, and this Tripp"—my father said the name as if it were a curse—"offers me a glass of wine. It's eleven-thirty in the goddamn morning, he wants to marry my seventeen-year-old daughter, and he offers me a glass of wine. Body odor to this guy was like a stamp of authenticity. He smells, she looks like a ragamuffin teenage runaway standing behind him, and their room looks like it belongs to a couple of four-year-olds. And how old was the guy, at least four or five years older than you, right?" He turned to me.

"He was four years older." I did it. I looked in his sprinkled yellow eye and answered him. He didn't seem to notice.

"Listen, for a father this Algonquin Hotel room may as well have been the seventh tier of Hell." My dad charged on. "She goes to New York wanting to be Virginia Woolf or Dorothy Parker or whatever, and she's not there six months before her aspirations have become to be the subject of his pissant photo sessions. This twerp's got some fancy-pants dream of being a *photographer*—right?—and now all of a sudden he's got my girl being a *model* and I'm supposed to sign some papers so she can work as an adult and this other set that are gonna let her marry this freak."

"I only invited you there so you would stop it," I said quietly. Looking at his face now, I was aware of how rarely he looked at me.

"That's not what you said at the time." He laughed, a big hearty chuckle. "Oh, boy, so that's the story now, huh? Jimmy, I'm sure you realize this, but to watch your daughter willfully hurt herself? I can't tell you." He threw up his arms like King Lear. "I know that's the weekend I lost you."

"You didn't lose me, you signed the papers," I said simply. Now I couldn't stop looking at him. I loved him, I couldn't help it. All I really wanted to do was kiss his cheeks. I didn't *want* to be angry. I wanted to see all the good he had done for me. I'd lived long enough at this point to meet individuals whose parents had truly scarred them. People who had been raped and abused, people who had been completely forgotten. My father had never done any of those things. We just misplaced each other. And now when our eyes met we didn't know where to hold on. He was what I was running away from, and yet he was a part of me. That, I realized, was why I'd invited him here.

"I signed those papers to try to keep you close," he said, meeting my eyes. "You may not remember, sweetie, but you were going to do what you were going to do. I just thought I'd stay closer as your ally than as your enemy." He paused and looked around the table for help but his eyes came back to me. "But I'll believe you if you tell me I did it wrong. You were very intimidating, even as a kid."

"Oh, Christ, Daddy, I wasn't intimidating, you just never knew how to listen," I said, trying to smile. "That's all you need to do." I was now holding his gaze full on and he was listening.

"OK," he said, his smile failing. "I can do that."

Under the table I grabbed Jimmy's hand, the way a pilot grabs the throttle.

"My mother used to say"—my father grinned, exposing the gap between his two front teeth—"'Frank has been successful at everything he's set out to do in life, with the exception of marriage.' I hope that's not a trait I passed on to you."

"Well, it isn't all up to her, sir." These were the first words Jimmy had spoken in what felt like twenty years. "It takes two. Isn't that the, you know"— he paused and smiled—"common wisdom?"

You could never predict Jimmy. He didn't give a shit about Tripp anymore—or my dad. He just seemed happy I was holding his hand. And for the first time in what felt like lifetimes, I was sitting still.

THE BLESSING ★

We were staying in your basic Mom and Pop version of a Motel 6. The neon sign out front advertised a pool and HBO in a bright blue light spilling out over Route 28. The pool was dead center in the parking lot, all tarped off for the winter. An Indian couple from Delhi owned the place. I don't know how they found their way to Ohio, but they kept the place super clean and seemed happy enough, very chatty and friendly. Christy was in the bathtub scrubbing her hair. She'd been so damn amiable lately. Her pregnancy had lifted a veil, a curtain of depression, that had often seemed draped around her. Most times she's quick to vacillate in and out of extreme irritation. For example, if I drop a banana peel on a table or pee on the seat, or if a cabinet door is left open and she bumps her head, that usually gets under her skin. But with the onset of the second trimester she was always scratching my back, playing with my hair, or rubbing my ears. She was almost constantly nice to me. If something annoying happened, like I took a wrong turn or we lost a pair of gloves, she'd laugh about it. She loved it whenever I touched her. We were boning twice a day. On the flip side, she could cry watching CNN.

Anyway, she always loved taking baths. She has a whole independent bag for bath stuff: salts, oils, bubbles, minerals, whatever. She'd been in the bathroom for over an hour. I was sitting on the bed with my shirt off, my jeans on, the television muted, and my nose buried in that prayer book.

The Lord's Prayer was always my favorite: *Forgive us our tres-*

passes as we forgive those who trespass against us. Reading all the blessings and vows got to me somehow. They were filling me up, like water collecting in a cloud, making me exceedingly emotional. I can't say it was honestly the mystery of Christ moving through me, it might've been the familiarity of the words or simple nostalgia, but these passages were searing through my chest. They seemed to come off the page and form a connective tissue between all the disparate moments of my life: my first communion, Christmas Eves, Sunday school, confirmation. Shit, I lost my virginity on a youth group retreat. The realization that Jesus had been there when anything big was happening to me made me feel close to him, or at least to his name. It felt good to be near these words again, like there had been some order, a constant presence in my life, even though I had been blind to it.

I thought of how my unborn child couldn't possibly understand the sounds she must be 'experiencing there in the bathroom, the twists of her mother's body, the echoes of the tile walls, the water sloshing, just as I can't understand the movements and sounds that shaped my life. Fuck, man, I was reading this book sitting on the bed listening to Christy splash around, and for a brief moment I felt held by God. I don't even know what I mean by God, but I felt held in a way that I knew I'd been held before, like I was moving with some deep hidden electrical current or an underground rushing body of water. I was on the road I had been born to walk, and I had never been away from it.

Stepping out of the darkness of the bedroom into the harsh fluorescent light of the bathroom, I shut the lid of the toilet and sat down. Chris was completely submerged underwater, but after a second or two she resurfaced. She wiped the soapy water from her eyes and smiled a goofy grin. There was a melon-sized bulge in her belly now and a thin dark line up the center of her stomach. Her breasts were large and seemed to float in the soapy bath.

"Can I read some of this to you?" I asked, motioning to the small prayer book in my hands.

She nodded and pulled her hair back off her forehead and behind her ears. Her giant toes were playing with the faucet, spinning the handle until the water shut off. It was quiet now. Only the slight rattle of the radiators and my voice broke the silence.

"This is the marriage blessing, OK?" I looked at her apprehensively, waiting for some reassuring gesture.

She nodded. With her hair all wet and flat against her head, her eyes were the large expectant eyes of a twelve-year-old.

" 'Most gracious God,' " I began, my voice thin and nervous, " 'we give thanks to you for your tender love in sending Jesus Christ to come among us, to be born of a human mother, and to make the way of the cross to be a way of life.' "

I didn't look up. I'm not the most tremendous of public readers, so I concentrated on trying to let her hear the words. " 'We thank you also for consecrating the union of man and woman. By the power of your holy spirit, pour out the abundance of your blessing upon this man and this woman. Defend them from every enemy, lead them into all peace, let their love for each other be a seal about their hearts, a mantle about their shoulders, and a crown about their foreheads.' "

I just loved this; emotion was percolating like boiling water in my chest. " 'Bless them in their waking and in their sleeping, in their work and in their companionship, in their joys and in their sorrows; in their life and in their death. Finally in your mercy bring them to that table where your saints feast forever in your heavenly home' "—I paused to make sure I didn't well up too much and start blubbering out of control; my vision was blurring like I was looking through an inch of water, but still I didn't look up from the page—" 'through Jesus Christ our Lord, who with you and the Holy Spirit lives and reigns one God forever and ever.' "

When I finished reading this, *blammo!* I was crying again. I can't explain what was happening to me, but I was ripping apart at the seams. It just all sounded so damn deep and profound: "A SEAL ABOUT THEIR HEARTS," "FEASTING WITH SAINTS." My eyes were all red and swollen. Like a sledgehammer, these passages were knocking me out. Christy and I were giving each other the only thing we truly have to offer: our time. We were going to give each other the living minutes of our life. Damn. I hadn't sincerely thought about God in so long, and now the ideas were cascading over me. I couldn't tell you what "the way of the cross" meant or define for anybody what the Holy Spirit is, but I loved this girl, we were gonna get married, and I was gonna BATHE IN THE HEAVENLY MERCY OF MY EVER LOVING FATHER.

"Jimmy, are you all right?" Christy asked.

I looked up from my red cloth-bound book, which I was now clinging to as a child hangs on to its security blanket, and Christy's expression shocked me. She was frightened.

"You're not like born again or anything, are you?" she asked me earnestly.

I thought for a moment. "Well, not really. It's just beautiful, don't you think?"

"I think it's—I don't know, it scares me," she said gently, moving her knees slightly back and forth in the bathwater, the ripples sending the soapy water high up the sides of the thin plastic tub. She sat up, her breasts hanging drenched and heavy on her chest. "That kind of language," she continued softly, "always makes me think that maybe in another lifetime I was burned at the stake." She splashed her face with water. "That stuff gives me the creeps."

I felt like she'd sucker-punched me. "It's kind of pretty, though, don't you think?" I asked weakly.

She shrugged her shoulders and dunked her head under the water again.

Suddenly my vision clouded over. It was like I was blind. I couldn't see my hand in front of my face. Without saying anything I stood up and stumbled out of the light of the bathroom and found my way down onto the gushy hotel bed and the darkness of the muted TV light.

"Are you OK?" she called from the bathroom. "I'm sorry if that passage gives me the heebie-jeebies, sweetie, but it does. Talking about God just seems so pointless." There was a pause as she figured out what she meant. "It's like drilling a well right by a river, you know?

The water's already there; you don't have to dig for it. Whatever is good or valuable about religion is always around us. You don't have to go to church for it. To be honest, churches give me the willies. Whenever I go inside one, I feel like the whole place is pleading to some outside force, you know? Like God or whatever is outside of us, withholding the goods. I don't really buy that idea—that someone up on a hill is doling out favors, but only if we ask in a really really nice way. I don't buy it, do you?"

I was staring into space listening to her voice, cringing more and more with each new statement.

"I guess I believe in God," I said, dazed. We hadn't ever talked about this kind of thing before. This should be important; it surprised me that the subject had never come up. Through the slightly open bathroom door, I could see the sink glowing brightly, but I couldn't see anything else, just the shiny wet floor and the glowing white sink. Amazing, I thought, how instantly I could feel I didn't know Christy at all, and how little I felt she knew me.

There is this place deep inside where I feel I am connected to everything, not just trees and grass and dogs but buildings and stairways, rocks and sidewalks. It's a deathly quiet place that I guess I've never shared with anyone and probably couldn't, a place that is cold sober when my body is stumbling drunk, another consciousness that sits still like an antenna in tune with some other part of the galaxy. It was this part of me that I wanted to bring to our wedding, a centered space from which I could send out my oaths. I imagined that this secret antenna was my connection to whatever eternity might be and was the part of me that Christy alone perceived and loved. It was that same magic timeless part of her that I wanted to marry. But in the dark of the motel room, I realized that whether I was married or not, no one would ever know all of me; my truest self would always be estranged and alone. I was incapable of expressing my limited screwball faith and I knew that, even if I could, I'd box it in so dramatically it would be trivialized. I began to feel the familiar swell of numbing anger.

"Look," Christy said, unplugging the bath, "I don't care if you believe in God. It just seemed a little scary, you reading that scripture like you were Moses or something."

"Moses?" I snarled, listening to the water draining out from the tub. "What are you talking about Moses for?"

"You know what I mean."

"No, I don't." Sometimes she acts so much smarter than me. I wanted to smack her head through a wall. I was dizzy thinking so many thoughts. My stomach hurt. My religious ideas were so half-baked they couldn't stand the cursory inspection of a five-year-old, and that pissed me off. I rubbed my forehead, digging painfully into my eye cavity to relieve some of the pressure building up inside my cranium.

"If you and I are going to commune with the Holy Spirit," Christy said through the doorway, "it's you and me who are going to do the communing, and I don't think any self-respecting God gives a horse's ass what rituals we enact, as long as our intentions are clean, you know?" She was getting out of the tub, wrapping a scrappy thin motel towel around her chest and another one around her hair. Through my obscured vision I could make out a glimpse of her reflection in the mirror above the white-hot glare of the sink. "My point is, I'm not gonna swear my everlasting love on a bunch of crapola creeds I don't believe in. I can't. You know what I mean, Beanie?" She was trying to maintain a demure, unthreatening tone.

I was silent, turning my eye to the flickering blue light of the television. Commercials were spinning by.

"Sweetie . . . are you out there? Sweetie?" She poked her head out of the door and looked at me.

"It's not crapola," I said, feeling the need to stick up for a religion I had basically paid almost zero attention to for the whole of my adult life. To not do so, I worried, would be a betrayal of where I came from and of all the thousands of little prayers I secretly pray. I kept forgetting to breathe.

"I'm sorry I called it crapola, all right? I was trying to be funny," she said earnestly. "You understand that blind faith in this kind of

thing causes wars and gross atrocities, right? You understand that?"
She had her very serious, no-bullshit manner about her that I find very
condescending.

"People do those things," I said.

"Yeah, people reading out of little red books." She made a move to
go back to the sink.

"Give me a fuckin' break! I thought it was beautiful! Call a fuckin'
lawyer. I felt good for ten seconds; *shoot me!*" I screamed, punching
myself so hard in the head I thought I might fall over. Sometimes I do
that, I wanna hit something so bad I just smack my own face. I paused
momentarily and tried to control my voice. There was the same frightening placid silence coming from the bathroom that always follows one
of my outbursts. I've said it before but, man, it's no joke: Christy hates
to be yelled at.

"It's like a song, you know?" I tried to present a new calm exterior.
"You've forgotten about it, but then it comes on the radio and you still
know all the lyrics and it makes you so happy that somewhere it's still
being played and now you can sing along, like your life isn't passing
you by at a zillion fuckin' miles per hour."

"I wish you wouldn't curse so much" was all she said.

I skulked around for a minute or so not looking at her, unmuted
the television, and sat in silence for probably over an hour. There was
an old episode of *Babylon Five* on that I watched while Christy got
dressed for bed and slammed some suitcases shut.

Zoning out there on the bed, I started thinking about my first girlfriend, Lisa. God, her smile was a knockout, all crooked and sarcastic!
She was Catholic and a good time. I remember kissing her out on our
high school parking lot while snow was falling on us. The skin on her
neck was hot, and I was feeling her breasts through her blue down vest.
She'd just gotten her driver's license and was standing outside her
daddy's green Chrysler station wagon. The snow collecting on top of
our heads like funny hats made us laugh. She was so adorable: auburn
hair, very petite—not like Christy at all. She loved me as if her whole
life depended on it, like her heart would split in two if the world ever

disappointed me. Later on that same snow day, we went back to her parents' house and goofed around on her living room couch while *The Terminator* was playing on HBO. She gave me her body—to play with, to touch, to kiss—as a gift. I don't mean that sexist or anything. It was her gift to me. My hand slid inside her, making those squishy sounds of wetness, but she didn't smile or look away embarrassed, she just soaked me in. I can still see the depth of her brown eyes. As I entered her, she whispered in my ear, "Is there anything else I can do for you?" and I came instantly. It felt like the fluid from my spine emptied out completely, leaving me paralyzed in her arms. Fuck, man, I miss her. I'll always miss her. Sometimes it hurts bad. The longing for the past is like a tangible physical torture. Oh, God, I wanted to remember every moment of my life. I didn't want to forget anything. If I could remember, then the passing seconds might have some meaning or be amassing into some definition or purpose. But I dumped Lisa, I knocked her up, and she got all turned around and confused about the abortion. She cried and cried, called the house for weeks, but . . . I let her go. Once every other year or so I still spoke with her. She had two kids. She told me she hated her husband, but she probably just said that for me. No one will ever love me like that again. The burden of all those memories creates in me a yearning for the quiet I imagine would come with a giant heroin overdose or if I shoved my skull under the wheel of a moving bus.

Bam! All of a sudden my daze of nostalgic reverie was smashed as Christy threw open the door, rushed out of the motel room, and walked onto the parking lot with no shoes on. I leapt up.

"Where you going?" I shouted after her.

"Just getting some ice," she called back, seemingly not angry anymore, and scampered off toward the front office, her feet hopping along the cold ground like a little bird.

That was her only true pregnancy behavioral oddity; she had a voracious appetite for ice. All day long we'd be hustling around town running errands, setting up the wedding, and the whole time she'd be chomping ice like a hound dog gnawing on a T-bone. *Crunch, crack, slurp. Crunch, crack, slurp.* I thought I'd pull my hair out. I'm not exaggerating, she was always munching it. She'd order big Styrofoam cups full of ice from every store we stopped at. It started the same day she quit smoking.

I was glad she quit, but now I was supposed to quit too, and she was cracking ice like a friggin' polar bear.

"Oh, Jimmy, ohhh, Jimmy!" Christy said abruptly, as she dashed back in the room, opening and closing the door quickly behind her.

"What? What? What?" I said, whispering for some reason. I stood up, panic snapping through my body like the crack of a whip. The whole time Christy was pregnant, the mysteries and concerns of her health invaded my waking moments.

"Look, look!" she said, and promptly fell flat on her back on the bed, hiking up her shirt to expose her naked belly. I moved up and knelt over her.

"Turn on the light," she insisted, whispering now as well. I leaned over and flicked on the dim yellow light of the bedside lamp.

Now, I won't be able to describe what I saw anywhere near as gracefully or beautifully as what it's like to witness it, but I'll give it a shot.

Once, right after my dad's suicide, when I first enlisted, I got stationed outside of Scagway, Alaska, for four months as part of a base-dismantling operation. Several times out there in the cold dark January nights, I could see the Aurora Borealis, the Northern Lights, and that was the BOMB. Light dancing across the sky, the stratosphere rippling, like a still lake hit by the first drops of rain, or billowing, like when you throw a clean cotton sheet over a mattress. The sky above me was literally at play and it was awesome, humbling, and funny. Those are the only words I have to describe watching my baby spin inside her mother's womb.

"You can lead us, you know," Christy said quietly. My hand was still on her belly, feeling for my child.

"What do you mean?" I asked. I could see all these yellow speckles far inside her green eyes.

"I'm not always going to agree with you or know what you're talking about, but that doesn't mean you're wrong. You need to believe in yourself. You've got a great heart, Jimmy, a heart like a horse, and I believe in it. I just believe in it more than I believe in little red books, OK?"

Now I have a theory that if a woman wants to keep a man she only needs to say two things: She believes in him and he's got a big cock. That's all it takes. It doesn't even have to be true.

"We'll write our own service," I said, "in a way we both like. All right?"

"Now you're talking," she said. "You know something, Jimmy? And don't get mad when I say this."

Whenever she prefaces a comment like that, I know I'm gonna get pissed.

"Sometimes I think you worry that if you surpass your father— you know, as a man—that you'll be showing him up or betraying him in some way. But you won't. If he was the good father you remember, he'd be proud of you."

She paused, looking at me to make sure she wasn't hurting my feelings.

"That doesn't make me mad," I said, as she snuggled down next to me on the mattress.

"Well, good." She sighed, closed her eyes, and pulled herself closer.

I turned off the lamp by the bed and held her close, proud of the muscles in my arms. She was right, I figured: God didn't care what words we used, it was our aim that mattered. An hour might have passed when I felt her weight increase with the onset of sleep. I was still smiling about seeing our little baby kicking around, and then easily, like a reflex, I spoke out loud.

"Dear God, I pray for my child and I pray for Christy." I said it lightly toward the window and the flaring lights of the parking lot, my voice fragile and slight in the echo of the empty room. "Watch over them and teach me how to love them always."

I stopped for a second and wondered if it felt like anyone was listening to me. I couldn't be sure either way. Indian music from the front office was filtering through our walls. Then another thought popped out of my mouth.

"I pray for all mothers and all their babies. I pray for all people who are lonely, all people who want children." I paused again, smiling, maybe 'cause I felt stupid or maybe 'cause I felt better. A horn was impatiently honking outside.

"I say a prayer for all dead people, too, and for the fathers. All dads; I pray for them." I added, more formally, "My dad too, please."

Grace the cat hopped up on the bed, frightening me for a second. Then she climbed up over Christy's slumbering back and onto her dark hair. The cat rubbed her wet nose against my shoulder. Christy rolled over, and the cat scurried to the edge of the mattress, careful to avoid some carelessly tossed limb. Christy nuzzled her face down into my ribs. It was clear to me then, easy as looking at the road from the windshield of an automobile, that I didn't choose any of this; from my birth forward, everything was just happening, like a string of firecrackers. My father, Lisa, Christy: we were all just falling. I didn't choose Christy, she happened to me. I happened to her. Shit, man, I like petite girls with high voices and small hands who laugh all the time; that's my type. I could've fallen for someone like that, someone Catholic like Lisa, or someone who liked muscle cars or someone I was smarter than, but I didn't. I fell in love with Christy. The cat crawled up over my chest and positioned itself directly atop my head. Slowly she began kneading my hair like a baker does bread. A purr of immense pleasure vibrated from her chest. Her claws dug into my scalp, hurting a little bit but not too much. The bliss the cat was experiencing seemed too great to justify shaking her off.

Then silently, in case Chris was still half awake, I said a little prayer for Lisa and how I hoped she was well. Then for good measure I even half said a prayer for Christy's first husband, that prick.

Next, I surprised myself—it was probably something I heard some preacher say once, but it felt like I was making it up—"I give you my life," I said. "I give it all away. I'll take whatever comes."

When I woke up I was naked. I have this one oddball idiosyncrasy: Sometimes in my sleep I take off all my clothes.

CHANCE ❧

You'd like to think that you go through something like marriage as a couple, but you don't. No matter what kind of ceremony you have, you still experience everything as an individual. At least that's been the case for me.

I was sitting in one of the chamber rooms of the largest cathedral in Cincinnati, with my best friend Chance doing my nails. To my right above me was a portrait of a bludgeoned Jesus hanging from a cross. Looking at his anguished face I thought of his line, "The kingdom of heaven is like a mustard seed," which always sounded more Buddhist than Christian to me. Heaven is right here all the time. There's nothing you need that you don't already have. Expectation, that's the killer. I couldn't think of one event that I'd loaded up with more expectation than my wedding day.

"Your hands are shaking," Chance said. Her bleached-blond hair hung over her eyes. She had driven in the day before with the dress, her husband, Bucky, and their eight-month-old son, Griffin.

"I know," I said. "Give me another one of those things." I motioned to the pile of peppermint patties she had stuffed in her purse.

"You don't need any more of those," she replied calmly.

"Yes, I do," I pleaded, and then added, "Do you think I should wear a veil?"

"Definitely," Chance said, giving my hand a yank to encourage me to stop moving but not making any move toward the sweets.

"I don't think I should." Truth be told, I was scared to get married. The idea of *two* failed marriages was petrifying, but it was a real possibility. Inside me lived a Gypsy, a powerful woman with dangling bracelets making a hell of a racket.

"Stay still," Chance whispered, as she continued painting my nails.

"Please give me one of those candies," I said again. Chance just continued working with a determined expression. Outside the door I could hear the church organist playing some kind of prelude.

"Can you believe how huge I am?" I asked, referring to my fatness.

"Hey, cowgirl, it's my dress you're wearing. You're not that big." Chance laughed, pulling my hands up so she could blow on my nails. "You look beautiful."

"You really think so?" I asked, my arms stretched out toward her. "You don't think people are going to feel sorry for me?"

This white gown wrapped around my growing belly was making me feel shy.

"I don't feel sorry for you, I'm happy for you. You deserve it, Christy. You deserve every good thing that happens." The anteroom we were seated in was pleasant and warm, full of candles and knick-knacks. A radiator in the corner was practically glowing. The skin of Chance's face was healthy and flushed. "Stand up," she ordered.

"Why should I wear a veil?" I asked again, rising as I checked out my finished nails. The engagement ring around my finger lit up like the torch of mortality. The point of marriage, I thought, must be something more than to stay together forever, because we will ultimately be redivided. One of us, Jimmy or I, would die first. Maybe it would be me. My credit card would be canceled. My driver's license would apply to no one. There was no finishing line, no competition to win. The point must be something else.

"Why do I have to cover up my face?" I asked.

"Because it looks pretty that way," she said, standing up now herself. She was wearing a royal blue gown I'd never seen before that was very flattering; it matched her eyes.

"You think?"

"I really do." Chance adjusted the dress around my shoulders. In that moment I felt the possibility of marriage as a kind of holy state, a space from which to rub away my narcissism and deepen my capabili-

ties of giving. I'd spent all this time and energy over the years searching for a home—and home for me, I was realizing, was simply being
close to my own ability to love.

"Do you think they have any beer in this place?" Chance said, as
she walked over and picked up the veil from a nearby chair.

"I doubt it," I answered.

"Outa beer, outa here." Chance grinned, reciting a familiar refrain.
"It's about time, sweetie. Are you ready?"

My father was waiting impatiently outside the door, anticipating
our cue.

"Can you believe I'm going to be somebody's mother?" I said,
looking down at my belly. "It happens so quick."

"What does?"

"I don't know . . . life." As I was growing up I discovered the harsh
fact that fairy tales were not true: trees didn't talk, eagles didn't pick
you up and fly you away, fairies didn't dance in the forest. There was a
deepening sadness in the realization that the fantastic was all myth.
Everything was just as it seemed. But recently, perhaps with the idea of
marriage, or maybe pregnancy, there was a returning childish magic in
the air. Was I positive that birds weren't winged messengers from
heaven? that whales weren't space aliens?

"Motherhood is not what you should be worrying about; that at
least comes naturally," Chance said, as she fiddled with the veil. "Being
married, *that* is what I call unnatural."

"What's it like?" I asked. "Is it OK?"

"I'll tell you later." She grinned secretively. "How's my lipstick?"

"Tell me now," I demanded.

"It's utter agony," she began, in complete earnestness. "You will
give all you have to give, and it won't be enough. You will resent him
and feel he has single-handedly ruined your life, and—worse than
that—you will be correct." She flipped the veil around in her hands
and moved toward me. "He will resent you and take all your gifts for
granted. For the life of you, you will not be able to remember how you
could've fallen in love with this lazy self-absorbed creep. At night you

will cry from loneliness, just as you have your whole life, only now someone will be lying in bed right beside you and that kind of loneliness is ten times worse than anything you've ever known before." She paused to let out a deep sigh and continued. "And then one Christmas you'll be driving slowly through a snowstorm, both of you not speaking 'cause you're petrified the car is gonna slide off the road, but you'll make it home. You'll start laughing and kissing, and then you'll realize that all this time while you've been grouchy and complaining you haven't actually looked him in the eye, and when you do you'll recognize the best friend you've ever known and you won't be able to believe that all this time he was sitting right beside you."

"I think you should tell me about it later," I said.

Chance stepped back, still holding the veil, and looked at me. "Your mom should be here, Christy," she said. "I wish she could see how beautiful you are today."

"Yeah, me too." I'd been thinking a lot about my mother these days. What if I run away from my daughter as she had run from me? *I will not,* I promised myself, but the oath echoed hollowly in my chest.

I remembered a Sunday early in my courtship with Jimmy when we ate a handful of magic mushrooms and pleasantly tripped the afternoon away. The day was long and full of adventures. We went to the movies and to the park, we laughed on the children's swings and ate spicy Ethiopian food. We were falling in love and it was springtime: that one week in late April or early May when all of Albany's trees bloom and flower petals fall like rain onto the streets below.

We wound up back at my apartment that evening, and Jimmy sat on the floor in the middle of the entranceway with the door open. Looking out at all the cars passing by, letting the spring air wash his face, he fell into a trance. A half hour might've gone by with him just moving his head back and forth with the traffic. I made myself some tea and was in the kitchen sipping it, waiting for it to cool, when I had a vision. From where I was standing I could see the doorway, only when I glanced over at Jimmy on the floor, he was gone. There, in his place, was a massive gray wolf swishing its tail in the entrance to my apartment. I didn't look away and just patiently breathed, waiting for the hallucination to dissipate. The wolf looked over at me, and inside the yellow irises of this wolf's glowing eyes I could clearly recognize Jimmy. The animal was not foreign to me and I was not afraid. He was guarding me. I watched his belly rise and fall. I watched his ears twitch with the wind. Minutes passed, and still the hallucination remained. Finally I looked down, and where my feet should've been I saw two gray paws. My body, too, was covered in a beautiful gray majestic fur coat, and my sight, I noticed, was void of color.

Jimmy and I had known each other for a very long time. I felt that the first night he touched me, and now I knew it to be true. I carried this vision of him and me as wolves through the whole of our affair, enjoying the fantasy that he and I had traveled through time together and met in different manifestations.

"Now I know you don't want to wear this thing," Chance said, as she placed the veil on my head and began fixing my hair around it. "You want to be open and clear, not hiding or masquerading or pretending to be anything you're not." She met my eyes and smiled. "I.e., a virgin." Chance was a physical therapist at the hospital where I worked, and she knew how to touch people. Her hands were calm and soothing.

"You think it's OK to wear white 'cause that's what's expected and it's pretty, but you know in your heart that you're not innocent and you're not a little girl and you think a veil is trying too hard or, worse, a lie—and you don't want to be lying when you're up there at the altar. Am I right?"

"I need another one of those candies," I said, not answering her question.

"No, you don't," she said quickly. "But here's the rub: First off, a veil is sexy. That's a fact. I don't know why but the whole virginal thing is a turn-on. And when the priest says"—she affected a deep stately voice—"*You may now kiss the bride,* you want your husband to have to lift up the veil to kiss you." She surreptitiously lifted the veil from my face. It *was* dramatic.

"Can I please have another candy?" I asked.

"No," she said curtly. "Heaven knows you're not innocent. Believe me, I haven't forgotten what a little slut you are—and there's a couple boys up there at Syracuse University that I'm pretty sure also remember what a huss you are—but here's what I know that you don't."

She brought the veil back down over my eyes, giving me her best coy expression. "It is this: You are a virgin. I know you've got a four-month-old little baby in your belly." She tapped my stomach. I tried to suck it in, but it was impossible.

"I didn't think I was a virgin when I got married either," Chance said. "But having sexual intercourse does not a hymen break, my friend."

Chance knew how to talk. We were roommates for a year, before she got married, and there was no easier person to talk to in the world.

"Having sex with a man you love is not how you lose your virginity, and consummating your marriage tonight is not how you will lose it. You will lose it by biting from the tree of knowledge, am I right?" She didn't wait for a response. Instead, she lifted up my arms, tweaking some part of my dress while she went on. "All the horsing around you've done in this life, you've done without any knowledge—we know that. If you had knowledge, you would have married that Jason character three years ago like I told you and you'd have a million bucks in the bank and you could have thrown out that zebra rug he had, or whatever it was you found such a turnoff. But you didn't; instead, you ran around and fell in love like a silly girl and that's why I love you and why you are still a virgin."

She brought my arms down, turned me around again, and began primping the back of my dress.

"You will lose your virginity after you've given birth and have healed, when you take your man into your arms and make love to him again. That is biting from the tree of knowledge." There was a bouquet of flowers from my father over by the door. The faint lovely smell of peonies was beginning to permeate the room. "When you find him sexy again after you know what it means to have his seed gestate in you for ten months—and it *is* ten, not nine; I don't know who started that rumor—when you make love with that wisdom in your brain you are a full-grown woman. That is when you will look around and realize that you're naked in the Garden of Eden. Until then—a girl."

Chance walked around me now, circling, scoping out all the angles. I stood self-consciously in the center of the room, trying to read her expression.

The future was coming on, hard, fast, and furious, like a steam engine howler racing through a tunnel with me standing on the tracks staring into the headlight. The future wasn't kidding around. There was no turning back; this pregnancy was an open door. I knew it and I wanted to walk through, but I felt my bones shifting their weight. Everything I could see seemed only the shadow of what I could not. My marriage was imminent, and with it my childhood would be over.

SIX CROOKED HIGHWAYS

IT WAS THE DEEP DARK BLACK OF NIGHT. I'd been driving for seventeen hours. The coffee on my breath, the glaze over my eyes, the subtle vibration of the engine moving through my legs—I loved it all. Christy was beside me, asleep, her gargantuan feet splayed out across my lap and her head snuggled tight on a pillow against the passenger-side door. The Nova rattled on as the miles clocked behind us. I couldn't tell if Christy had been asleep for twenty minutes or ten hours. Another set of headlights hadn't appeared for what was beginning to feel like days. For me driving is a passion, as sensuous and hypnotic as anything else I've ever experienced. I can drive twenty-four hours straight, no problem.

Focus and attention to detail, that's the key. You have to watch the road ahead of you while incorporating your knowledge of the road behind. Mark the cars, count them. An old woman in a Cutlass smoking a cigarette, 62 mph. Two Caucasian males approximately twenty-five, drinking large cups of soda and laughing in a '96 blue Dodge pickup, 72 mph. Always be aware of what the cars around you are up to. It takes two bad drivers to have an accident; we all know that. Stay ahead of the police. Use your brain. A good driver can see a speed trap before it happens. Stay alert and engaged in what you are doing. Never pass on the right; that causes more wrecks than any other highway infraction. No emotion. Fast song, slow song, good day, bad day: no difference. The world is still turning and you're still watching three cars ahead and two behind. Note the landmarks as you go. That way if you get lost or need to return, you'll be able to find your way. Trust your instincts and make your decisions instantly. If you make a mistake, acknowledge it and keep on truckin'.

Shaking my head like a horse with a long mane, I pushed the Nova up to 95 mph. It rests easier there than at 70 or 80. That's the other thing: Know your car.

Christy looked pretty when she slept. The muscles in her face completely relaxed into a madonna-like expression of calm, her cheeks and lips flushed red with blood. The gold wedding band wrapped around her finger flashed and glittered, reflecting the green dashboard lights. The matching ring on my hand was tapping the steering wheel. We had been husband and wife now for twenty-nine hours, and the panic that would arise momentarily had not yet arrived.

The wedding had gone off fine. Before the service I'd been assigned to wait in a little cloak/dressing room with Father Matthew to the left behind the altar until the set music cue, at which time we would both step out and the service would begin. Christy's father and stepmother had flown in from Houston for the service. Chance was there too, with her nitwit husband, Bucky, and their kid, as was my mom; they were pretty much the only ones in the church. I just stood in the dressing room bouncing my johnson around in my pants, nervously waiting while Father Matthew arrayed himself in all his priestly regalia. The tuxedo on my back was rented, but it was an antique wool beauty hanging off my shoulders perfectly. Father Matthew started off handily, talking to me about the perils of jealousy as he unbuttoned his black oxford shirt, revealing a thin worn white V-neck over his barely living skin. I didn't want to read too much into what he was saying, but it seemed like he was hiding some kind of lesson or metaphor inside his idle chatter. Maybe he was just trying to distract me from my nerves. He talked about what a source of pain jealousy had been for him. It was surreal listening to the old guy talk like this as he slid on his robes. The priests, he said, were always bickering over who got appointed bishop and things of even lesser significance.

"All this ridiculous jealousy. Why aren't people satisfied with who they are?" he asked me.

"I don't know," I answered, my hands still deep in the pockets of my tuxedo.

"To know who you are and then to accept it—that is life's journey," he said, dropping a mammoth silver crucifix around his neck.

He was reminding me of a game I sometimes play with myself at the gym. I stare around at all the other guys lifting weights and try to figure out in what ways I'm better than each one of them. It usually makes me feel buoyed in superiority until something happens like Captain Powers'll come in: He's Special Forces Airborne, a great bowler, his wife is both smokin' hot and nice, he's got two boys and combat experience in Desert Storm, he saved some new recruit from blowing his brains out in a barracks bathroom—the guy is awesome. He can drink a fifth of vodka and still shoot the bottle from fifty yards. His parents both died in a plane crash when he was only fourteen, so it's not even like you can think he's spoiled and hasn't suffered. The game doesn't work with him. I'd sit there and watch him bench 240, and the burden of the world's unfairness would fold in on me. I know I should use him for inspiration, but the physical discomfort I felt, as if somehow his excellence was piss on my face, made any warm feelings I could muster evaporate.

"God loves you better than your best friend, sees and loves your soul better than any lover, and he always will," Father Matthew said. "He also loves everybody else. It's important to remember that."

I couldn't figure out why he was gabbing to me about all this.

Then, rather sharply, he turned to me and said in an irritated tone, "I got passed over for bishop again. Can you believe that?"

I shook my head in disbelief, my hands still deep in my pockets.

Driving south, parallel with the Mississippi River, I was in a state of steady untroubled bliss. A honeymoon in New Orleans and then onward to Texas to deal with the military and get settled in for the birth—that was the plan. I'd had so much sex in the last day or so, my mind had reached a rare tranquil calm like that of a patient recovering from hours of intense electroshock therapy.

Christy's feet were so damn big they made me laugh. She was still asleep as we passed the state sign for Missouri, her toes lightly squirming in my lap. I looked again at the gold wedding band around my finger. It was a fraction too big, but I liked it that way. After I was dead, I figured, my kids would keep the ring and believe I had large mythic powerful hands. Not that my hands are girlish or anything, it's just sometimes I wish they were a little more commanding.

The cathedral had been glorious. We did it like Christy wanted: at night, lit by candles. The place was glowing amber as she walked down the aisle, her pouchy belly pushing out the bright luminescent white dress, her father holding her arm with this monster of a smile. Yes, she looked ravishing, and yes, she looked delicate, but more than anything else she looked confident.

That's what breaks my heart when I think on it now.

Glancing over at her spread out on the Nova's front seat, lit in the dim green glow of the dashboard lights, I could see she was still sound asleep. She had a thick wine-red wool sweater on, with several different-colored scarves wrapped around her neck and my blue knit hat on her head. Sharp gorgeous locks of her dyed black hair were shooting out across her white forehead. Grace the cat was asleep beneath my seat. A faint smell of Kitty Litter filled the car's interior. We kept a small box in the back, cleaning it religiously, but even the smell of fresh Kitty Litter is less than appealing. The radio was off, but even without it the Nova was anything but silent. That bad bitch makes a hell of a commotion. The odometer creates a loud quick clacking sound, the heater has a deep rumble, and whenever you're traveling above 65 mph the whole front console jitters and shakes like it might drop off. When the music is cranked it's no problem (I put in a sound system that requires its own battery supplement), but with the tunes turned down you may as well be rattling along inside a B-52 bomber.

Still wide awake and traveling at about 85 mph, I tried to concentrate on my driving but sometimes my mind would drift away. Time was so different for adults. I missed junior high: first period, second period, and the clear structure of days, months, and years. First semester, second semester, seventh grade, eighth grade: It had all been clearly drawn out, pass or fail. Now I was floating, rudderless really—across the country, across space. The army was probably over for me now. Anxiety sifted down on my shoulders as I remembered my lieutenant yelling at me over the phone, telling me to get back on base. He'd threatened dishonorable discharge; I figured that was the worst thing that could come out of this whole stunt. My buddy Eric was submitting me for an emergency leave of absence, and his dad was the colonel, so maybe some kind of pardon could be worked out, but there was credible skepticism as to whether or not I'd handled my departure in accordance with the proper military protocol. I didn't give a shit, but what was I gonna do next? An uncle of mine made a million dollars in meat processing back in Cleveland; he always said he'd hire me. I'd be a good stockbroker or a cop, maybe; it's easy to get a job on the force coming out of the military. On the other hand, dishonorable discharge might botch that up.

Oh, my God, I thought, I might have just fucked up my whole life!

The best thing about being young is that you can be "promising." By now, however, a big chunk of my life had already gone by and it was almost all undistinguished.

I know it's an average dream, but I did want to be an athlete. If I could live my life over I would dedicate myself to swimming. Some people thought I could've gone to the Olympics—I mean, if I'd really applied myself. I held the Ohio state record in the 50-meter butterfly for a couple of years. Ultimately, I guess, I really am too short, and even athletes seem kind of feeble and depressing when they get older. It's not like accomplishment is a ticket to being a significant person. All I wanted, my life's goal, was to be a person I could admire; it was that simple. I thought marriage would kick-start that for me, but I was surprised how vulnerable I felt now without the army.

Christy wanted me to sell my car—it was not "baby friendly"—and I knew she was right. To her this automobile was the full expression of my all-encompassing inability to mature. If the damn thing even made it to Texas, I'd have to sell it. Who would I be then, some dweeb with an '89 Taurus? I know things like cars and clothes are external and frivolous, but it was difficult to picture myself in a civilian domestic lifestyle. The good thing about the military is it keeps you young. It's a young man's world, full of young men's toys. Snowmobiles, firing ranges, fast cars, fast boats, strippers—they were all amusing, but it was the long-standing promise of adventure that was gonna be so hard to live without. Not that there ever was any adventure, but still. Man, life was so much more subtle than I'd anticipated. All I wanted to do was love a girl right, and the next thing I knew everything I understood about myself was blowing away like leaves.

We were still in Missouri when the black night sky started shading its way toward navy blue. New Orleans was probably ten hours away. I'd have to sleep before we got there. Christy was starting to wake up. She squirmed uncomfortably for a moment and then sat up and rubbed her eyes. Her face was squashed up in the grumpy expression of a two-year-old. She reached down onto the car floor, pulled up Grace, and situated the gray cat on her lap, gently stroking her, as all three of us silently observed the beginning stages of the dawn. I couldn't believe we'd done it. We were married.

. . .

The most nerve-wracking thing about the actual ceremony for me had been the whole consummation aspect. I can't explain it, but from age eleven or so on I've had this nightmarish paranoia that I wouldn't be able to get it up on my wedding night. A shadow of inadequacy and failure would fall over our memories of the big day. We'd throw the pictures away. A mental block would form and I'd go permanently impotent except with hookers and weird kinky transvestites.

I've been playing out that scenario for as long as I've been thinking about marriage. So you can imagine the dark annals of anxiety I'd reached by the time I was saying "I do." I wasn't focusing on my vows or thinking *Oh, I'm so happy!* I just had my hand in my pocket, lightly shaking my johnson back and forth through my tuxedo pants, making sure the old boy was still vital. By the time we were done kissing I was so jacked up I gave Christy the business in the church lavatory right before we did the pictures.

Now, usually when I was having intercourse with a girl I'd wind up daydreaming about another scenario that I'd find even more titillating, a sexier girl or a more electrifying situation, but looking into Christy's face with the wedding dress spread out over the porcelain sink and the white skin of her naked legs wrapped around me, I knew I was living right then a moment I would dream of and long to return to my whole life. There was no fantasy better than right now. Life would no longer be defined by the maybes—maybe at this party I will meet the love of my life, maybe at this new job I will be introduced to my soul mate, maybe that girl behind me on the train will be my blazing eternal love. No, my blazing eternal love is sleeping in the car right beside me with ludicrously large feet, my eternal love is four months pregnant and addicted to ice munching, and my love wants to know why I'm having such a problem maturing.

Peering out into the highway in the distance, maybe two hundred yards ahead, I could see the dark shapes and yellow eyes of deer darting into the trees. I could still hear the sound of Father Matthew's Massachusetts voice.

"If you are to love one another well, you must first love the truth. You must seek the spirit of God breathing inside each other, you must somehow enter deep into the mystery of God's love for all of us." This was the only sermonlike advice Father offered up at the altar. He didn't do any preaching during the service, for which I was grateful. It was a brief ceremony that Christy and I had mapped out with him, and we all felt good about it. But with his lax relationship to the scriptures it wasn't too hard to understand why the higher-ups weren't rushing to make him bishop.

I thought the service was heartfelt and touching. My mom, however, thought it was "short and goofy," and she got testy when she noticed the continual omission of all the more didactic language. She'd been such a bitch. I don't want to be mean—"Honor thy mother," right? and I do—but this whole event taxed her. Christy thought it was important to invite her to the wedding so I did, but her attitude was atrocious. It was a hassle, the timing was bad, she had a business trip the next day.

I drove her to the airport the morning after, and she didn't have one nice word to say.

"Too bad you didn't have any music.

"Why was the service so short?

"Boy, Father Matthew sure has gotten old."

"How much weight has Christy gained?"

She felt our brief ride to the airport was the opportune time to inform me that she didn't really believe in marriage and her only advice was not to get too "stressed out" if everything didn't turn out like I hoped.

"Marriages seem to work out well, at least from my perspective, when the two people involved don't have any real desire to live a deeply explored life," she said, holding her purse uncomfortably in her lap. "People who are really interested in appearances—those are the ones marriage seems to be most successful for. I worry that you're not that type of person. Maybe you are; I don't know." She was sifting through her bag for her ticket. "Well, I should say, I've never enjoyed being married but I have enjoyed the ceremonies, so I hope you guys had fun." And she looked up, not at me but out at the flat Ohio landscape.

"Don't you have anything positive to say, Mom?" I asked, trying not to be oversensitive.

"Oh, don't take this the wrong way. It was a beautiful service and I'm very happy for you, I really am." Her voice was clear and musical as always. "It's just, frankly, I hope you don't feel rushed into anything. You have to be careful. Pregnant women don't always think too sharply."

"What's that supposed to mean?" I said, both hands firmly on the wheel.

"God, Jimmy, I don't know why you're getting so uptight. I wish you guys the best, I really do."

"You keep saying that, Mom, but that's not what it sounds like."

"Look, I'm just not the biggest advocate of marriage, I hope it works out better for you than it did for me. If all you want is the sunshine report, maybe I'm not the right person to be talking to. Sharing your life with somebody is not what it's cracked up to be." She was doing her lipstick now, studying herself in the tiny mirror I'd glued to the visor. "In my experience one person seems to get larger and the other gets smaller, and I don't want you to be the one who shrinks."

"You don't like Christy?" I asked.

"I don't know her, sweetheart. If you love her, she must be terrific." She kissed her hand to get rid of the excess lipstick.

"You know something, Mom? I don't think I'm gonna talk to you for a while, all right?" I was trying to stay calm, but I felt like I was turning inside out.

When we arrived at airport Departures, I helped her with her bags and kissed her good-bye.

"Do yourself a favor, will you?" she said, before stepping away. "Get rid of that car."

Watching her walk through the mechanized departure doors, I rubbed the muscles around my navel to try and settle my nerves. I'd never felt so much like an adult. There was no doubt about it, I thought. The umbilical cord was gone.

My mother was spot-on in regard to one subject, however: that car. With all the praying that'd been goin' down in the last week, I'd forgotten the only thing I should've been praying for: that sack-of-shit Chevy Nova. For every mile we passed, I tried to be grateful. For every turn up ahead, I braced myself. If it rained we were done for; there weren't any wipers. I took them off to replace them with better ones, but you know how these things go.

As we left Missouri and entered Arkansas, almost immediately the highway we were driving on ceased to be any kind of main throughway. The road was narrowing and beginning to wind and ascend a large slope. I couldn't figure out how this had happened, I didn't remember exiting and the incline was becoming so steep that I was terrifyingly aware of the engine's rpms revving into a high-pitched whine. Christy wasn't worried yet; she was playing with Grace's collar, spinning it around and pushing back her ears. How did I make a wrong turn? I thought to myself. I'd been so careful. I wanted to remedy the situation before Chris realized we were lost. Maybe everything was fine, I tried to reassure myself.

We arrived at the peak of the hill and immediately began a descent. The pull of the brake pad against the wheel was discernible in my intestines. Needless to say, I don't have power brakes.

At the bottom we turned and immediately began the ascent of another steep hill. Christy reached over and flipped on the radio: static. The SEEK button spun all the way through the dial without stopping once. She clicked it off and put on her seat belt, situating the strap comfortably under the bulge of her belly.

"This car better make it to New Orleans, cowboy," she said quietly.

"Or what?" I asked.

"Or you're in trouble, Ratskin!" she said, licking her finger and pushing it into my ear. I tell you, the more pregnant she got, the harder it was to bring her down. Progesterone happy head, she called it.

"Give me a break," I moaned, leaning away from her. I was edgy about where the hell we were headed and how far off the track we might be. It was still dark; dawn was not coming as rapidly as promised. A truck was barreling toward us, its high beams blazing. I flashed my lights at him but he didn't respond. I dimmed mine anyway, acquiescing; one blind driver is better than two. For a moment I could see nothing, not even the line marking the center of the road, my eyes whited out in the glare, but the moment passed and we were still traveling, rattling like a bag-a-bones forward up this old country hill.

I snapped my brights back up.

A WALK IN THE SUN

WE HAD BOOKED THE HONEYMOON SUITE at the Fairmont Hotel in New Orleans. The room was lavish, with high cracked ceilings. A hundred years ago the Fairmont might have been called extravagant. Rich red velvet carpets lined the hallways, the lobby was gaudy with giant crystal chandeliers, and beautiful intricate murals were painted on the open walls, but like all of New Orleans stains on stains had washed and beaten the colors down to a muted version of what they had once been. The city seeemed dipped in a film of alcohol.

After we checked in, I undressed and began preparing for my nightly bath. I could see Jimmy doing push-ups while he watched the end of a basketball game on TV. He would pause for a minute or so at a time and nibble on a slice of pizza left cold in a box on the floor.

"Can we listen to some music?" I asked, as I heard the announcers discuss the final score.

There was a radio inside the television set, and Jimmy flipped off the game and spun the radio dial. With the overhead light out, the TV off, and no lamp on in the room, a dim yellow glow from the city seven floors below poured into the honeymoon suite, giving the air a sepia tint. Sitting on the thick ravaged hotel carpet, Jimmy already looked like an old photograph. He was wearing only boxers, and the skin tone of his legs and chest was glorious, sweet and golden like a malted milkshake. He stood up and walked purposefully toward me. I could tell he wanted to dance, but dressed only in my towel and fully sober, I wasn't ready. Dancing makes me self-conscious, unless I'm drunk. Some old Frank Sinatra melody crackled through the television speaker, and I guessed from Jimmy's response that he loved this song. He pulled me toward him, mouthing the words along with the music. He grabbed my hands formally and we began to dance as if we were at the high school prom. My towel fell from my chest onto the floor, leaving me naked. Jimmy refused to let me bend over and pick it up and waltzed us to the center of the room.

All right, I decided: one nude dance.

Jimmy loved dancing. His father had taught him some old school moves and he'd probably used them on every girl he met, but they were fun and cutting the rug with him was always comfortable and easy. Frank Sinatra led us around the room, as I looked for the still point inside our dance. Against my stomach I felt Jimmy getting an erection.

I imagined myself a willow tree, flowing and supple but ultimately strong and rooted. With his erection pressed tight against me, we moved more slowly, just holding each other. As the song ended and another began, he slid down to his knees, kissing my stomach and tickling my navel with his lips. Then he moved under me, his mouth between my legs. I stood awkwardly in the center of the dark room. I wanted to sit down and hide from the windows but I couldn't bring myself to step away.

Feeling Jimmy in between my legs, kissing, lapping, and loving me, I felt sorry for him. Would he really be happy as a married man? It's a boyish and silly quality, but Jimmy's lust for adventure was one I admired. His eyes were full of a desire to prove himself. I wondered whether fatherhood and husbandry would be enough.

Did my mother and father ever dance like this, newlyweds holding and licking each other with aspirations of a lifetime together? Probably.

Jimmy picked me up and set me down on the bed. Sometimes when we made love, I would do a kind of invocation of ancient gods, Apollo or Aphrodite, beckoning them into the room in hopes of casting a spell.

Waves of sexual pleasure began beating back the busy patterns of my brain. My body was now resting on the cotton sheets of our bed and Jimmy's head was buried between my legs, while his hands gently reached up to cradle my swollen breasts.

As a child, I'd been obsessed with the events around my own birth. All the stories that collected around my parents' meeting, my conception, and my birth were molded in my mind into the stuff of legend. A couple times with my dad I would meet someone in a bookstore or in line at the movies whose name I recognized from an anecdote, someone who was intimate with my parents when they were in love, and it felt like shaking hands with a fictional character from a favorite novel. I was now aware of myself as a player in some larger epic.

Only four months earlier, Jimmy had insisted on taking me fishing, and inside a gas station near Lake Ontario we'd asked an old clerk, Wayne Sheffle, if he knew any sweet spots. He told us of a secret cove where the fish were bountiful out on his land; we were welcome to camp there if we liked. "I always like to help out lovers," he'd said, winking at us. For three days we camped there, swimming naked in a freezing-cold pond, picking flowers, and making love inside our blue two-person tent while it rained. Either during the rainstorm or later that second night our child had been conceived. On the third night, two locals came by the little cove, blasting shotguns and yelling at us to get off their land. They were obviously drunk and dangerous. Jimmy went out of our tent and walked over to them. The larger of the two stepped forward and shoved the shotgun right in his face.

"Get the fuck out of here," the man slurred, the barrel of his gun at Jimmy's chest.

Jimmy stood silent for a moment and then held out his hand. "I'm Jimmy Heartsock. What's your name?"

The man looked confused for a moment. "Don't worry about who I am, just get off my damn property."

"Wayne Sheffle told me we could camp here," Jimmy said, leaving his hand outstretched with the gun still in his face.

"Wayne Sheffle is an asshole, and he stole this land from me."

"He seemed like an asshole," Jimmy said.

The man slowly lowered his gun and begrudgingly shook Jimmy's hand. Slurring some drunken monologue involving deeds and parents, the man went on about how Wayne Sheffle had ripped him off. Finally they left, telling us we were cool to camp there another night, but if we saw Wayne again to let him know that their business wasn't done. We packed up and left at the first light of dawn, but Jimmy had unknowingly succeeded in his first challenge as a father: protecting me and our fertilized embryo from a couple of drunken rednecks.

My child's poem was intertwined with mine now. Someday the child might ask questions. "What did you love about Daddy?" "Why did you get married in Ohio?" Perhaps we would drive by this hotel ten years from now, pointing out this honeymoon spot on the way to drop our child off at summer camp. Perhaps we'd be divorced.

Be still, Christy, I told myself.

Twisting on the soft hotel mattress, I invoked the gods and tried not to worry too much as Jimmy moved on top of me. Careful not to crush my belly he kissed me, his mouth wet with my own salty taste, and entered me. Whatever the cards dealt us, it was a relief to acknowledge myself as simply a supporting player in a much longer, ever-expanding, rhyming verse. Rolling over, I sat on top of him. Jimmy was gorgeous. This whole marriage business was exhausting. If things went well, I realized, we would probably keep on at this pace for the rest of my life.

I woke up at five-thirty the next morning, got dressed, and ventured out while the entire metropolitan area was just beginning to go to sleep. The bellmen in the lobby were all dark black with strong sexy accents in over-the-top gold and red uniforms. They nodded and smiled silently, as if they were guiding me back into an earlier moment in the century. I was hungry and wanted some ice.

Enjoying the silence, I strolled through the wide empty hotel foyer and made my way downstairs and onto the street. The air outside wasn't hot yet, but you could tell it would be; it had been the hottest Mardi Gras in sixty-seven years, or that's what we heard the day before on the radio. Ice, I kept thinking. I need some ice.

Like the city, I smelled of sex. The main boulevard outside the Fairmont was lined on both sides with metal Louisiana State Police barricades, stretching side by side far into the horizon. At the moment, however, no floats were passing and no people were screaming or cheering; there was only masses and masses of garbage covering the ground: half-eaten sandwiches, bright red pizza boxes, thousands of beer cups, cigarette packages, and green Heineken bottles rolling back and forth in the gutters. Transparent plastic bags billowed and floated; newspapers lay abandoned over the asphalt along with the remains of crawfish and shrimp, crushed into the seams of the sidewalk. PAT O'BRIAN'S HURRICANE cups were stacked on top of each full garbage can on every corner. Broken under my feet were millions and millions of beads: yellow, red, green, purple, and orange string necklaces. They were in every crack and crevice; they hung from tree branches, street-lamps, and statues. The day before, when Jimmy and I had arrived, this entire boulevard had been a sea of human beings thousands deep. Children, adults, and elderly of every race were lined up, grabbing and begging for these little glass-bead necklaces being thrown from passing floats. Now there was almost no one around at all. A young black man in navy slacks and a white button-down shirt was standing outside a place called the Picadilly Lounge. He had two rugs laid out over parking meters and was beating them lethargically with a broom.

As I walked across the street and made my way toward the French Quarter, I stepped over the dried white skull of a ram with purple and yellow beads wrapped around its horns and hanging loosely out of its eye sockets. It was inexplicably lying in the gutter beside a crushed green sixteen-ounce plastic soda bottle and some red Styrofoam hamburger packaging.

Direct sunlight had yet to climb over the low buildings of the Quarter, but rays of bright warm orange light shot between the buildings, creating long thin shadows. A young woman appeared from around a corner dressed in a short black miniskirt and a loosely done lace-up top, her hair cockeyed and crazy and caught under the elastic of the cat mask she was still wearing. Her legs were bare and her stockings were in her hand. She passed me by without acknowledging me, floating like a ghost.

On my left and right in the closed-down shop windows were advertisements of sex shows: LUST IS LIFE: BOTTOMLESS MEN OR WOMEN. Pictures of naked girls were spread out in the glass, black squares covering their genitals. On the side of a brick building was a large decades-old faded green hand-painted advertisement for GINGER-MINT JULEP. I wanted some, with ice. A man was sleeping on a bench in a brand-new jeans jacket, with hundreds of different-colored bead necklaces around his neck. The section of sidewalk around him smelled pungent with vomit.

Making a left onto Dauphine, I passed two men dressed as the Tin Man and the Cowardly Lion from *The Wizard of Oz*. I wondered what had happened to Dorothy and the Scarecrow. Perhaps they were still passed out on a couch in a ballroom full of other sleeping fictional characters.

I was beginning to love being pregnant and was already experiencing a sweet nostalgia, aware that I would yearn to return here and that this morning in particular was a golden hour of my life. Waddling a little, I kept moving forward, noticing the beauty of the empty streets. I had been to New Orleans once before, as a child, although I didn't remember much, only the photos. Shortly after Christmas one year my father took me to a tree-burning ceremony somewhere in the center of the French Quarter. On a grassy island between two large boulevards, families piled their dead trees. Little kids stood around drinking hot chocolate in the balmy wet air as the trees went up fast, like books of matches. Tinsel was melting and lifting up into the sky. The scent of singeing pine tickled my nose as I watched silk-wrapped balls warp and melt. There was a picture of me on my father's shoulders from that night with a small white crown on my head and a fairy's magic wand dangling loosely from my hand. No tangible connection to that little girl existed in me. Someday soon, I thought, I will have no connection to the woman I am now. It's amazing how permanent I always feel each moment is, as if the person I am at any given instant is someone constant. When I was seven I vowed never to have sex, it sounded so revolting. At eleven it seemed unfathomable that I would ever be married or have a job. Now I cannot imagine death. I realize it will probably come just as effortlessly as sex, or present itself as unavoidable as adulthood, but I can never quite feel its reality. Walking down the morning streets of New Orleans, I felt closer to the afterlife than I'd ever been; the whole of the French Quarter smelled as if it had passed away forty years ago. Mortality was palpable here. I sensed that it too would be as passing and impermanent as being seven had been.

The sun crept over the buildings and daylight was complete. In an instant with this one hit of light the whole mood and composition of the city altered. About twenty yards away a young woman laughed boisterously as she rode the shoulders of her boyfriend, who was galloping like a pony toward Bourbon Street. They were oblivious. With this sunrise somehow I felt I was exactly where I was supposed to be: on this street, at this hour, with this child in my womb and my newlywed husband still asleep in our bedroom. I couldn't help but grin at the crystallizing realization that, no matter what happened, everything was just as it was supposed to be.

Have faith, the light seemed to announce.

What if always, every day, no matter what you did, you were in exactly the right place at exactly the right time?

As I reached the end of the French Quarter I could see that a fast food restaurant was open across one of the main drags. I walked in and bought a large orange juice with tons of small perfect cubes of ice.

I walked back toward the hotel down Rue Dauphine, the New Orleans sun climbing higher with every step I took. Already it was almost hot.

As I went up the steps of the Fairmont Hotel, pleasantly swishing shards of cool ice around my hot mouth, I felt a tickle of wetness in my underwear. In the privacy of the empty elevator I reached down under my dress and touched myself. Pulling up my hand I could see unmistakable dark red drops of blood.

FAT TUESDAY

"ALL RIGHT, listen to me very carefully. I don't want to alarm you, we need to do some more tests, but I am very concerned about your health. At this point I'm unable to find your child's heartbeat, which at or near twenty weeks should be quite clear."

Dr. McCarthy paused and looked up at Christy, over to me, and then back to Christy.

"You are bleeding," the doctor continued. "If the placenta is pulling off the wall of your womb, you could bleed very heavily. The more active you are, the more you'll bleed. We don't know for sure, but the baby may already be dead. We have to worry about you first. If you start to bleed a lot, we need to empty the uterus as quickly as possible and you may need a transfusion."

Christy and I were both motionless as we listened to this overweight alcoholic-looking doctor. He was a real southern gentleman, the kind who look slightly ill at ease without a martini. Christy was fully clothed now and seated in a red plastic chair. I was standing behind her with a magazine closed in my hands. The doctor spoke in a voice so gentle and quiet I felt I was reading his lips. His name, McCarthy, was printed in neat white letters on his ID badge. We were in a small not very impressive hospital about an hour north of New Orleans. Originally we'd gone to the inner-city ER, but the place was too over-run with stabbings, drug overdoses, and other incidents resulting from the chaos of the festival. This hospital was exactly the same, only less well equipped. We'd arrived here at 11:50 A.M. It was now almost 9:45 at night. In the seven hours we'd spent in the waiting area, I'd felt I was slowly observing the deterioration of mankind.

"I'm very worried about you, Christy," the man said, in a sincere daddy-will-take-care-of-everything voice.

"Why aren't you worried about the baby?" she asked quietly, her body in a controlled spasm of anger.

"Even if the baby is alive, it can't survive on its own for another six weeks. That's a long time from now." He paused, scribbling a few more notes on the paper in front of him. "We need to admit you formally." He looked up at her. "We won't be able to complete the tests until morning."

"Why not?" she asked.

"Unfortunately, we only have one ultrasound machine, and our radiologist was sent over to Andrew Jackson Memorial this afternoon. The festival has taxed the resources of the entire area."

"Well, then, I'm afraid we'll have to go somewhere else," she said, the muscles in her forearms flexed in a tight grip around the plastic arms of her chair. She turned to me. "I want to go home."

"I understand how scared you're feeling," the doctor droned, "and I understand your wanting to go somewhere more familiar, but I can't emphasize enough how much I believe that would threaten your situation."

"I've never seen that device before," Christy said, pointing over at the apparatus the doctor had pressed against her abdomen to listen to the baby. It was a bizarre tool that attached to the doctor's head.

"I've been using this fetoscope"—he held up the contraption—"for a long long time. It's very reliable."

"It's not what my doctor in Albany used to check the baby's heart-beat," Christy stated.

"No, they were probably using a Doppler device. That's a more sophisticated piece of equipment. We don't have one here."

"What, are we in Istanbul?" She was getting aggressive.

"There's no harm in resting until tomorrow." The doctor paused and shuffled through some more papers. "Let me ask you just a few more questions. Could you tell me a little bit about your diet?"

"What do you mean?" she asked, looking nervous and uncomfortable.

"How many meals a day have you been having? How much protein, how much iron? How much water have you been drinking? How much caffeine? Have you been paying attention to those things? They're not minor details."

Christy just glared. The guy was probably in his mid-sixties and smelled like bathroom disinfectant.

"I don't know," was all she could say.

"Have you been eating three meals a day?"

"No."

"Have you been taking prenatal vitamins?"

"No."

"Do you smoke?"

"I've had a few cigarettes." She looked over at me.

"Do you drink?" he asked.

"No." She paused. "I mean, I've had a couple glasses of wine."

"Have you been drinking coffee?"

"Yes."

He looked up at me in disbelief.

I don't exactly know why I did it, mostly because at the moment I was a basket case, but for some reason I laughed.

He didn't smile back.

This whole day was going unbelievably badly. I'd woken up that morning alone for the first time since our wedding, and neither the shower, the television, nor the radio could stop this one thought: *I don't want to be married. I want to be alone.* Believe me, I knew it was too late for this kind of thinking, but it just kept blitzing me from out of nowhere. Arriving in New Orleans, Christy and I'd passed by little taverns and sports bars, and I wanted so badly to be inside one with a shot of whiskey and a beer, talking about pro basketball, I would've chewed off my own leg to get there. There was this unmistakable clamoring inside me. I felt trapped. And the more I thought about it, the more I realized I didn't *feel* trapped, I *was* trapped.

"I want you to know that as a doctor and obstetrician I feel it is imperative that you spend the night here. Leaving is not an option. I need you to let me take the time to do the necessary tests. You might be at serious risk, Christy. I'm going to give you an intravenous feed, to bring up your blood sugar and make sure we have access, in case we need to give you fluid, blood, or medicine. You realize at this moment we are unable to ascertain the status of the fetus." He was trying to get to her by scaring her.

I couldn't process this information. Doctors shouldn't be as overweight as this guy. New Orleans, I'd read, has the highest rate of obesity in the United States, too many beignets and po-boys or something, but his weight didn't instill a great deal of confidence. The little room we were in smelled salty like saline solution. I don't like hospitals and I wasn't particularly enjoying my first few days of marriage. I felt like a Siamese twin. This room, the pompous doctor, and his horrid fuckin' news were all like icy fingers clamping down around my throat.

"And why is that?" Christy asked calmly, standing up and beginning to gather her purse.

"Why is what?" the doctor responded.

"Why are you *unable to ascertain the status* of my child?" Christy looked up at the doctor, speaking clearly and precisely, but her face was expressionless.

"I told you. Unfortunately our radiologist is assisting in New

Orleans tonight. With all the hysteria resulting from the festival, it's been difficult to make local care a priority."

Christy laughed incredulously.

"He'll be here first thing in the morning," the doctor continued. "But if the fetus has miscarried, you are in danger and should not be walking around."

"I think we should wait and do the tests, baby," I interjected. "I mean, it's still possible that the baby is all right? I mean, is that correct?" I turned to the doctor nervously, looking for a place to set down the magazine.

"Yes, there is a chance, but it is not a reason not to take the appropriate precautions."

"Well, I'm leaving," Christy said quietly, taking off and folding her tortoiseshell glasses and placing them inside her purse. Then in two quick steps she walked out the door.

I don't know why, but I seemed to have no reaction to anything going on around me. By the time I got my ass out into the hallway she was already halfway toward the elevator.

"Hey, come on! Hold on a second!" I shouted after her.

Catching up to her, I grabbed hold of her arm. She turned around and punched me awkwardly in the chest.

"Let go of me," she hissed, in a loud controlled whisper, and stormed down the sparkling-clean hallway.

"Christy!" I yelled, trailing right behind her.

"Take my side, you shit," she said, turning and slapping me in the chest again. "Why would you laugh about *that?*"

I grabbed hold of her and put my arms around her, but she yanked herself away. The doctor was approaching, his heavy old limbs jostling with each stride.

"I don't feel safe here. My baby is fine," she said, pulling away and leading me toward the elevators. She pressed the little circular button.

"Please, Mr."—Dr. McCarthy looked down at his form— "Heartsock. It is extremely foolish of you to leave. We should keep you here. Your wife is in serious danger."

The elevator door opened and Christy stepped in. For a second I delayed, knowing we should stay, but then I stepped in after her. The doctor and two nurses stood dumbly watching the door close after us.

Alone in the elevator, Christy slapped my face hard. The skin rippled with an electric ring of pain. I held my cheek, looking down and away from her. My whole body, every nerve, every cell, was vibrating with the desire not to leave this hospital.

"What the fuck are you doing?" I mumbled toward the elevator floor, still holding my cheek. I knew what Christy needed me to do; she needed me to keep her here. But then another part of me thought maybe I should just back her up, foolish or not. There was reasonable skepticism as to this doctor's grasp of the current standard of care. We stood in silence for a long minute as the elevator descended.

"How could you laugh when he talked about my diet?"

I looked up at her. "You're freakin' out, all right? You need to calm down right now!" I was trying to be firm.

"Don't speak to me like that," she spat.

The elevator door opened and Christy was off down the hallway, passing through long corridors, sets of swinging doors, people on crutches, soda machines, a black guy in a tuxedo, a woman holding her bandaged eye, a kid with a cut finger, all kinds of battered individuals waiting in a large square room staring at a fuzzy television. She passed underneath several clocks, with all their second hands ticking in unison. Speakers above trickled out a Top Forty radio station. She passed the registration desk and the gift shop and then blew out through the automatic glass doors. She stopped dead as she hit the silence of the parking lot and the sea of automobiles. I followed about ten paces behind her. The warm night air was stifling; the black asphalt of the hospital parking lot was slick with humidity. All colors of the rainbow were lit up and glowing off the hundreds of cars parked in the bright halogen light of the streetlamps. For a moment Christy paused, lost and confused. She struggled to orient herself, looking for the Nova, then charged off in the right direction. As soon as she found the car, she swung open the heavy silver door, slid inside, and shut herself in. I opened the driver's-side door, sat down, and reached for the keys although I had no intention of actually leaving. Surely, I thought, the doctor, nurses, a security guard—*somebody*—would follow us out here. The leather seats were still warm with heat from the day's sun and smelled stuffy in a way that I normally find comforting. Sliding the key into the ignition, I gave it two or three tries and it started up. I kept my eyes on the dash as I pretended to wait for the engine to warm up.

"You gotta calm down," I said. I knew I should not allow us to leave this damn hospital.

"You want an annulment or what?" she said.

"Give me a break," I said.

"The baby's dead, Jimmy. Are you awake?"

"The baby's not dead. The guy just wanted to do some tests. Everybody goes to the doctor and gets tests. You were bleeding; we should figure out why." I was trying to retain an air of coolness.

"Look, I'll get treated faster by driving to Houston than I will sitting around waiting for these idiots to get their act together." Christy bit her lip like she might chew it off.

In the silence I looked over and saw Christy close her eyes and slowly begin to breathe. After a moment her inhalations became more and more rapid until I was worried she was going to hyperventilate.

"Let's go, Jimmy, let's go." She opened her eyes and looked over at me. "What are you waiting for?"

I put the car in reverse and turned around to look where I was going. Fuck it, I'd take her to Texas, but I knew I was doing the wrong thing.

"Oh my God, oh my God, oh my God," she kept saying, breathing quickly in and out. Her eyes were closed and her arms wrapped tightly around herself as she rocked back and forth. The Nova rolled gently backward. I took the car out of gear, stepped on the brake, and reached over to touch her shoulder, but she flinched and I withdrew my hand. We sat there in silence with the car half in and half out of its spot.

One of the bright lights of the parking lot was hanging directly above us, lighting up Christy's face and her closed eyes. She tried to regain control of her breath by pressing hard on both temples.

"Let's go to the hotel, get the cat, pack our shit, and drive to Houston," she pleaded.

"You sure you don't just want to go back inside?" I took a deep breath myself. Then, speaking as if I were going formally on the record, I said, "That's what I think we should do."

Christy looked over at me. "Give me the keys. I'm not going back in there." The anger in her voice grew as she continued. "I want to go *home,* Jimmy. I've been trying to go home since I left Albany. I don't have confidence in those doctors or in the attention I was getting. I don't feel safe here. Please take me home."

I threw the car back into reverse and headed to the hotel.

It was the last night of Mardi Gras, Fat Tuesday, and driving silently through New Orleans I could feel the swell of excitement in the air as crowds massed together like flocks of birds. What seemed like two thousand Harley-Davidsons began passing us on both sides. All day I'd been struggling with the desire to drink. Watching drunk people stumbling in and out of restaurants, clubs, and bars wasn't helping.

I dropped Christy off in front of the hotel so she could start getting our gear ready while I went off and parked the car. Alone in the Nova, the engine kicking and vibrating uncomfortably as I idled through the Mardi Gras traffic, I felt as lost and disoriented as a child at a state fair whose parents have ditched him. The neon haze of the French Quarter painted the crowds with ghoulish red and green faces. All the festivities were culminating in a parade that would shut down abruptly at 12 A.M.

"Don't get caught on the street when the party stops," the clerk at the hotel had warned us. Apparently, at the stroke of midnight, with the onset of Ash Wednesday, Mardi Gras ends, and the New Orleans police force takes back the streets.

I parked the car illegally only three blocks from the hotel and found myself literally sprinting to get back to Christy. People were bumping and banging into me. With each minute that passed there seemed to be a thousand more bodies on the street. A young man in ripped blue jeans and a SAINTS T-shirt was thrust spread-eagled over the hood of his red Honda Civic while two uniformed policemen dragged another guy out the passenger-side door. For a moment in the swirling undertow of the crowd I felt I'd lost my way, but quickly scanning the sea of bobbing heads I saw the steps of the Fairmont Hotel. I fought back the fear that I knew would release absolute pandemonium inside my brain. The thought that Christy had miscarried jerked my stomach up into my trachea. Almost certainly we had done the wrong thing by leaving that doctor.

The door to our hotel room was open when I arrived. I stepped in and found Christy sitting fully dressed on the toilet with our packed bags at her feet and the cat in her carry case purring calmly on her lap. She turned, looked up at me, and spoke in her softest, clearest, most childlike voice.

"Why couldn't I have eaten right? Is that so hard? Do you think it was the smoking? What kind of neurotic person am I?" She paused and looked back down at her knees.

"You do the best you can. You can't do anything else," I said, slightly out of breath, standing impatiently by the bathroom doorjamb.

"It's too late," she said, as if she had already seen our future.

"It's not too late," I said quickly. "Walking up here I got this feeling, all right? A very clear feeling that everything is OK. If we just get you to a doctor, get you home like you want, everything will be fine." I hadn't had that feeling at all, in fact pretty much the opposite, but I was struggling to say something that might be helpful.

"What did the doctor tell us? I can't remember what he said," she whispered.

I didn't answer her. There was no way I was going to repeat any of the nasty shit he said.

"Let's go, baby, I want to get you taken care of."

She stood up slowly, holding the cat carrier with one hand and straightening out her dress with the other. For some reason, she'd taken time to apply makeup and was dressed in one of her most expensive outfits, a burgundy dress made of a thick cotton and embroidered with wildflower patterns that fell to her calves.

"There hasn't been any more bleeding. Don't you think that's a good sign?" she asked, tugging on her little opal stud earrings.

"It can't be bad," I said.

"Oh, boy." She sighed.

I thought about all the action of my life that has taken place in bathrooms.

"Nice honeymoon, huh?" she said, trying to smile.

"It's OK, baby, it's OK," I offered. "It's all gonna be fine. We just gotta put one foot in front of the other and play this thing out." I'm always placing everything in the context of sports metaphors. You'd think I'd grow out of it.

"I wanted it to be a great honeymoon."

"I know. I did too."

Taking one small step forward, she bent to pick up her bag, but I reached for it, hoisted it over my shoulder, and moved into the bedroom to pick up the others.

"Let me take some," she said politely.

"I'd prefer it if you didn't," I answered, hefting up the fourth and last bag.

We walked out of the hotel without saying another word. I was loaded down with luggage, and Chris was carrying the cat carrier.

Outside, the crowds were now so dense it was difficult even to step out of the hotel. The pulse of the city was being rhythmically beaten out by drums and brass horns. Every high school jazz band in the state of Louisiana was marching by, slapping their drums and belting out squealing attempts at "Dixieland" and "When the Saints Go Marching In." I tried to hold Christy's free hand and fight my way through the crowd, but it was awkward. One of the bags kept slipping from my shoulder and falling down to my elbow. I could see Christy say, "Let me help you," but I couldn't hear her voice at all. A forty-year-old guy directly to our left was holding a sign high above his head and shouting out its message, HUGE-ASS BEERS. People were swimming around us, struggling to get to him. After wriggling ourselves a few steps forward, new sounds took over. A man was preaching through a megaphone, his arms desperately extending out into the crowd. People covered their ears as they tried to get away from him.

"When God looks out to our world he weeps, he weeps because lust for power has corrupted human dignity!" the man screamed in a hoarse voice through the electronic amplifier. Three assistants in black suits stood by his side handing out pamphlets.

Still holding Christy's hand, I tried to make our way to the corner, only twenty paces away. Behind me Christy's eyes were watching the world around us with a resigned despair. Hundreds of shirtless fraternity brothers were in the balconies above us. To the left was another long terrace, this one elegant and beautifully crafted with sashaying men and women in tuxedos and ball gowns.

"One, two, three, show us your tits!" the fraternity brothers shouted in unison, exploding into heaving showers of laughter. Two girls in front of us lifted up their shirts and shook their breasts up toward the men. Their tits were painted like eyeballs, with nipples as pupils. Beads by the thousands came raining down on us. One of the necklaces hit Christy's upturned face and she stumbled forward, barely holding on to Grace and grabbing a swelling welt on her brow.

I met her eyes. Sometimes I'd catch it, an odd glance while we were in line at the movies, a dark empty stare while driving, some simple inadvertent expression of a blistering resentment. It was clear in these moments that she hated me. At certain other times—making love, obviously—Christy's affection for me was easy and effortless and I was aware of her sincere desire to hold and care for me, but with equal frequency it seemed that the affection was only a momentary confused compassion and in reality she felt me more as a cumbersome weight.

People don't want to hear what really being in love is like, 'cause it sucks. It's like a diamond; it looks pretty from the outside but inside it's hard, angular, and sharp. Truly loving somebody else should never be confused with a good time. Loving somebody is just as painful and disappointing as it is getting to know yourself. It's probably the only thing worth doing, but that doesn't mean it's gonna be a picnic.

"I shouldn't have left the hospital," Christy said behind me.

I could've punched her in the face. Every friggin' step I'd taken today had been wrong.

Grow up, I screamed at myself as we continued pushing our way forward through the crowd. Straps from the bags were digging into my shoulders. There are a lot of people in the world, and it seemed that most of them were shmooshed together in the French Quarter. When I was a teenager, my father told me the reason I was turning into such a prick was that I didn't really believe that everyone was equal, and that was going to be my major source of suffering. I looked around me in the chaos of lights and floats and wondered, Could we all really be equal? Don't I get any special help?

The whole time we had been in the hospital waiting area, the whole time the doctor was speaking to us, Christy had looked to me and seemed to ask, Do you offer any assistance? Her every glance implied that a real man would handle this better, would make things right. I provided nothing but my own insecurity. I should've made some calls to other OB–GYN clinics or something. There's got to be someplace closer than Houston. Christy's hand was limp and cold in mine.

In the maze of streets and people, I got turned around and couldn't remember whether the car was to the left or the right. My hands were shaking; I was totally powerless. In front of me was a young woman in a beautiful long black evening gown, her hips, her back, and her ass all curved like a panther. I couldn't see her face. "Everyone is an oracle of God." I remember my dad telling me that. What the fuck did that mean? The woman turned around, and she was older than I thought but still seductive as hell. She went left and, hoping it was the direction of our car, I swung after her.

"Hey, nice pussy, babe," I heard. I turned around and saw some preposterously skinny redneck laughing hard directly to Christy's left. The dude was shirtless with about fourteen tattoos spread across his arms and chest. Chris tried to jerk away. The guy was laughing his fool head off, as were two of his cronies.

"What did you say?" I said, turning around.

"I was just telling your lady what a beautiful pussy she's carrying." His friends were all losing their lunches with laughter. And I can't tell you why, it was the first time in several years I'd done it, but I dropped the luggage, hauled off, and nailed that guy three quick times in the face: *bam-bam-bam.* Blood from his nose splattered on my clothes, and I could feel two or three bones in my hand break. He dropped on one knee and I grabbed his long hair and hit him one more time hard across the temple. My whole arm from my wrist to my shoulder went absolutely numb. One of his friends hit me hard across the back of the head. A thrill of adrenaline shot through my veins and I felt ten fuckin' feet tall: my vision was keen, colors were bright, my reflexes sharp. Oxygen was flowing into my lungs like a drug. For the first time all day I was feelin' good. I went to hit his buddy before he thought about hitting me again, but somebody else clocked me from behind. I went blind but I didn't fall.

"Don't fuck with me!" I remember yelling, over and over. Then I tackled the motherfucker. People were tripping and falling and pushing and trying to separate us. Christy was shrieking in a voice several frequencies higher than all the other noise. I just kept throwing punches, not knowing anymore who I was hitting. Somehow a couple of older men came in between me and this redneck asshole. Everybody was yelling and cursing. Christy was standing in front of me, yelling, *"Stop it, stop it, stop it!"* like a screaming eagle.

Our bags were all spread out on the ground getting kicked around. But that stupid cat case was tucked under Christy's left arm like a football. My face, my arms, my knees: Everything was cut up. I must've looked terrifying. One of the guys came at me again, but as he got close

Christy got right up in his face and released some unintelligibly witch-like shriek that came up from her intestines and scared the piss out of anybody who heard it.

"Fuck off!" She grabbed one bag, I grabbed the others, and we split, leaving the assholes behind.

As we got away from the crowd, the realization of what an idiot I was started flooding in.

"Where's the car?" Christy kept asking me. I just pointed, hoping, still unsure of the direction. Christy led us forward while I stumbled behind, trying to hold on to our bags while keeping the other hand in a tight grip on my nose, where blood was flowing like from a faucet. We moved much more easily through the crowd now, my appearance frightening and scattering people in different directions.

"This way?" Christy asked.

I nodded. Through a break in the crowd I could see the Nova. Green, red, and purple lights were glittering in the chrome and reflecting off the windshield. The poor cat was terrified. Desperately the three of us made our way to the car. An explosive noise broke out from behind us. I turned around and could see a faint swirl of red and blue police lights accompanied by frantic shouting and running people. My first thought was that they were coming after me.

They weren't; it was only midnight.

Wild errant partyers were scampering around us with beaded necklaces and popcorn flying through the air. Cups of warm beer were being hurled at the cops. Eventually, through the crowds, sirens, and splashing water, I could hear the pleasant surreal clopping of a great many horses.

Blood was still dripping through my nose and over my hand, my head was as light as helium, and my vision completely blurred.

"Give me the keys," Christy said, reaching out to me.

"No, no, no," I said, my voice stuffed up and nasal. "I'll drive."

"Jimmy," she said, with her hand still extended, "don't be an asshole."

"Listen, I can drive!" I shouted out, as I dropped the bags on the sidewalk, fumbled with the keys, and pushed my way past Christy to the driver's-side door.

"You're gonna get us in a wreck. You don't know what you're doing."

There was no way I was gonna let her drive. For chrisssakes, the woman was experiencing pregnancy complications! I was driving; that was final. I sat down in the seat, dragging the bags in after me and hurling them into the backseat, just missing Christy and the cat. Christy settled in beside me. We both looked out as people moved by us, always in the opposite direction: some walking, some running, some dressed in outrageous costumes, others naked, everybody but us drunk, laughing, and playful.

I turned the key in the ignition. It always takes at least three tries. On the fourth I got nervous.

"Oh, Christ, Jimmy," Christy said under her breath.

On the fifth try I was miserable. I paused, giving the starter a chance to rest, and wondered if my nose was broken and how it would look.

On the sixth try the car started, and the muscles in my back relaxed into a more sustainable level of extreme high tension. The engine sputtered along for a few moments and then fell quietly into its normal gentle rhythm. We were now ready to roll and I threw the gearshift into first before I realized there was nowhere to go. About fifty yards ahead and coming straight toward us was the full procession of police. Bullhorns were calling out unintelligible announcements in a high electronic cadence. A light show of blue and red spinning sirens accompanied the mass of officers. Only now did I realize the full extent both of the police issuing forth to reclaim the streets and of the illegal nature of my parking spot.

Leading the armada of cops was a shoulder-to-shoulder row of foot police, each carrying a clear plastic shield covering his torso and face from the gallons of flying beer. Behind them was close to a full division of marching police officers, followed by another hundred or so cavalry officers on horseback. The horses, beautiful well-groomed animals, lifted their proud hooves high above the garbage and succeeded in being very intimidating. To the sides of the police force were scattershot religious groups using the situation as an opportunity to evangelize. Two large banners pronouncing GOD HATES SIN, PROVERBS 6:16 were being hoisted above the crowd by a local church group. One guy in his early twenties was moving with the flow of people carrying a fifteen-foot-high wooden cross belted and strapped to his chest. Sweat dripped from his pale face—it looked like any moment he would collapse and probably take a few people with him—but he continued stumbling forward, all the time balancing this giant mother-fuckin' crucifix.

There was no way I could move the car; people were flowing around us like a swarm of bees. I looked over at Christy. With her hands neatly folded in her lap, her hair barretted off her forehead, her skin shining with sweat, she looked like a little girl. How the hell did she get here with me? The cops marched steadily toward us. At odd times people would bang on the hood of our car or stand momentarily on the bumper to get a glimpse over the sea of heads. Christy finally looked over and made eye contact with me. The dress she was wearing was left open around the beautiful shape of her neck, exposing her elegant collarbone. She was twenty-six years old. It's amazing anybody lives to thirty.

"Move it along! Move it along!" the cops were shouting. They slapped the metal hood of the Nova as they passed. Where was I supposed to go? The horses clomping by the car were hypnotizing, the sounds of their hooves reminded me of being a kid: *clippity-clop, clippity-clop*. I reached over to take Christy's hand but she didn't even notice, she was so transfixed by the scene around us. About forty yards behind the horses came the fire department, idling their gargantuan red trucks forward. Men were walking alongside the fire engines, dousing the street with water and creating rivers of trash that coursed toward the gutters. Our windshield was splashed and sprayed by a fire hose that blurred our view as if we'd passed through a car wash. Still

the noises and shouts were coming from all directions around us. I withdrew my hand and set it in my lap. The inner channels of my sinuses were suffocating in blood; every breath I took was like a death rattle.

"Move it along! Move it along!" the fire guys shouted at us. I looked over and tried to offer Christy a consoling smile. She didn't smile back; she looked at me flatly without expression. I had no idea what she was thinking. After the fire department came another long entourage of marching policemen and a convoy of about a hundred squad cars, all of whom continued to remind us to *"Move it along!"* I would be happy to oblige, I thought, if there was anywhere to go. This whole procession had lasted almost half an hour. Then, as the last of the foot police passed, trailed by a few squad cars, the boulevard opened behind them, wide, empty, and sparkling clean.

I threw the car back into first, but I guess, because of my clobbered, swollen nose, I accidentally slipped into reverse and backed the car into the curb. Without saying a word or even looking over at Christy, I jammed the gearshift into first and we rattled off, leaving New Orleans behind us.

The clock in the stereo flashed 12:32 A.M. Ash Wednesday had arrived.

LOVE COOL LOVE

I LIKE IT WHEN THINGS BREAK DOWN. There's something about a flat tire, or a train getting stuck, or long weather delays at the airport—any time when the earth stops turning the way it's supposed to—that releases me. I am a child again, curious, confused, not knowing what will happen next. For a moment, a space, a breath, I'm not responsible. All I have to do is respond—until time catches up with itself, the tire is changed, the train starts rolling again, or the snow melts, and the weight of accountability is hoisted back up on my shoulders. Sometimes I wish for a tornado or a hurricane, even a war. Anything to stop the inertia for an instant. Being an adult, the awareness of opportunities that have been compromised, the stunted growth I feel in my bones, is simply exhausting. A disaster striking can be a relief—as long as it isn't your fault.

In this way there was something about the unyielding awfulness of this particular Wednesday that I liked: I didn't deserve this, it wasn't fair, and it wasn't my fault. From the back of the police sedan, all I could see was the flat landscape and billboards lined up like dominoes.

Advertisements from the Church of Christ were posted along the highway:

NEED A MARRIAGE COUNSELOR?

TRY ME,

GOD

I hated Texas.

The police officer was quiet. Through the chalky glass I could see the back of her neck. Little twists and curls of reddish hair were spilling down from underneath her hat. All around us I felt I could sense the molecules bristling, as if they too knew this was not where I was supposed to be. I could hear the temperature and feel the movement of light. I was aware of myself sitting numb in the center of a maze. There were many paths to take, but one was just like another and they all were part of the same larger pattern. The noises around me collected into a dull hum much like the static of a television with the antenna ripped out. Somehow I had failed our child. It's easy when sickness or weakness falls on you to feel that you are being punished. I looked out my window at the open morning sun. The sky was smiling in a mocking fashion. Only in Texas is it stark raving hot at 8:27 A.M.

I remember Jimmy ranting. "Listen to me. I don't care if this baby lives or dies, I love it—like I love you. Its dying doesn't change anything." I wasn't listening. I was petrified, watching the speedometer and holding on to the armrest as we shot in and out of our lane. Jimmy's silver Nova was flying like a comet.

"We can handle it. We're resilient motherfuckers, OK?" he was yelling over the rattling Chevy engine. "I gotta believe in this. You gotta believe in this," he continued.

"Watch where you're goin'," I said quietly. For about the last night-marish twenty-four hours I'd been resisting what I think might be described as a full-blown anxiety attack and I was exhausted.

"Who's driving, me or you?" he snapped.

"I didn't want us to get married, Jimmy, I never did." I wanted to hurt him like I hurt. He had tricked me into unbridled happiness. I had let my guard down, and punishment was the result. Jimmy's nose was crusted with blood. He still dressed like a teenager. Gray cords and a sheepskin-lined corduroy jacket was his everyday uniform. It was so terrifying to be alone with 100 percent of the responsibility.

"Why do you quit so easy, huh? What is your mental problem?" He was looking over at me, his brow creased and wrinkled with scorn, his expression unbalanced and deranged. The dawn light outside the car was just beginning to break across the horizon. He was so tired his eyes were frosted and glassy and his hands were trembling slightly with weakness. "You know what it is? You've got some major fuckin' self-worth issues, you know that? You are a goddamn *dynamo*! You are a goddess, a Thoroughbred! You are the Muhammad-fuckin'-Ali of chicks. But you don't know it. Inside your head you're like, *It's not gonna work out. Everything is shit.*" He mimicked me in a high whine. "That's why you don't eat right. That's why you smoke. You're proving to yourself how incapable you are. You're scared to say *Hey, everybody, I'm happy!*" He rolled down the window, wind rushing into his face as he screamed out toward the sky, "*My life is fuckin' awesome! I kick ass!* You think that'd be like tempting the gods with hubris or whatever, but that's bullshit. You are the most killer piece of ass I've ever seen. You're smart, you're wicked powerful, you scare the shit out of me. I gotta tell myself to buck up just to look you in the eyes."

"Would you please roll up your window?" I asked. The wind was spinning my hair in erratic circles and slapping me across the face.

"*I don't want any beliefs.*" He mimicked my voice. "I call bullshit on that." He struggled with one arm to crank up the window, still steering with the other as we barreled ahead at 80 miles an hour. "This baby dies and I still believe in love. I don't know why any of us are born. I don't know what the point of *me* living and dying is. But you gotta be accountable to something, and you are fuckin' accountable to me. We're pack animals. I need you and I love you!" He slammed his fist against the dashboard.

I flinched, turning my head away from him into the cool glass of the passenger-side window.

"Something has to mean something even if we have to make it up. Let's make it up: I love you; you love me. Let's stick with it. Let's take it across the goddamn goal line. OK?" Jimmy stared over at me, taking his eyes off the road for what seemed like a full minute. "Look at you, all arrogant and disapproving over there. You're disappointed in me, huh? You think *I'm* not disappointed? You think I like you all the time? I don't. *You* up there on your high wagon, focusing on all the shit I'm not. Well, guess what? *You're* not a lot of things either. And I think you don't respect me because I love you. 'Cause you think only a dimwit motherfucker like me would chase after you like a puppy dog." He started panting like a spaniel. "I'll tell you this right now: Sure as shit, I'm the best man you'll ever know. You want the dream, I'm your ticket. Pour water on me and I'll grow. Sit there and worry about yourself and keep a little tally about all the things that are wrong in your life, and you'll stay miserable."

"Please watch where you're going," I said, in as noncombative a tone as I could muster. He ignored me.

"Maybe this baby was conceived to bring us together and it doesn't need to do anything else. Bad shit is gonna happen. Listen to this: I'll say it. I'm gonna have affairs. I'll tell you that right now. As far as that goes, I got a cock and balls in my pocket, and baby they were meant to burn. We spend fifty years together and some shit's gonna go down. But you can't stop fighting. You can't let go. Take your shoes off. Stay awhile."

I couldn't even look at him. There was a raving maniac in the car.

He started imitating me again: *"Oh, he was some guy. Oh, my first husband. . . . Oh, my second husband, he was a* real *prick."* Right then if I had had a knife I would've stabbed him in the chest.

"One little trial; we can handle this. The world is mean," he went on. "I used to spend all this time walking around trying to convince everybody that I'm a good person, but I'm not good. I'm childish. I want everything my way. I want you to be the way I want you to be. Frankly, I want you to be exactly like me. I think the whole world should be exactly like me! I am manipulative as hell. I feel sorry for myself, I'm two-faced, I talk shit about people I actually like. I am not a good person and I don't want to be, screw that, but I'm not *bad* either." He was wagging his finger like a third-grade schoolmarm chastising a kid, and then he snapped his hand into a clasped fist. "I want to be a wolf and I want you to be in my pack and if this baby dies I'll nurse you back to health and if this baby is born I'll cut the friggin' cord and you're supposed to have my back. We're not alone. That's the idea; isn't it a relief?" He paused. "Would you *look* at me?" He banged repeatedly on the ceiling of the car.

"No, I don't want to," I said. I couldn't even listen to him. He was talking but I didn't know who he was talking to. "I want you to look where you're going."

"I know where I'm going. I'm going STRAIGHT AHEAD."

"Please just slow down."

He seemed to be only speeding up.

"Listen to me and the words I say to you now." He spoke deliberately. "You get what you give in this world. I know you think I'm a walking bag of clichés, but the reason clichés are true is that none of us is unique, all right? Our experiences are not in the least bit fuckin' exclusive." We whipped past a sign marking the city limits of Houston. "There are like eighty thousand women right now, worried that they're losing their babies. And you know what? Some of them will and some of them won't, and one of the lucky babies that does get born will be an ax murderer. A couple of months ago you weren't even sure you wanted this baby; now it's gonna ruin your life if you lose it. *Bullshit.*"

It was then that the police car appeared behind us.

"Oh, my God" was all I could say, staring at the spinning lights in the passenger-side mirror.

"Fuck me, fuck me, fuck me," Jimmy went on. We pulled over and sat in silence as the Nova cooled and rattled.

"I hated our wedding," I said out loud. I hadn't ever thought that before, but at that moment I felt somehow that marriage was responsible for all this misery.

"Shut up about the wedding," Jimmy said, not looking at me. "The wedding was tits, OK? It was the best time you ever had in your life."

The officers seemed to be taking an hour, most likely running our license plate through a computer. Every thirty seconds or so another car would rush by us on the highway, sending a shiver through our seats and my nerves.

"Has this thing been inspected?" I asked, referring to the Nova.

There was a long silence. I tried to see the cops' movements through my side-view mirror.

"What do you mean you hated our wedding?" he finally asked.

"It was lousy," I said, drained of emotion. "I wanted a big wedding outdoors with a band. I wanted to look pretty and not be pregnant."

"You looked pretty."

"I didn't want it to be in a church. I don't even believe in God."

"Yes, you do. Don't say that, it pisses me off."

"OK," I said to myself. I turned and looked outside at the dry plains. Little bits of garbage and high mangy-looking grass surrounded us. Houston loomed large in the distance.

Without warning, Jimmy launched into another tirade, mimicking me in a mock-serious childish whiny tone. " *'I don't believe in God. There's no reason for anything. It's all just stinky. I don't care if there's mountains or deserts or rain or snow—there's no point to it. There just happens to be oxygen for me to breathe, that just happens to be created by the sun hitting the trees, which just happen to be made from the minerals in the earth that just happen to be made by my decomposing ancestors. But there's no reason. Oh, sure, there's a moon that comes out to light the sky after the sun sets, but who cares? There's no purpose, there's just me and my pooh-pooh unhappiness. Oh, boo-hoo, there's no reason for seals and sharks and eagles and cows, it's just all a big coinky-dinky. Just me and my black hole.' "*

"You are such an asshole," I said. I was furious. "You punched a guy. We're on our way to the hospital and you punched a guy. What are you, ten? I have to take care of everything. We're trying to get to a decent physician and you're going two hundred miles an hour in a car that isn't safe at thirty-five. No, I don't believe in anything, least of all you."

We looked at each other across the seats of the Nova, and at that instant there might as well have been an ocean and ten thousand years between us. I hadn't imagined I could ever feel so distant from him. I didn't even recognize his face.

"Look at you: You're completely irresponsible. You know that?" I continued. The police were still sitting in their car behind us with their lights spinning. "Who's gonna take care of me? I'm *pregnant*, Jimmy." I was not so much angry anymore as I was just thinking out loud.

Jimmy shook his head. "I'll take care of you. You make it sound like I'm not trying."

"I'm always sitting in urine, Jimmy, do you know that? I'm pregnant, and I wake up in the morning—not that I ever sleep—and I go to the bathroom, which I do ten hundred times a day, and every time I sit in a puddle of your urine."

"Listen, I will never do that again, OK? I promise." He cut his hand through the air, making a giant dramatic gesture. "I swear to God I will never pee on the seat again. Is that cool? Can we stop talking about that?" Then, more quietly, as an aside to himself he added, "I gotta get you to a doctor." He turned impatiently around to get a better view of the cops.

"Well, you're doing a great job." It was like I was somebody else and I just said everything I thought. "You know, we just stopped for gas and you didn't even ask me if I wanted anything to drink. Some orange juice, some water, anything. It didn't occur to you to think, Hey, maybe she's thirsty?"

"I got a shitload of Gatorade in the backseat. You want some? Would you care for a glass, your highness?"

"It's warm, and I DON'T LIKE GATORADE," I said, and started crying. Hot salty tears were streaming down my face. "I want to call my father," I said out loud. I thought I would like my father to beat Jimmy up.

"You gotta tell me," Jimmy said, putting on this overly sincere, sensitive voice. "You gotta ask. You gotta say, 'Hey, I want some water,' and I'll get it, but I can't read your mind."

"I have to tell you everything: to shave, to brush your teeth, to take a bath, to wash your hair. How do you think you'll be able to take care of a baby? You don't take care of anything." I said this through streams of tears.

"Oh, for crying out loud. I gotta get you to a doctor." Jimmy scowled.

Just then a female cop with short curly reddish-brown hair appeared at the driver's-side window, with another cop, a tall skinny male, lingering behind the taillights. Jimmy rolled down his window.

"License and registration," she said, her hands placed confidently on her hips.

"Listen, my wife here is pregnant and we're experiencing some complications and we're a little desperate to get to the hospital in Houston."

"Why Houston?"

The question seemed to baffle Jimmy. "I don't know, that's just where we're going. We were at another hospital, but we figured Houston would have the best one. Christy's family lives in Houston." He gestured lamely toward my section of the car. The busted nose in the center of his face wasn't helping our cause.

"First give me your license and registration," she said, with no discernible level of empathy.

"Yeah, right. Hold on." Jimmy dug into his wallet, lifting up his butt awkwardly and reaching behind him. Then he leaned over and dug into the glove box. As he opened it I was the first one to see the small pistol Jimmy keeps there. Still wrapped in a brown leather holster, it plopped dumbly onto my lap.

Both officers started shouting *"Gun, gun, gun! "* as they pulled out their firearms and pointed one at each of us. Jimmy raised his hands in surrender but I just sat still, dumb to the world. I couldn't even move my arms. I hated Jimmy. I had no idea when I married him how painful it would be to be defined by someone else.

"That's a registered firearm," Jimmy said quietly, in a peaceful passive tone. "I have a carry permit. I am Staff Sergeant James S. Heartsock of the U.S. Army. There is no need to be alarmed. We will comply with full efficiency."

"Oh, God." Listening to Jimmy talk like an army goomba made me want to puke. I have nothing to do with this person, I wanted to say to the officers, but my mouth was dry.

"Step out of the car," the female said, while her partner reached inside the Nova, opening the door and seizing the pistol from my lap. Eventually we both stepped out. I don't know how I did it, I wasn't aware of controlling my limbs at all. We looked like a couple of delinquent deadbeat kids, Jim with his broken nose and wild manic eyes and me with my pregnant round face, worn and stained from crying.

"I know who you are, Staff Sergeant James Heartsock. I also know from my computer that there is a warrant out for your arrest back in the state of New York. Do you know anything about that? You are listed as AWOL, sir." Obviously they'd run our plates. That must have been what had taken them so long.

Jimmy paused momentarily as he registered this information. "My lieutenant is the biggest fuckin' asshole, ma'am. He knows I just got married, and he knows we're expecting a baby. I'm on leave. I've got a letter to the colonel."

"I don't like it when people curse at me, sir. I would appreciate it if you would refrain." She spoke in a cool detached voice.

If I hadn't lost the baby yet, the pounding fear in my gut was sure to kill it. I looked across the top of the Nova at Jimmy. I hadn't slept in a long time, and I've never been so terrified in all my life.

Jimmy and I were placed in the back of the squad car with Grace the cat mewing like she was in heat from inside her gray plastic carrying case. He did have a permit for the gun, in the state of New York. Eventually we were driven away, leaving the Nova alone on the side of I-10. Watching the car grow smaller against the flat barren Texas landscape, I hoped I would never lay eyes on that vehicle again. Jimmy had voiced more concern to the police as to the status and future of that vehicle than he ever had for my pregnancy. They told us they'd drop Jimmy off at the station and take me on to the hospital, while a tow truck driver would impound the car until his release.

"I'm really sorry," Jimmy whispered to me in the back of the squad car, his face swollen and blotchy red from holding in tears. "I'm really sorry." I sat there frozen. After a brief silence, in a voice barely audible to myself, I started speaking.

"Listen to what the lady said: You are AWOL. You don't know what you're doing. I hear the things you say to me when you adopt this Boy Scout I-believe-in-love-let's-stick-it-out attitude, but I don't believe you. They're words you learned, it's an attitude you've copped, but it's not true, it's not in your heart. You say the right things because you want to be on the right side, but you don't back it up with your actions. You're not ready for this responsibility. Either you don't want anyone to be angry with you, or you don't want to be the one to blame. I see it in your eyes all the time, your anger, your doubts about me. You give me these pep talks like a high school football coach, but you're only trying to convince yourself. You never wanted to have this baby. This wasn't your choice. You should go home, clear your head, sort your mind out. This trip, our marriage—it's been too fast. I'll have the baby or I won't, we'll take it one step at a time. I'll call you when things get settled down, after I talk to the doctors, but you should go home and sort things out."

"You don't know me at all," he whispered back to me. The police car was moving steadily ahead without the lights, no siren, just carrying us forward. "You think I'd go home? You think I'd leave you now?"

"I want you to. You're AWOL, Jimmy. I feel it in the way you touch me. Since the day after we got married you're like half a person with all that doubt you're carrying around." This was true. He'd rarely seemed present since the wedding. I'd catch him looking over at me as if I were a foreign object; then, as quickly as I'd met his eyes, his face would snap back into a smile. "The way you laughed at me in that hospital, like this was my fault, like it had nothing to do with you."

"Just 'cause I act like an asshole sometimes doesn't mean I don't love you."

"You act like love is a decision you made and then it's over."

"It *is* a decision," he said, in a volume just above a breath. The police in front of us appeared oblivious to our conversation. "You split up with me and a few years from now you'll meet somebody else and fall in love. The exact same thing that happened with us will happen again. You guys'll be all over each other for about a year, give or take six months, and you'll start to see he's got problems just like me, only, you know, a slightly altered variety, and you'll start to think just like you are right now about how disappointing this poor sap is, only you'll be older and most likely you'll be a touch more accepting and forgiving and you'll think, *God, why didn't I just stick it out with Jimmy? If I had I'd be somewhere new instead of the exact same spot.*"

"Where does this sunny mister self-help boy come from, huh? *Keep a positive attitude.*" I had raised my voice by accident but immediately brought the volume back down. "You can't just make up an attitude, it has to be true."

"Yeah, you can. I'm happy. It's a decision." Jimmy was starting to speak in a normal tone, not caring whether the cops overheard us or not.

"You don't seem happy."

"I'm not happy right now."

"Well, why don't you decide to be?"

"Fuck you, OK?"

"Watch your language back there," the female cop said into her rearview mirror. Again we were silent.

"Go home, Jimmy, I give you permission. It's my fault. Everything is my fault. Get your life in order and I'll get mine in order, and then we'll figure out what to do."

My body, my voice, my eyes—none of them were doing what I wanted. Couldn't he see my hands were shaking? Couldn't he see the muscles along my spine tighten and compress into steel cables? One part of me wanted him just to disappear; I couldn't be responsible for him. Then there was another part of me outside myself observing him and able to see and feel how hard he was trying. The cat continued to mew. My head splintered with grief. People can mean so well and want the same end results and still miss each other by such a cavernous margin. When we fell in love it was like I could only see the gorgeous top part of Jim, but now with the introduction of adversity I could only see his ugly pulsing sinewy underside. I knew they were both true, but I could never see them both at the same time.

I wanted to be able to give more than I take, to carry more than I'm held. But I felt so weak. I could have wept with disgust at my own ineptitude. We paused in front of the police station for maybe ten minutes before the male officer led Jimmy in. We didn't even say good-bye to each other. It was only just before the car door slammed shut behind him that I heard Jimmy say, "I'm gonna come after you. You know I will. The question is, Would you come after me? That's what you gotta figure out. 'Cause one day I'll stop chasing." The door closed and I was alone.

The policewoman behind the wheel announced that she personally would be taking me to Sam Houston Memorial Hospital. We drove
on, passing roads I had driven often as a child. I was sixteen the last
time I was in Houston. Summers when I was a kid, on our way to
Grandmother's, Daddy and I would pull over at a watermelon stand,
sometimes twice if it was ridiculously hot. In the winter we would
stop for coffee and orange juice at the White Elephant café. From
Grandmother's bedroom you could hear freight trains rumble through
late at night if you were still awake. Texas is a true-blue mythological
place, at least it is for me. Maybe I left too young. It was strange watching the familiar landscapes pass by with no remnants of me as a child
to be found anywhere. We passed the Doll's House, a large building
designed like a fairy-tale home of Hansel and Gretel. When I was little
I thought that was where I wanted to work, until I turned about twelve
and realized it was a strip club. Now I kept expecting to see myself
come strolling around a building carrying a frosted angel-food cake
from the Snow White bakery, but all I saw were more parking lots and
modern glass and metal architecture.

Sam Houston Memorial Hospital was where I had been born
twenty-six years earlier, January fifteenth at exactly three minutes after
midnight. I would call my father as soon as this policewoman dropped
me off, I decided. Somebody would need to be there with me if things
turned out as badly as I was anticipating. Ever since I'd seen my dad
at my wedding I'd been missing him tremendously, which is funny
because I don't remember ever missing him in Albany. A wash of forgiveness and love for him had arrived out of the unknown. For so long
I'd been angry with him, telling every new friend I made what a selfish
prick he was. Now—maybe from working at the hospital and seeing so
much real abuse, or maybe it was the baby, or maybe it had to do with
time—I was realizing how much I had to be grateful for. Recently I'd
even begun admiring him. His life had been so focused. A life seems to
hold much more substance when it's been deliberate and purposeful
than when it's been scattered. I wish I had found something to do

much earlier in life and stuck with it. I've bounced around like one of those off-center balls that dogs love to play with because you can't predict where it'll go next.

I poked my finger inside Grace's little case and let her rub her wet nose against my fingernail. I'd never told Jimmy the reason I left this animal back in Albany was that cats are notoriously bad for pregnant women. They can carry some peculiar germ in their claws. At least that's what I'd heard.

It's funny. I had had this notion that when you were married you could put to rest all the insecurities and musings about whether you should really be together, but it didn't work that way. Marriage just seemed to have loaded the relationship with responsibility and fear of failure. I knew I had to stop caring whether it was a *good* marriage or a *bad* marriage, the *right* decision or the *wrong* one, and realize that it was gonna be all those things. It almost made me angry, the effort and courage it takes to keep slogging through. There's something familiar about despair; it's like a soft old blanket. I know depression; I feel welcome there. To believe that my life may be full of joy, laughter, and understanding fills me with so much fear of disappointment that I would prefer to smoke a cigarette and not believe at all. I either want everything to be magic and mythic or I want it to be dead. But I can't take the everyday living with small disappointments and fragile victories, the grayness of maybe-it'll-work-out and maybe-it-won't. I always feel the end is right around the corner, so why even try? I can't look at a calendar without wondering if I am looking at the date of my death. But then I will arrive at a perceived end, only to find it was a turn and the road goes on.

At that moment, just minutes before I arrived at the hospital, I felt my baby move. As if I'd been given a shot of adrenaline to the heart, I awoke. That baby moved, and the heated glass walls of depression around me were once again splashed with hope.

The simple action of that child moving let me know that I was gonna have to keep plodding forward, trying to do the right thing, trying to understand, trying to be understood, trying to pretend to be mature, trying to learn, trying to fake being strong. I could've laughed. You think something's over but it's not. You gotta exhale to inhale. I clearly, distinctly, felt my baby spin on some internal axis of my belly— and more than anything else, I instantaneously longed for Jimmy. He was the only one in the world I wanted to tell.

THE MIDDLE WAY

"LISTEN TO ME: *no, no, no!*" I was shouting into the sheriff's department pay phone. "For two seconds, all right? Just listen to me." Like I've said before, my lieutenant was a fuckin' prick and he'd been talking to me like I was his twelve-year-old son. "If marrying my pregnant girlfriend and taking her home is suddenly *dishonorable,* then go right ahead. If that's the truth, that's what I want."

Dishonorable discharge. It had a terrible ring to it. I definitely wanted out of the military, but not this way. I wasn't sure what kind of long-term ramifications this would have on the rest of my life—I couldn't imagine much—but I hated the sound. "I am a *terrible* soldier," I said. "I would never deny that. But I am not *dishonorable.*" I glanced over at the two police officers working the phones at the desks behind me while my lieutenant lectured me further. Being patronized by someone with an extraordinarily low level of intelligence is an indescribable humiliation.

"Maybe you're right," I answered him, "and I haven't been thinking too clearly." I wasn't sincerely doubting myself; even as I spoke I knew leaving the military was one of the most clearheaded decisions I'd ever made. "There's no war going on. I didn't let anybody down. The only people I could've let down were me, my wife, and my child, OK? They were the only people I might've failed in this situation. I saw the priority and acted accordingly, all right? Give yourself a little credit, buddy, you taught me that."

I shouldn't've said that; it pissed him off.

"Relax," I said. That was another bad move. Never tell anyone to relax; it doesn't help. "Listen, you taught me a lot. Mainly that I was never meant to be in the military." My situation was deteriorating with each sentence. "So please release me, OK? I don't mind, discharge me if you want, and you will never have to have another conversation with me again. But in one regard be generous, all right? Don't fuck up the rest of my life with a *dishonorable,* OK? Nothing bad happened; nobody got hurt; I didn't leave anyone in the lurch."

That was when he brought up Kevin Anderson and his mother and the assignment I completely botched.

"That was *your* job!" I screamed into the pay phone. Everyone around me was now openly staring. "Kevin Anderson was your job, you know that." Apparently, Mrs. Anderson had filed a complaint. Of course she complained; she should complain. Despite the anger I felt toward my lieutenant, there was a swell of shame inside my chest. For that action alone I probably did deserve all this shit. Actions have reactions; that's what Christy would say.

"Is there anything I can say so you won't do that?" I asked, following one of my lieutenant's longer monologues about my inadequacies and further threats of a dishonorable discharge. "You know what?" I asked. "I take that back. I deserve it and I'll take it. Do whatever you want. God bless you." And I hung up the phone. I couldn't fight any longer.

On the pay phone was a sticker with the familiar image of the

Christian fish. It was an advertisement for the United Protestant Foundation of Texas, accompanied by a phone number. My dad hated Protestants. Jews, Buddhists, even Muslims, were more popular with him than Protestants. "They're weak-minded and uncommitted!" he would say.

I need a new mentor, I thought, as I stared at the police desks.

Seven months after my father died, I'd joined the army. Searching for some kind of order in my life, I was attracted to the regimen of the military. I wanted someplace I had to be. The chaos and freedom of adult life were overwhelming. Also, I could see now, I had been pursuing some kind of definition of *manhood*. It sounds drippy if you talk about it, but it was something I needed. Nobody was going to prop me up, I knew that, and I needed something to orient myself around. Six weeks in, it was clear I'd made a mistake. I stuck with it, though, hoping against reason that if I put in the effort the situation might right itself and I wouldn't have to face my idiocy; but now that was all over. For a short period of time you can pretend you don't know the truth. It's like holding your breath. Eventually you have to come up for air. The deeper you bury a lie, the greater the pressure when it explodes.

Officer Parks looked at me; he was a pleasant enough guy. We'd gone through the process together of fingerprinting, picture-taking, the whole nine yards, and he'd made it as undegrading as possible— which was still pretty degrading. I was so tired I could barely walk as he escorted me back to my holding cell. It doesn't get much worse than this, I thought, as he locked the door behind me.

For some reason I thought of July 4, 1976. Lying on a Navajo blanket in the open trunk of my father's old yellow Plymouth, the sky exploded with fireworks around me. I was in the bull's-eye of the universe. My father and I both wore Cincinnati Reds baseball caps and whooped and hollered and tossed them around as blue and white explosions rat-a-tat-tatted over the Ohio River. We were hiding in the woods by the river where you didn't have to pay. The dull hiss of the flaming embers sifting into the water was like the sound of applause. This was my cleanest moment. This was pure grace. I was five years old and my dad's best friend. My childhood seemed light-years away as I walked back into the holding cell.

The cell was larger than I would've imagined, a rectangle with bars on one wall and benches on the other three. Two other guys were in there with me, one of whom was pretty much of a lunatic. He was scroungy and bearded, about sixty years old, sitting completely at ease in the far corner of the cell. The old torn tweed suit he was wearing was so large it hung on him more like a robe. Officer Parks had explained that every year the old guy tries to spend all of Lent in prison emulating Christ. Ash Wednesday, apparently, was the day Jesus himself was put in jail. Some people like to give up chocolate or maybe quit drinking, but this guy vandalizes property till he gets arrested and then stays in jail, refusing to pay the fine. He didn't want to have to do any more property damage and pleaded with the officers just to leave him there in prison till the day of resurrection. He smelled like a homeless person. The cops were gentle with him. It was his third year in a row of pulling this stunt. They kept trying to explain to him that the taxpayers didn't want to subsidize his peculiar faith habits.

The other guy in the holding cell was a chatterbox named Steve McNally. About forty-five and a redhead, he was super nervous, pacing around the cell talking pretty much nonstop. He had been arrested for driving through a toll booth without paying, and he was complaining bitterly about being arrested for such a trivial crime. He had already come up with the fine and was anxious as hell to get released.

"McNally," a heavyset police officer called from his computer.

Steve quickly snapped up his head. "Yeah, man, what's the status?"

"You checked out, you're cleared, you'll be outa here in a minute."

"All right, all right, all-right-a-rooney!" Steve shouted. "Open these doors, Long Arm, this bird's gotta fly."

"Relax. I have to finish up the paperwork; it'll still be a minute," said the officer.

"I told you, Long Arm, you can't hold me—check all you want—my record is squeaky clean." He turned around to us, singing Lynyrd Skynyrd's "Free Bird." Then he looked at my ring. "How long you been married?"

"Three days," I said, my nose still killing me. I sat on the aluminum bench just holding my face.

"Good start." He laughed. "Rock on, cowboy, you're doing great!" He kept pacing back and forth, dragging his fingers along the bars. "Don't be fooled, Tex, that ring around your finger is a tracking device; it's a matriarchal society out there." As he spoke, he was stealing glances over at his arresting officer, trying to see what was taking so long. "You're gonna be in trouble!" he sang. "Women run everything, and they're so goddamn good at it they've even snowed people into believing they're the victims."

"Oh, yeah, but it's really you, huh? You're the victim?" I mumbled, not wanting to talk to anyone. There was a kind of magnetic rattle in my balls telling me I had to get out of this place and back with Christy.

"No, man, I'm nobody's victim. I'm just saying, don't you go thinkin' it's a fair ball game out there in the world. Chicks make all the rules. One day you're hanging out drinking, carousing, havin' a good time in the local bar, right? Ladies think you're sexy, you've got a good sense of humor. You're a good guy, not doin' anybody any harm, just enjoying life, takin' it as it comes. Then you knock up one of them gals and you try to go back out to the bar—to laugh, to get a little play, throw some quarters in a jukebox—same old you, only now you're a fuckin' asshole." He pointed his finger in my face. I really had no energy at all and just sat and listened. " 'Cause you should be at home. You should be taking care of the baby. You should be gainfully employed. Grow up, all the women will tell you—but they want you to grow up on their terms. They want you to turn into the person they want you to be, and if you don't, *shame on you!*" He brushed one index finger against the other, taunting me like we were in a schoolyard.

"Don't listen to him," the homeless guy in the corner interjected, scratching his cheeks through his thick beard with both hands. "As long as we secretly adore ourselves, our own deficiencies will remain to torture us," he added, as if he were quoting from scripture.

"Shut up, you're a crazy person." Steve waved his hand at the man as if brushing away a horsefly. "You think you're Jesus, right? I mean, you lose all credibility right there." He cupped his hands, imitating a loudspeaker, and continued, *"You are totally out to lunch!"*

"I am Jesus," the man said, still scratching his face as if he had fleas.

"Well, if you're Jesus what's that make us, the two thieves?" Steve laughed, amused with himself.

"We are all Christ in our own story. Both of you are Christ as well."

"Oh, brother." Steve sighed and turned back toward the police desks. "Hey, Long Arm, get this guy a straitjacket, OK?" he shouted. "He doesn't belong here with the healthy criminals of the world."

I rubbed my eyes with my wrist, trying to avoid contact with the pain in my nose and in my hand.

When Christy and I were first going out and my father had only been dead a little while, I had a dream where he appeared to me with a blank look in his eyes and asked me if I had found Jesus Christ. That night in Christy's bedroom, I wept my living guts out, like blood would come from my eyes. Christy held me but I couldn't stop crying. "I won't let go," she'd said, and I just howled.

Steve took another quick peek at the cop and then turned back to me, speaking more quietly. "I like young girls, right? I'm comfortable saying that. But I don't like young girls for the reason my wife thinks I like 'em, not 'cause their tits are perky, not 'cause their pussies smell fresh like a spring day, because—I'll be candid with you, and I'd be willing to bet you already know this—young chicks can smell just as bad or as good as their moms, and there are plenty of twenty-year-old girls out there with saggy tits. Are you following me?"

I remained expressionless, wondering how Christy was and what was going to happen to us tomorrow.

"I don't like young girls because they're cute, and I don't like them because I *secretly* still want to be eighteen myself; I'm comfortable getting old. I'm happier now than I've ever been. I like young girls because they laugh." He paused for effect. "When women get older, they forget how to belly-laugh. It's like responsibility is their one fuckin' line, their be-all and end-all."

Christy had a wonderful laugh.

Steve sat down next to me. "Responsibility," he hissed. "Screw a woman over thirty-five and she'll give you the ride of your life—makes an eighteen-year-old look like a blow-up doll. I'm not talking about sex, I'm talking about a sense of play. My wife, man, she doesn't understand that. She's forgotten how to laugh."

"Maybe you never say anything funny," the bearded man blurted out from his corner.

"Oh, I'm funny, don't you worry about that."

"Funny to an eighteen-year-old maybe?" the old guy suggested.

"No. Funny, *period*," said Steve.

I've heard guys talk like this my whole life. I didn't want a young girl, I wanted my wife. I wanted to be in her arms and cry my fuckin' guts out.

"I don't know, man," I said, and then out of exhaustion I added, "Listening to you and the bullshit coming out of your mouth has fucked me up my entire life, and I don't want to hear any more."

"Bravo," the old guy said, finally giving his beard a rest and clapping his hands. Having this character as an ally didn't make me feel any better.

I remembered being fourteen years old and my father driving me back to my mom's house—the same house that used to be theirs together. We had just spent the weekend goofing around and were both sitting inside that same yellow Plymouth Duster. He took the opportunity to inform me that the reason my mother and he had split up was that she'd begun sleeping with his best friend shortly after I was born. "I know it's been hard for you," he said, sitting there jiggling with the radio, "and I probably shouldn't be unloading this crap on you, but your mom—man!" He shook his head, exasperated. "She's what some men would call a project." He looked up at me intensely and thumped me hard on the chest with his forefinger. "Watch your ass! Women, they don't want to love you, they want to make you very small so they can fit you in their pocket."

"No, no, no, you're misunderstanding me," Steve said, sitting down next to me. "I'm not selling you any bullshit. My wife, man"—just mentioning her was stirring him up—"she's a top-notch ball-buster. I should've never married her." He reached into his back pocket and pulled out his wallet. "But she gave me these three little guys, so I guess she's not all bad." Inside his billfold he had a picture of three small boys. "These guys are great, but their mom—that's another story."

"Why'd you marry her?" I asked, holding the picture of his kids. They were handsome blond boys, about two, five, and seven.

"Can I see the picture?" the old guy asked from the corner.

"No, don't give him the photo," Steve told me. "He'll get his crabs and scabies all over it."

"Come on, let me see it," the old guy said again, and I handed it to him. "Thank you," he said, taking the photo.

"All right, take a look," Steve relented, "but wipe your hands first."

Next Steve took out a picture of his wife and stared at it. The picture was at least ten years old, but she was clearly an attractive woman.

"I married her 'cause she'd scratch my head to help me fall asleep. I get headaches, you know? Real bad ones. And she started making these long faces every time one of her friends got an engagement ring . . . so you know? *Whammo!*" He slammed his fist into the hand with the photo.

"How you doin' over there, Long Arm?" he said, placing his face between the bars.

"Relax," the cop said, not looking up from the computer.

"There's a little tiny window in a man's life," Steve continued, turning back around to me, "when you're actually a man and can do as you please, but the rest of the time you're working for Mommy. Either yours or your kids'." He paused.

Sitting there, I vowed that if I got Christy back I would never allow her to become my mother. That was my job. Treat her like a woman and she would treat me like a man.

"We're men, we have peckers, we want adventure, to get drunk, fight, go to whorehouses—and there's nothing wrong with that. It's livin'; you gotta feel the blood move in your veins. My wife she holds her nose in the air like I'm a boy. But I'm not a boy."

"The lady doth protest too much," the old guy quoted again from the corner.

"Shut up, asshole," Steve snapped. "Women are the protectors; we just protect the protector. We operate outside the family circle, like lions. We're warriors, man, hunters and outlaws, and if you deny that inside yourself you're livin' half a life."

"Now you really sound like a boy." The old man was scratching his beard again. The action seemed to give him an inordinate amount of pleasure. "We're not warriors, we're men of God, children of God, and if you can't pursue a more noble action than fighting and fucking, you're just gonna cause misery to yourself and everybody around you. Humility is the only thing worth learning. Shatter the ego. Dance in the perfect contradiction of life and death."

I noticed the old guy's ankles, how swollen and disfigured they were. He wasn't wearing socks, and the fungus and filth of his skin made my stomach queasy.

"If you want to fight something, fight yourself." He rambled on, getting more zealous as he spoke. "Everything that's born dies, right? We all agree on that; the only thing we don't know is when. Today, Ash Wednesday, is the day our Father set aside for us to acknowledge that our death is coming and could arrive at any moment."

"Oh, that's a real upper," Steve muttered under his breath.

"It's uplifting if you listen," he snapped. "We carry that truth with us so that we can engage in life more deeply and with a richer sense of gratitude. Dust to dust," he proclaimed. "The word of the Lord is the spoken teacher. Death is the silent teacher!"

Finally there was quiet in our cell for a moment. I hoped the conversation was finished.

Steve looked over, staring at me with an almost melancholy expression. "What are you, almost thirty?" he asked me, after a long beat.

I nodded.

"Fuck, buddy—YOU'RE IN THE PRIME OF YOUR LIFE!" he whined. "You shouldn't've gotten married. What are you, crazy?" He leaned in front of me, his blue eyes bright and pleading. "Go out and score as much as you can. Shoot the moon. This old dude's right: We all get older. Believe me, cowboy, it'll happen to you too. I used to take off my shirt every chance I got. I mean, I had abs for miles"—he sucked in his gut and punched himself hard with both hands twice in his fat belly—"and chicks would drop for me. Now I leave my shirt on even while I'm screwing. Look at me, I'm falling apart." He stood in profile and let his gut hang. "You're a good-looking pup, panties will drop for you, but it'll stop. I shit you not; it will stop. Go out there and get some ass, cowboy, quick as you can. Listen to the old man, someday you'll be dead. But"—he paused, forcing me to look in his eyes—"don't ever let them see what you got inside, in here." He thumped his hand against his chest. "That's you, baby, don't show it to nobody. They'll use it against you and burn you alive. Trust me on this one."

"Give your heart to everybody you meet," the old man chimed in quietly. "The rest is pretense."

"Super, so you go sit up there in heaven and hock luggies down on the rest of us, good for you. We're livin' on earth, OK?"

"I'm on earth right now, but when I go to meet my heavenly Father, I hope he will say, Bruce, your entry fee has been paid."

"McNally," the cop called from behind his desk.

"Yeah, boy." Steve spun around.

"Does Arizona mean anything to you?"

"FUUUUUUUUUCK." Steve gave out a Comanche death cry that shook the foundation of the building. "You can't do that, man. You said I was good to go! You can't go back on your word like that. *You can't do that!*"

"Oh, yes, I can." The heavyset cop smiled. "Looks to me like you should sit down. You're not going anywhere. Except maybe back to Arizona."

For a full minute Steve looked out in dumbfounded silence. The back of his red head was perfectly still. Then slowly he turned around.

"Don't look at me!" he yelled at us. "Don't either one of you two motherfuckers look at me." He kicked the bench I was on and threw himself down on the floor to sit with his head buried in his hands. Turns out he had escaped from a correctional facility outside of Phoenix two weeks earlier.

For the next five hours I sat there waiting.

Ever since I'd met Christy I seemed to have lost all my friends. I didn't want to, I loved my friends. I loved drinking and talking about ass, bowling, driving fast, basketball, chatting up eighteen-year-old girls with their heads full of air; I loved all that with a passion.

I just loved Christy more.

I wondered if I would really be able to be a faithful husband. I hoped so. One day at a time, I figured, like an alcoholic.

She told me she loved me after the second time we slept together. We were lying in bed watching the Knicks like we always used to do. "I love you," she blurted out. I couldn't help it, I burst out laughing. It seemed so kamikaze. We barely knew each other.

Finally the officer called my name and opened the door to the cell. A court date and a fine had been set for the speeding. Officer Parks let the illegal concealment charges slide, partly because of the unspoken alliance between the military and the police and partly because he was a good old boy who didn't want to harness me down with a felony. The gun was confiscated. It was an old Colt of my grandfather's but it was no big deal. I didn't want the damn thing anymore. My car was waiting for me in a lot on the other side of town. And I had been formally discharged from the U.S. Army, the conditions of which were still outstanding. All I could think about was getting back to Christy.

Steve didn't even look up as I stood up and moved out. The bearded religious dude in the corner waved. Stepping out of there, I was hell bent on spending the rest of my life figuring out a new, more accurate definition for being male. I didn't want to be a monk or an outlaw. There had to be a middle way.

In the waiting area of the sheriff's department, I dialed Christy's dad and the hospital: no luck at either place. I switched to Plan B: Go directly to the hospital. I called a cab, stumbled outside, and waited.

There was no activity whatsoever in my brain as I sat on the front steps of the police station. It was now about four in the afternoon and the sun was still bright. Looking up at the clouds, staring into the sun, I sighed. Everything was so different from what I thought it would be.

When I was nine I shot a bird, a red-tailed hawk sitting on a telephone wire in our front yard. I started thinking about that. Squeezing the trigger slowly, I popped him square in the chest. He didn't fall. His talons had instantaneously clasped the wire, and he hung there upside down. I promised myself right then that I would never kill another living thing. Holy shit, I was glad to be out of the army. I didn't *ever* want to kill anything. I'd be the first guy down in a war. That dead hawk hanging in the sunlight was what I thought of whenever I thought of love. So much regret.

As my taxi pulled up, I stood and started down the steps. Before I reached it I saw Christy step out, pay the driver, and turn around. She looked up at me, just as surprised as I was looking down at her. We were about twenty paces apart. I could barely see with the ten thousand thoughts racing through my mind. She shrugged her shoulders and gave me a faint smile, placed both her hands on her belly, and without speaking nodded her head yes.

Floating down the front steps, a fresh gust of wind at my back, I felt new, like one or maybe all of us had been resurrected.

ACKNOWLEDGMENTS

In the creation of this novel there are so many people to whom I am indebted. First off, for his conversations and ideas, the playwright Keith Bunin; my editor, 2x going, Jordan Pavlin, for cutting out all the boring parts; my staunchest ally, Jennifer Walsh; also I must thank her husband, Patrick, for his friendship; Bryan Lourd, for his unflinching support; everybody over at Knopf and Vintage, particularly Sonny Mehta and Marty Asher; Dr. Gae Rodke, for the medical tutelage (not to mention for delivering both my babies); Jann Wenner for his early encouragement and advice; Patty LaMagna, Angela White and Sam Connelly; the late Thomas Merton and Allen Ginsberg, for the inspiration; Quentin Tarantino, Greta Gaines, Frank Whaley, and Jason Blum, for listening as the story unfolded; Richard Linklater, for meeting me down in New Orleans; Charles Gaines; John Starks; Spencer Tweedy, for his insight into the nature of dogs; my family, most notably Leslie Green Hawke, Howard and Mary Green, Bronwyn Hopkins,

Patrick Powers, Sr., Patrick Powers, Jr., Heather Powers, James Gay, and Matthew and Samuel Hawke; and of course, Bob, Nena, Ganden, Datchen, and Mipam Thurman. I am so grateful to you all.

And finally, Uma, Maya, and brother Levon, without whom there would be nothing.

A NOTE ABOUT THE AUTHOR

Ethan Hawke is best known for his starring roles in the motion pictures *Dead Poets Society, Reality Bites, Gattaca, Before Sunrise,* and
Training Day. He was the cofounder and artistic director of the
Malaparte Theater Company, based in New York, and is the author of
the novel *The Hottest State.* He lives in New York with his wife and
two children. He is thirty-one years old.

A NOTE ABOUT THE TYPE

This book was set in a typeface called Bulmer. This distinguished letter is a replica of a type long famous in the history of English printing which was designed and cut by William Martin about 1790 for William Bulmer of the Shakespeare Press. In design, it is all but a modern face, with vertical stress, sharp differentiation between the thick and thin strokes, and nearly flat serifs. The decorative italic shows the influence of Baskerville, as Martin was a pupil of John Baskerville's.